HAPPINESS UNDER A SUMMER SKYE

LISA HOBMAN

First published in Great Britain in 2026 by Boldwood Books Ltd.

Cover Design by Alexandra Allden

Cover Images: Alexandra Allden and Shutterstock

Paperback ISBN 978-1-80557-006-6

Large Print ISBN 978-1-80557-007-3

Hardback ISBN 978-1-80557-005-9

Trade Paperback ISBN 978-1-80635-011-7

Ebook ISBN 978-1-80557-008-0

Kindle ISBN 978-1-80557-009-7

Audio CD ISBN 978-1-80557-000-4

MP3 CD ISBN 978-1-80557-001-1

Digital audio download ISBN 978-1-80557-002-8

This book is printed on certified sustainable paper. Boldwood Books is dedicated to putting sustainability at the heart of our business. For more information please visit https://www.boldwoodbooks.com/about-us/sustainability/

Boldwood Books Ltd, 23 Bowerdean Street, London, SW6 3TN

www.boldwoodbooks.com

To all my fellow myasthenia gravis warriors. We are capable of achieving so much in spite of our perceived limitations. Don't forget that.

PROLOGUE

2015

Angelia 'Angel' MacAuley's knees trembled beneath the black leather trousers she had been styled in, and she hoped her juddering wasn't visible to the rapt TV studio audience. Her long dark-chestnut hair had been styled to perfection and fell in loose waves over one shoulder but the makeup on her face felt cakey and tight under the bright lights. It wasn't something she usually wore and had meant she hardly recognised her reflection in the dressing-room mirror, but it had been necessary for the studio lighting.

Her right hand was almost numb thanks to her fellow competitor squeezing it so hard that the circulation had begun to slow. Her fingertips tingled now, and because of this she absently wondered how on earth she would be able to accept the consolation handshake she was about to receive from rising star movie actress Ruby Locke, who had been tasked with the job of presenting the grand prize: a gold microphone trophy mounted on a Perspex stand; and, of course, the best job in the world.

It had been six months since Angelia's first nerve-racking audition for the TV talent show *Scotland Rocks*. This was followed by shortlist auditions that she had no expectations of being selected from, but only a week later she was called back and informed she had made it through to the TV series. Initially she presumed it was a prank call, but when the producer had finally convinced her it was really happening, she was invited to a costume shopping trip in Glasgow's Barras Market where there were a number of cool vintage shops, and a further fitting in Edinburgh. After that there were choreography meetings in Glasgow and dress rehearsals, followed by prerecorded heats filmed at Pacific Quay on the south bank of the River Clyde. But it had all ultimately culminated in *this* night: a live television broadcast to the whole of the UK – and maybe beyond – where the new lead singer of The Fallen Angels would be crowned.

The Glasgow-based band had been established ten years ago, after meeting while studying at various universities across the city. Their original vocalist, Lorelie Dean, had sadly passed away a year before the competition after a six-month battle with illness. Lorelie had left the band with two instructions: one, carry on in her memory and two, make an unknown singer's dreams come true when choosing her replacement. The band had taken time to mourn and had then set about fulfilling her final wishes. So now, after performing a variety of songs over a six-week series, and seeing new acquaintances knocked out of the competition at the end of each episode, twenty-year-old Angelia MacAuley stood, quaking, backstage at the TV studio, with the other four finalists; two female, one non-binary and one male; a shaky smile plastered on each of their faces as the camera slowly scanned them in turn. There was literally nowhere to hide.

Angelia's eyes stung and she blinked rapidly, trying to usher away the threatening tears. She didn't want to ruin the perfectly drawn winged eyeliner seeing as the camera was up close and rather too personal for her liking. The tears were a mixture of sadness and relief. Sadness that the process was almost over, meaning she would probably not be seeing her newfound friends as often any more, and relief that she would soon be able to go back to university and finish what she'd started; a BMus (Hons) Performance at Glasgow's prestigious Conservatoire, the starting block for many famous actors, musicians and writers.

To say she was on an emotional rollercoaster was a vast understatement. How the hell had she got this far? She really didn't know. From day one, even though the camaraderie had been immensely positive, the competition had been ridiculously tough, and Angelia hadn't expected to even be a contender, let alone end up on the live final. She had only entered because her university besties had badgered and cajoled her until she had eventually capitulated.

* * *

They had been watching TV in the communal lounge area of Angelia's accommodation block on a *dreich* Saturday evening, when the ad for the future show had appeared on screen. It had featured The Fallen Angels' drummer, Angelia's star crush Josh Baron, and the lead guitarist, Heath Lennox.

Fiona, a fellow Scot, had gasped. 'You have to apply, Angelia! You'd be *soooo* good!' One of her best friends, Fiona had gripped her arm, shaking it and whining like a toddler in a tantrum. 'You're just what they're looking for.' At the time Angelia had been a little distracted by Josh's vivid blue eyes. He had the looks of the stereotypical bad boy and Angelia had a poster of him on her bedroom wall at home. Fiona pulled her from her daydream. 'Earth to Angelia! I'm being serious about this, you know. You have *the* most melodic voice, and it would be perfect for a rock band. Look at Amy Lee from Evanescence.'

Angelia had met Fiona Morton at the university's audition preparation day, and they had kept in touch ever since. Fiona, a native Glaswegian, was a rare one; unlike most of the other attendees she had no dreams of bright lights and stardom. All she wanted, she had told Angelia, was to study at the best university in order to achieve her dream job as a music teacher. Angelia had liked the mousy-brown-haired woman with smiling hazel eyes right away, because she was the perfect balance of empathetic and a little bonkers – in the best way, of course. 'Plus,' Fiona continued, 'and it's the thing I most envy about you, you can play any instrument you pick up. How the hell you do that I have no idea, but what band wouldn't want you?'

'I'm too soft and folky though,' Angelia had insisted. 'And anyway, what would be the point? I could never compete with the talent Lorelie had.'

'Fee's right,' the third member of their friendship trio, Ed, had said. 'You don't have to sound like you eat gravel for breakfast to sing in a band like that. Avril Lavigne, Gwen Stefani, Ann Wilson, need I go on?'

Edwin (aka Ed) Halsall, somewhat a musical prodigy – he'd been writing symphonies since he was twelve and had dreams of playing with the New York Philharmonic – had literally bumped into the pair on a night out during freshers' week. On that night the girls had taken pity on him as he was akin to a deer in headlights after what would later transpire to have been a fairly sheltered upbringing by strict religious parents. He was a tall, dreamily handsome dark-haired young man with piercing green eyes and the most gorgeous smile Angelia could recall on an 'in real life' person. He had gone a little mad with the freedom of living away from his family home in Hampshire for the first time and it was evident he had consumed rather more than his limit of alcohol so the two young women had taken him under their wings to make sure the well-spoken, friendly, drunken guy wasn't taken advantage of and got back safely to his student digs.

Angelia had fallen hard for Ed from the start. But she knew she would never feel the same about anyone else and that her heart was his alone when she saw and heard him perform Debussy's 'Clair de Lune' at a university concert. She had been mesmerised, her eyes filled with tears as he played the piece by heart, eyes closed, head back. It had been the most beautiful sight she had ever beheld.

Ed was talented, funny, sweet and very considerate and so, aside from crushes on famous people, he had been the first *real* love of her life. But, and much to her dismay, he showed no signs of reciprocation. In fact, he always seemed to make a beeline for Fiona, so Angelia did nothing about her unrequited feelings, and instead, henceforth he became the third wheel of their tricycle from that first night; the three had been inseparable ever since. The Three Amigos. The Three Musketeers. The Terrible Trio. And apart from one drunken kiss they had shared, he and Angelia had been the best of friends.

'And anyway,' Ed had continued, pointing at the TV screen where Heath and Josh were talking to the camera, 'you're not competing with Lorelie. She left the door open for her replacement, remember? Bless her.' He shook his head, suddenly lost in a touch of melancholy for his new favourite band.

Angelia loved her friends' confidence in her, if only she believed in herself as much. 'Ughhhhh! If I agree to enter, will you just drop it?' she had whinged. 'You're as bad as my folks. They've been messaging me the application link for two weeks now.'

Ed had got up from his armchair, stood to attention, blown his floppy chocolate-brown fringe out of his face, and saluted. 'Scout's honour.' He had kicked Fiona's leg and given her a wide-eyed glare.

Realising her input was needed, Fiona had nodded and pointed up to him. 'Oh... erm, yes. What he said.'

Angelia had rolled her eyes. 'Okay, fine. I'll do it.'

Her two friends had dragged her up from the sofa, grappled her into a bear hug and begun jumping up and down chanting, 'Angelia's gonna be a rock star, Angelia's gonna be a rock star!' It had garnered more than a couple of strange looks from students playing pool across the other side of the room.

'God, you guys are so immature,' Angelia had said, giggling as she flushed cerise with the embarrassment of the situation.

Of course, at that time Angelia knew she was unlikely to be selected, never mind win the damn thing. Things like that *didn't* happen in real life. Not to people like her, anyway.

Angelia had grown up in the north of Skye just outside Portree with a bank manager dad who had played the guitar in various bands since he left school, and a bookshop-owning, Richard Marx-obsessed mother; hence her name, which was taken from a song on her mum's favourite eighties album *Repeat Offender*.

Music was the family's shared passion, and they often spent evenings at the local pub partaking in music nights. On these occasions, Angelia would nervously sing traditional Scottish songs to the accompaniment of her father's acoustic guitar, while her mother rhythmically tapped away on the *bodhrán*, a handheld Irish drum, and someone else played the accordion or fiddle. When they weren't performing, they gathered together in the living room of their converted and extended bothy listening to their extensive, and eclectic, vinyl collection, often jamming along on the variety of instruments they had acquired over the years. Her dad used to laugh and say they were like a mini Von Trapp family only without the outfits made from old curtains, and her mum would usually respond with a good-humoured laugh, saying he shouldn't joke because if he kept spending money on guitars, using the curtains for their clothes might end up being necessary.

The decent-sized white-painted house was situated along a track that led off from the main B885 out of Portree leading towards Bracadale. It was situated at the top of a slope and had spectacular views over the surrounding farmland. Her parents had chosen it for its solitude, which meant they could play, and listen to, music as loud as they wished without causing a disturbance to others, while being close enough to Portree so that they had access to all the amenities a family could need. It was a beautiful place that Angelia would always call home.

Angelia's final performance for *Scotland Rocks* had been a song that was very special to her; 'Martha's Harbour' by a nineties band called All About Eve. She had loved the band and the melancholy of the song since she could remember, and her mother had once informed her that the affinity with the song had probably come about since she used to sing it to her in the womb.

* * *

Angelia was snapped back to her present-day terrifying situation by a drumroll that echoed around the backstage area over the speakers. The studio audience fell silent. And Ruby Locke took to the microphone as the group of finalists stood against a glittering backdrop that featured the show's logo and watched the stage on the monitor.

'This has been an amazing night, hasn't it?' Ruby asked with a wobble of nervousness to her voice as she addressed the audience. They, in turn, dutifully rumbled their assent. 'Our five finalists are waiting backstage and I'm sure everyone in the studio and those of you watching at home will all join in me in thanking them for their incredible, heartfelt performances.' Thunderous applause, whistles and whoops travelled around the dimly lit room. 'I'm happy to say that the band and their management team have made a unanimous decision tonight. After putting these young people through their paces, they have chosen the vocalist who they think is the best for them. I have to say I wouldn't have wanted to be in their shoes tonight, don't you agree?' More rumbles from the audience ensued. 'I'm just going to get straight to the point because these guys have been waiting long enough.' Despite her words, there followed a pause, and another drumroll as Ruby fumbled with a golden envelope. Eventually she pulled out a card with the show's logo visible on the face of it. 'The winner of *Scotland Rocks* and the new lead vocalist for The Fallen Angels is...' (another annoyingly long pause followed, clearly a tack by the production company to build tension) 'Angelia MacAuley!'

1

TWO MONTHS LATER

Angelia MacAuley stood on the riser beneath the stage, heart pounding, mouth dry. It was her first gig with the world-famous Fallen Angels, and even though she had rehearsed almost daily since the final *Scotland Rocks* show, she was plagued with imposter syndrome. How the hell was she here? How had this massively well-known band with their gazillion fans across the globe chosen her, a nobody from the Isle of Skye, to be their new front person? This was the stuff dreams were made of. Perhaps she would wake up any minute now and find none of it had been real. It wouldn't have surprised her. Although if it was a dream, it was bizarrely real. Her heart kept a steady, if a little fast, beat against her ribcage and her breaths came rapidly through the space between her parted lips and as she closed her fist around the microphone in her right hand, she noticed the sheen of sweat on her palm. Tears needled behind her eyes, and she wasn't sure if their presence was out of fear, excitement or a combination of both.

'Come on, Angelia, you've got this,' she whispered to herself as she tried to inhale and exhale a little slower.

She could already hear the fourteen-thousand-strong crowd in the packed stadium as the build-up to the first song began. Initially it was a low rumble, but it built and built with every chord and every beat, the pace matching the increasing tempo of her heart until she could feel it vibrating, first through her chest, and then throughout her whole body. In her ear the rhythmic tick, tick, tick of the metronome track was somehow reassuring, and she tried to focus on nothing but that.

Lead guitarist Heath Lennox, bass player Baird Munro, aka Bear because it suited his size and bushy beard, and keyboard player Dom Holyhead were already on the stage, as was Josh Baron, behind his drum kit, and their female rhythm guitarist who originally hailed from the Loire Valley in France but had lived in London for fifteen years and could speak better English than most people Angelia knew. Anouk Barbier had also been Lorelie's long-term partner and Angelia had worried most about being accepted by her, but her fear had been unfounded. Anouk had been so supportive and lovely, making sure Angelia felt at home from the start of her time with the band.

Angelia's entrance had been planned this way to make a huge deal of her first-ever official gig. But the fact that it was taking place at Glasgow's SSE Hydro was what made it special for her; all of her fellow contestants from the show and the friends she had made during her own, somewhat brief attendance at the prestigious Conservatoire had been given complimentary tickets. Her besties, Fiona and Ed, were there too, of course, along with her parents in the VIP area with the other family members and girlfriends of the band. She could imagine her dad chewing his nails and her mum pacing up and down as she told him to stop it. She smiled. They were no doubt more terrified than she was.

As she stood there on the riser, waiting, she had a flashback to earlier that day when she had been standing on the stage at their dress rehearsal, and how she had been completely awestruck at the magnitude of the auditorium. Heath had excitedly told her the show was a sellout and that everyone was coming to show their support for their new lead vocalist. Unfortunately, this news had been counterproductive and had terrified her. After some unpleasant recent events she was aware that, amongst the people who would be there for good and positive reasons, there were also bound to be people who were there hoping to watch her fall flat on her face. Since the live final of the competition there had been posts on social media claiming that the show had been fixed and that Angelia was talentless. Her parents and the rest of the band had tried to reassure her that these were jealous idiots, and she needed to ignore every single negative comment.

'You do deserve to be here, Angel,' Josh, the band's drummer, had told her with a reassuring squeeze to her arms. He had been the first to call her 'Angel' and the rest of the band had simply followed suit, and it had stuck. She hated that Josh was even more gorgeous up close, and she chastised herself for noticing. After all, she knew business and pleasure should never be mixed so it was a waste of time swooning over him. In addition to this, unlike her, he wasn't even single.

Heath had added, 'Josh is right, Angel. We chose *you*, remember? We wouldn't have done that if you weren't good enough. You're *more* than good enough.'

She'd wished, at the time, she could've believed them. And more so now she was on the verge of stepping out onto the stage for her first gig. But deep down she knew from firsthand experience that a certain cohort of the fans could be obsessive ones who would only ever accept Lorelie as the lead singer, even though the beloved singer had expressly said on social media that this was her final wish, to have an unknown singer take her place; to make their dream come true. She was grateful to Lorelie and wanted to protect the former singer's legacy after being the one to have this amazing opportunity bestowed upon her. So Angelia had tried to push all the negative thoughts to the back of her mind as she had stared out at the empty seats under the stark bright lights, knowing that in a mere few hours she would be looking out at a whole different view.

She had been in the studio rehearsing with the band almost every day for eight weeks since the live final of *Scotland Rocks*. As a huge fan she had, of course, known the songs already but now she was learning harmonies and stage marks too. It was a lot more complicated than the band had made it look. Anouk had been amazing, so encouraging, even though it must have been so much harder for her seeing someone taking her girlfriend's place. Rehearsals had been gruelling but exhilarating all at the same time and tonight was the night it all became a reality.

No more pinching herself when she woke up, no more checking and rechecking the copy of the signed contract she kept on her phone so she could look at it when she needed to prove to herself that it hadn't all been an elaborately realistic dream. No more worrying about the bridge in the third song where she kept getting the lyrics wrong.

It was now.

It was happening.

It was real.

If she didn't know it now, she never would.

* * *

Back in the present again, Angelia's heart skipped as a voice said, 'Riser up,' in her earpiece, and sure enough, the platform on which she stood began to ascend towards the stage. Dry ice surrounded her as white strobe lights illuminated her silhouette. As she reached stage level, pyrotechnics fired off at the front of the stage, making her jump, and a unified, almost deafening, cheer travelled through the stadium. With a confidence she didn't know she possessed, Angelia strutted towards the audience and sang out the first line of the first song, aptly called 'Now I'm Here'.

Only two years before, Angelia and her friends had been in the audience at this very venue as Lorelie had sung that same line while pointing out at the hordes of adoring fans singing right back to her; marching around the stage as her long auburn hair flew behind her. For a petite-framed woman, she'd had a huge personality and an even bigger pair of lungs. And now Angelia was walking the same steps.

This feeling was surreal.

As if Lorelie's spirit had possessed her body, Angelia stomped around the stage as the lyrics flowed easily from her lips – even the bridge in the third song. It was hard to see all the faces of the people singing back to her but the ones at the front were pretty clear and she made eye contact with smiling fans who reached out towards her as she sang her heart out. It felt a lot like acceptance for the twenty-year-old who had been terrified of backlash for stepping into such a role.

During his guitar solo, Heath walked towards her, and she leant her back on his shoulder as he moved his fingers deftly up and down the fretboard. It was like a scene from a movie and Angelia couldn't believe it was real life. *Her* real life. He turned to face her and beamed, giving her a wink before he made his way across the stage to Anouk.

The whole night whizzed by like a fever dream. Angelia didn't miss a step, her voice sounded like it didn't belong to her. The PA gave her tone a richness she had never realised she was capable of, and the rest of the band were incredible. They all interacted with her as if she had always been a part of them. Not for one second did she feel like a replacement or an afterthought. The imposter syndrome had left the building, taking her anxiety with it.

At the end of the night, after the final encore, Josh came down from his kit and addressed the audience. 'You guys have been incredible tonight!' Of course this was met with a raucous cheer. Then he turned to Angelia. 'And so have you. You stepped into the shoes of someone we love and instead of trying to be her, you've made this band yours. Isn't she amazing, guys?' Again, the thousands of fans in attendance cheered and whistled. Angelia's eyes filled with tears, and she blew kisses to the audience. 'We've loved Angelia MacAuley since we first saw her perform on *Scotland Rocks*, she has this big heart and truckloads of talent, don't you all agree?' More cheers. What came next, however, almost knocked her off her feet. 'In fact, we love Angelia – or Angel as we call her because that's what she is to us – so much so that we've decided to change our name to... Angel and the Fallen!' Angelia gasped and covered her heart with her hand as panic flooded her along with a wave of heat. They hadn't mentioned this. *What was happening?* The fans would hate her for this sudden change, surely. Her mind spun and the stadium appeared to join it.

What's wrong with their original name? Bands just don't go changing their name like this. Queen are still Queen after Freddie Mercury passed, Alice in Chains is still so called after the death of Lane Staley, so why this? Why now? So many questions stampeded around her brain without an outlet.

The stage lights flickered, and Josh dramatically shouted, 'Whoa, guys what's happening?' as he turned to face the back of the stage. The rest of the band acted shocked and shared over-emphasised shrugs and wide-eyed gawps as they all turned to face the back of the stage too. It was all very 'high-school drama production' and Angelia couldn't help giggling. She followed their lead and turned to see the digital backdrop pixelating as the stage lights continued to flicker, and then there it was, the band's new name emblazoned on the screen in six-feet-tall gold letters. Much to her shock, the audience seemed to lap this up. The noise was immense. *How was the roof still in place?*

Josh turned to face her and spoke into his microphone again. 'Angel, you've made it possible for us to carry on doing what we love and we're eternally grateful. Lorelie would've definitely loved you. And she told us that we should rename the band if it worked so that the new singer didn't feel like an outsider in someone else's place.' As he spoke, his eyes welled with tears and he took her hand. 'It just so happens that your parents were bloody awesome and gave you a name we could *really* work with!' A rumble of laughter reverberated around the vast space as Josh laughed, too, his eyes crinkling at the corners. Tears spilled over from Angelia's eyes and Josh pulled her into a hug. He whispered into her ear, 'Thank you, and I mean that wholeheartedly. Now why don't you speak to your audience.' He passed her the towel from over his shoulder, and she wiped at the escaped tears.

With Josh's hand on her shoulder, she turned to the audience and huffed out a long, shaking breath as she shook her head. 'What do I say after that? After tonight?'

A loud cheer erupted again and as it died down, she heard someone from amongst the crowd shout, 'We love you, Angel!'

'Dad—?' she asked with a laugh and the audience joined her. 'Seriously though, wow! I love you right back!' she said, as relief flooded her veins. 'This is like a dream. I've loved this band since I first heard their music and Lorelie's voice was just... transcendent. I think I'll wake up every single morning from this day onwards pinching myself to check if it's really happening.' A rumble of 'Awwws' met her ears. 'I want to say my own "thank yous". First of all, to this incredible group of musicians.' She turned to face the band who were now all standing together just a few feet away, arms draped around each other's shoulders. 'You guys took me under your wings and made me feel like a part of you from day one. Thank you for making my dream come true and for making this transition so much fun.' The rest of the band applauded her, and she blew kisses to them before turning to the audience once more. 'And thank *you* so much to each and every person in this place tonight. You've made me feel so happy and accepted and I'm so grateful.' One by one the members of the audience in the seated sections stood and applauded as the house lights illuminated, showing Angelia, for the first time, the enormity of the band's impact on the world and this was only *one* city. The rest of the band walked to stand beside her, and they all joined hands to take their final bow of the evening.

* * *

Backstage, Angelia was engulfed in hugs from the band who congratulated her on a brilliant first gig.

'You're a bloody natural!' Josh told her. 'We definitely made the right decision, eh, guys?'

'Damn right we did,' Heath agreed.

Anouk wrapped her arms around Angelia and hugged her tightly. 'Lorelie was watching over you out there tonight. I could feel her there. You were wonderful.' Angelia loved Anouk's French-tinged accent. She was softly spoken and shy unless she was on stage.

Angelia pulled back and looked into Anouk's eyes. She saw a little sadness but a whole lot of sincerity too. 'I can't tell you how much it means to hear you say that,' she whispered.

Anouk simply smiled and nodded, her eyes glassy with tears now. She patted Angelia's arm, turned and walked over to the drinks stand.

'Aye, bloody brilliant,' Dom said. The gay Glaswegian had always been the heartthrob of the band, to both male and female fans, with his bright blue eyes, thick black hair and stubble-covered chiselled jaw. 'Lorelie would be so proud.'

She spotted her parents standing with Fiona and Ed, waiting patiently across the room, and she made her way over.

Her dad pulled her into his arms. 'We're so proud of you, darlin',' he said with a wavering voice. 'You just belong up there.'

'Your dad's right, sweetheart,' her mum said with tears streaming down her face. 'You were amazing. Nanny and Grumpa would have loved tonight.'

Hearing mention of her grandparents made tears well in Angelia's eyes. 'I wish they could have been here. Thank you for coming, it means the world to me.'

Her dad cupped her face in one hand. 'Wouldn't have missed it for the world, *Angel*.' He winked.

'We'll wait over by the barrier while you speak to Ed and Fiona. I think they're both bursting to talk to you,' her mum said, glancing over to where her friends were waiting.

As she approached Fiona and Ed, excitement got the better of her, and she squealed as she jumped up and down on the spot and they joined her. In her periphery she saw her bandmates watching her and laughing. Josh looked on with a handsome smile that melted her heart. She really would need to work on *not* having a huge crush on him.

'Oh my *God*! You were incredible!' Fiona said as she grappled Angelia into a bear hug. 'I can't believe I'm best friends with a rock goddess!'

'Fee's right, Angelia. Or should I say *Angel*? You rocked everyone's world up there. I couldn't take my eyes off you,' Ed said as he put his arms around the two women.

'What happens now?' Fiona asked. 'Are you going straight on the road?'

Angelia nodded. 'We're going into the studio for a week or two first to record and write some new songs. It's a studio in New York where loads of famous people have recorded. I still keep thinking I'm going to wake up and find out this is all a dream.'

'Nope. It's all real. We were right, you're gonna be a rock star,' Fiona said, grinning like the Cheshire Cat.

'So... we erm... won't see you for a while then?' Ed asked, a hint of sadness to his tone.

'Well, no, but we can video call. And I'm sure I'll be coming home from time to time. Don't worry, I'm not going to disappear from your lives. You're stuck with me.' The thought of not seeing her friends every day was weighing heavy on her, but she didn't want them to worry so did her best to make light of the situation.

'We'd better be. We're going to be lost without you, aren't we, Ed?' Fiona said, giving him a nudge.

He nodded. 'Yeah, yeah, we really are.'

'Look, I'm busting for the loo. Don't run off to New York until I get back, okay?' Fiona said as she darted off down the corridor.

Ed rubbed at his chin. 'Look, Angelia, can I say something?'

His serious expression concerned Angelia and she frowned. 'Of course you can, Ed. What's up?'

He glanced over his shoulder and took a step closer. 'The thing is... I mean... here's the thing...' He stepped from one foot to the other and his gaze darted around, anywhere but on her.

Angelia gave a small laugh. 'Come on, Ed, it's not like you to be lost for words. Spit it out.'

His jaw clenched and unclenched beneath his skin, and he shook his head. 'Okay... I'm only saying this because I'm going to miss you and... I might regret it if I don't say it. But I'm also worried about ruining things between us. We've been friends for two years and I don't want to lose you but—'

Angelia scowled. 'Ed, you're worrying me.'

'I'm back!' Fiona rushed over. 'What did I miss?'

Annoyance briefly swept across Ed's face as he abruptly stepped away. 'Oh, nothing much.'

'Not nothing, Ed, you had something to say?'

He gave a dismissive wave and what appeared to be a disingenuous smile. 'Nah, really, it's nothing. I'm just being daft.'

Before Angelia could push Ed further, Heath arrived beside her. 'I hate to do this to you, Angel, but we're heading straight to the airport tonight, so you need to say your goodbyes for now.'

Angelia nodded and her throat tightened. 'Okay. No worries.'

He walked away and Fiona grabbed her and hugged her again. 'I'm not jealous of you being surrounded by all the hunky musos, honest.' She giggled. 'Go and be astounding, my gorgeous friend. You know we love you, right?'

Angelia sniffed and her eyes stung. 'And I love you too.'

Ed hugged her next and whispered, 'Sorry,' before pulling away. 'We'll get going and let you speak to your folks.' He smiled but his eyes were tinged with sadness again.

'Okay, if you're sure,' she replied, very much aware, thanks to his crumpled expression, that there was something he'd very much wanted to say.

She watched them walk towards the exit, arms linked. Fiona rested her head on Ed, and he glanced back over his shoulder one last time.

2

TEN YEARS LATER – 2025

'I don't believe this, he's dumped me by text message,' Angelia said in disbelief as she stared at the screen on her phone and shook her head, her heart sinking. 'Coward.' She huffed as she crumpled her brow, willing away the tears stinging behind her eyes. Her chin trembled and she sniffed, biting the inside of her cheek as disappointment and hurt flooded her. At moments like these, the only thing she wanted was to bury her face in her little dog Scrappy's fur, inhaling the sweet, familiar scent of home and make the whole world go away. Scrappy made everything feel better and she missed him terribly. Clearly, he had been a good judge of character too as he had growled the first time – and all subsequent times come to think of it – he had met her latest beau, Dane.

Don't cry.

Do. Not. Cry.

The words – if you could call them that:

DANE

Its jst not wrkn out Angl but I wsh you all the bst 4 the future lv D

were followed by a sad face emoji shedding a single tear. It was an assault on her eyes – *what does he have against vowels? And punctuation for that matter?* It all felt a bit childish and patronising if she was honest. Or like she was being fired, or turned down for a job, by a teenage boss. The accompanying emoji, even though it appeared to show emotion, felt a little too light-hearted for the situation. Too comedic. But she wouldn't cry. She absolutely wouldn't. She had shed enough tears over men who didn't stick around. She would simply chalk this up to yet another bullet dodged.

The tour bus was winding its way north on the I95 to New York where they would play a charity gig in memory of Lorelie and to raise money for the foundation she implemented before her death. It would be the last gig of the current tour and Angelia, and the others she guessed, were looking forward to a well-earned break. The scenery on the route from Philly, where their last gig had taken place, was a mixture of industrial landscapes, suburban districts and a smattering of historic locations. The architecture changed regularly, telling the story of the towns and cities they travelled through.

The band's drummer, Josh, slid into the seat opposite. 'He hasn't! No way! You're joking? What a piece of shit,' he said as he placed a mug of coffee in front of her. 'Sounds like you're well rid of him, if that's how he treats people.'

It was a dreary March day, and the gloomy grey clouds overhead matched Angelia's plummeting mood. *Why does this keep happening?* she thought as she stared out at the endless expansive stream of concrete factories on this present chunk of road, the same washed-out shade as the sky, so it was hard to tell where the buildings ended, and *it* began.

'How long were you guys seeing each other?' Josh asked, his Glaswegian accent softened slightly after years of being on the road.

'Six months,' Angelia said with a sigh. 'I really thought he was in it for the long haul. But of course, I was wrong... as always.'

Josh reached out and squeezed her hand. 'He didn't deserve you, you know. I've seen it time and again with the other guys. These outsiders all think they can hack it until they realise what fame can do to a couple.'

She rolled her eyes. 'Says the man with the perfect relationship.'

'Aye, but me and Nancy were childhood sweethearts, Angel. I've been with her since I was fourteen. She knew me before all this,' he said as he gestured around the luxurious vehicle they were travelling in. Its shiny black surfaces and chrome detailing screamed *high-end man cave*. 'I'm just *me* to her. Just Joshy. I'm not *Josh Baron, drummer for Angel and the Fallen*,' he said in a voice that mimicked the dramatic MC voiceover at one of their shows.

Angelia crumpled her brow as she glanced down at her lock screen at the image that showed her with her now *ex*-boyfriend, soccer player Dane Bakker. The epitome of handsomeness with his dark hair, chocolate-brown eyes and chiselled jaw. The centre back for the New Jersey Stallions had been at one of their shows around eight months earlier and had been introduced to her by a mutual friend. They had chatted for a while via WhatsApp and then had begun dating. In this particular photograph they had been at Disney World in Florida and were both wearing Mickey Mouse ears, grinning like idiots. On the face of it they seemed happy. She had certainly felt that way.

'He's famous too though, Josh,' she said, 'that's what I don't get. I felt sure that *that* fact would mean he understood.'

Josh paused and seemed thoughtful as if choosing his words carefully. 'I think it's a different kind of fame. I mean, sports stars are treated like heroes, of course, but rock stars are treated like gods. Our fans can be a lot to handle as you know. They get quite possessive over us and some people can't deal with that. And...' He paused again and chewed his bottom lip. 'If you think about it, soccer isn't as big a deal in the US as American football so he isn't quite as well-known as he could be if he was playing in the UK. If I'm completely honest, I got the feeling he was a wee bit jealous of the attention you get. Like he thought he deserved more, you know?'

Angelia widened her eyes. 'And you never thought to say anything?'

Josh held up his hands. 'Hey, you were crazy about the guy. I didn't want to be the tosser who ruined that for you; you're my best friend.'

Angelia flared her nostrils and snapped, 'Exactly!' She immediately felt guilty. It wasn't Josh's fault that Dane's ego couldn't cope with the adoration she received. She could hardly cope with it herself and it had been ten years. 'Sorry, I shouldn't be taking this out on you.'

He shook his head. 'Hey, it's okay. Like I said, you're my best friend, Angel.' These days, being known as Angelia was a distant memory. Everyone, even her parents, had resorted to calling her Angel and for the last ten years that's who she had become. Initially she had loved that it had been Josh that had coined the name because she had harboured a crush on him since long before she even joined the band. These days she was happy that those feelings had mostly subsided. He sipped his coffee before adding, 'I don't want to be the reason you're upset. I wouldn't hurt you for the world. You know that.

And you *will* meet someone. I have every faith that the right guy is out there, waiting in the wings for the right moment to rock your world.' He smiled.

If only I believed that was true, she thought as another wave of melancholy washed over her.

After countless romances that had ended in tears, Angelia just wanted to meet someone who didn't care about the fame. Someone down-to-earth who wanted to be with the real *her*. Someone who didn't want to compete with her, who she could just be herself with, who wouldn't mind seeing her without makeup, and with her hair all messy. Someone who she could watch sad movies with, and who would cuddle her and pass her tissues as she ugly cried, undeterred by the snot and red eyes. Someone who adored Angelia the person and not her Angel persona. Because underneath it all she just wanted to be loved.

Most of the time it was the fame that put an end to things. Either the fact that she was shadowed everywhere by security, or that she couldn't just go home to meet his parents or attend a family wedding or birthday party at the drop of a hat, or that her schedule took her away for months at a time. And then there were men like Dane who, now she looked back on it, were trying to hijack her spotlight so they could have it shine directly on them instead. They would be welcome to it really. It could be very tiresome. Exhausting even.

She thought back to some of the dinner dates she had been on with Dane, and how he stopped to pose for the paparazzi at every given opportunity, when all she wanted to do was get into the car and go home rather than be dazzled by camera flashes and subjected to calls of, 'Angel, darlin', look this way!' or 'Give us a smile, sweetheart!' when she really didn't feel like it. And how Dane would do interviews with newspapers and magazines without her knowledge and would divulge private things about their relationship. At the time she had put it down to love. He wanted to tell the world how much he loved her, and it was so sweet that he wasn't embarrassed to talk about the things they did together. But now, maybe with thanks to Josh's insights, she saw that he was fame hungry and would do anything for attention. And then it dawned on her; he had never actually said he loved her out loud.

She could have slapped herself. How had she not seen it? Josh was right. And her anger being aimed at him was actually a deflection from the one who deserved it – *herself*. Because if she really thought about, truly reflected on their six months together, deep down she had known all along he was in it to advance his career. But she had told herself lies for so long in a desperate bid to feel wanted and loved.

God, she was pathetic.

'What's up with yous two?' the band's lead guitarist, Heath, asked as he slid into the seat beside Angelia.

'Dane the pain's dumped Angel by text message,' Josh said before Angelia could respond.

Heath scoffed. 'Ugh! No way! The dick. Never liked the arsehole anyway,' he said with a sneer. 'He was a vain prick and he *wasnae* good enough for our Angel,' he added for good measure, nudging her with his shoulder. 'I'm sorry though, Angel. Break-ups suck.'

It's all right for you, you're married and head over heels in love, she thought but she forced a smile. 'Thanks,' she said, hoping she sounded more positive than she felt.

He pointed at her. 'You know what you need to do, don't you?'

'Go find someone and have revenge sex,' Josh interjected, wagging his finger at his bandmate and nodding emphatically as if it was the most obvious solution. '*Lots* of revenge sex.'

Heath glowered at him. 'That's not what I was going to say at all, dipshit.' He turned to Angelia. 'You need to write about him in a song. Let all your anger and vitriol out in poetry. But be subtle about it. Use only things he would know about so it's like a secret message. A secret middle finger at him.'

Josh smacked his hands on the table and then gave a single loud clap as his eyes widened. 'Aye! Like Taylor Swift! That's a grand idea. You should totally do that.'

'Who should totally do what?' Bear asked, yawning and scratching the curly mass of hair on his head that resembled a bird's nest, as he walked over from the direction of the bunks. He was wearing shorts and a crumpled T-shirt, and his face was red and puffy with sleep.

'That arse of a second-rate footy player, Dane, dumped Angel by text message,' Heath informed him.

Bear scrunched his nose as if a bad smell had arrived beneath it. 'Oh my God, I've been looking for an excuse to punch that *bawbag*. Now I have the perfect reason!' He squeezed his huge frame in beside Josh.

'You'll do no such thing, *Baird*,' Angelia told him in a warning tone.

Bear's eyebrows shot upward. 'Ooh, shit, Sunday name, she means business, lads,' he said in a theatrical whisper as if she couldn't hear him.

It was like having four overprotective big brothers, including Dom, the band's keyboard player. Thank goodness for their female rhythm guitarist, Anouk, or she might drown in all the testosterone.

'I appreciate you caring about me, guys,' she told them. 'But I'm a big girl and I can look after myself, thank you.'

'Speaking of looking after yourself, how are you feeling now? How's your throat?' Heath asked. Angelia had been having a few issues in recent weeks, her voice had seemed weaker and she had tired easily. Notes she could usually belt out had been harder to achieve but she had put it down to general fatigue; it had been a long tour, after all. She'd had issues swallowing food and her eyelids, arms and legs had felt weighted down, too, but she hadn't mentioned that to anyone. And thanks to encouraging audience participation, she had managed to get away with the bizarre situation for the most part. But Heath was very observant. Annoyingly so.

'Oh, I'm fine. Just ready for a break like we all are, I suspect.' She was aware her reply was a little curt, but she didn't want to dwell on it too much because she was known for overthinking and panicking herself unduly. 'Now if you'll excuse me, I'm off to have a nap.'

Heath moved out to let her pass. 'You sure you're okay, Angel?' There was a look of sincere concern in his expression.

She nodded. 'Perfectly fine,' she lied.

Josh said, 'We're going to go through the set list for the Radio City charity gig. Don't you want to have some input?'

She smiled. 'No, it's okay. I trust you. Keep the noise down though, eh?'

Once out of her seat, she made her way up the narrow corridor towards the bedroom she shared with Anouk to a chorus of, 'Yes, boss!'

Thankfully Anouk must have been in the shower, meaning Angelia had the room to herself, for a short while at least. She closed the door behind herself and slumped onto her bed. The tears she wasn't going to shed began to flow and she angrily swiped them away with her sleeve. She would cry it out and then get on with her life. Because this was just a little blip. She would get over it. She wouldn't give up on love. Because Josh was right, there was someone out there for her. There had to be.

But she had been dumped so many times in the last ten years that she was getting a complex. Was it really the fame or was it just her? Was she unlovable? She sincerely hoped not.

3

The night of their charity event at Radio City Music Hall arrived and Angelia was excited to be back in New York, her second home since joining the band, to play their acoustic set. The Lorelie Dean Foundation had been set up prior to Lorelie's death in order to further research into the rare type of heart condition that had taken the singer's life too soon. The band's record company Blue Demon Records had arranged the gig with guest performers, and upcoming stars, The Errant Brothers, a trio of actual brothers from New York who played funky rock music. Heath had discovered them on a rare night out in the city a year before and had recommended their management team sign them. He clearly had a good eye for talent. The brothers were extremely talented guys and had snapped up the chance to support Angel and the Fallen so the high-end black-tie event was publicised and had completely sold out within an hour of tickets going on sale.

Now the night had arrived, Angelia stood in front of the full-length mirror in her dressing room and smoothed down the black velvet of her fitted gown. It was strange to be wearing such formal clothing when the band was so used to jeans and leather, but she liked the change. She wasn't so sure the guys would feel the same, however.

'You look stunning, Angel,' her Welsh personal assistant, Meghan, told her, adding, 'But I hope you can breathe because wow, it sure is fitted.'

Angelia pursed her lips and crumpled her brow. 'I can't say it's the most comfortable thing I've ever worn but it's a really lovely dress. And anyway, deep breaths are overrated.' She giggled but then turned to face her assistant. 'Although, you don't think it's *too* tight, do you?'

'Oh, heck no! That's not what I'm saying at all. You look incredible. If I looked like you, I'd be wearing that stuff all the time. No, you look absolutely gorgeous.' Meghan, originally from Cardiff, was a pretty woman in her late twenties, around five feet five inches tall and curvy, with shoulder-length brown hair and thick-rimmed glasses. She had studied PR at university in London and remained there for work once her course had finished. When she had first been employed by Den at the management company to assist Angelia, the guys had nicknamed her Velma after the *Scooby Doo* character which Angelia had chastised them for. They soon grew to respect her, however, when it became evident that she was a black belt in Judo, a part-time certified Krav Maga instructor, and an all-round tough cookie. In addition to this, she was incredibly efficient and very good at her job. Where Meghan was concerned, looks were definitely, 100 per cent deceiving.

There was a knock on the door and Meghan answered it. 'Oh, hi, Ms Locke, I had no idea you were here. Come on in,' she said as she stood aside.

Angelia and the Yorkshire actress had been friends ever since *Scotland Rocks* and they would meet for dinner when in the same city, which sadly wasn't as often these days since Ruby had drastically reduced her Hollywood commitments once she had become a mum.

Ruby stepped into the room and gasped. 'Bloody hell, Angel, you look incredible!'

Angelia giggled, her outspoken friend certainly didn't mince her words. 'Thanks, Ruby. It's so lovely to see you.' She hugged her tightly. 'It's been far too long.'

'It has. And I'm so sorry to hear about that rat dumping you by text message. I couldn't believe it when you messaged me to tell me. What an arse. I hope you know you deserve so much better.'

Angelia scoffed. 'So people keep telling me. But I'm yet to believe it.'

'Hey, it's true. The right man is out there.'

'Hmm, well, I think I'll be swearing off dating for a wee while. I'm sick of getting dumped.'

'Not all men are as immature as Dane Bakker, you know,' Ruby said. 'In fact, you'll have to let me know when you're up for dating again because I know someone who I think would be *perfect* for you. He's an actor you'll no doubt have heard of. He's gorgeous, sweet and I think he could be just what you need. No rush though. But I know he loves the band and has a crush on the lead singer.' She gave a theatrical wink.

Angelia smiled. 'Thanks, but I'm still smarting a little from what happened with Dane. It may be a while, I hope you don't mind.'

Ruby waved a dismissive hand. 'Don't be daft. He doesn't know I'm talking to you about him so it's not a problem.'

Angelia wrapped her arms around her body and tried to eradicate thoughts of her footballer ex. 'Thanks, Ruby. I was really excited when I found out you were in New York. So, what brings you over this time? Another premiere?'

'Actually no. Mitch is with me this time, and for once it's a romantic weekend away instead of a work thing. My mum and dad are looking after Rosie so we're making the most of the "us" time.'

Angelia pictured the pretty little girl with her fiery red curls who she had seen and chatted to on video calls. 'Oh, I bet they're loving that, getting to dote on their granddaughter.'

Ruby rolled her eyes. 'Hmm. Let's just say she may only be a toddler, but she knows how to wrap them around her finger. Mitch keeps suggesting we call her. He misses her so much.' She shook her head and smiled. 'And of course she's such a daddy's girl.'

Angelia couldn't help wishing she had a Mitch in her life. He and Ruby were simply meant for each other. 'That's so sweet. It'll be lovely to see him. It's been ages.'

'He said the same. We'll have to meet up for dinner before we leave. Anyway, I'm missing the support act, so I'd better go. See you after the show.' They hugged again and Ruby left.

Tickets for the Radio City show had, in Angelia's opinion, been sold for extortionate amounts of money. But regardless of that fact, people were keen to be there, all dressed up in their finery, to see Angel and the Fallen and their supporting guests, The Errant Brothers, play their acoustic sets. Special merchandise had been designed with all the profits going straight to the charity. The band were in high spirits because, not only was it a very worthwhile cause, but it was to be the last gig of their latest tour around America which had been incredible, but incredibly draining too. Angelia was mostly looking forward to a few weeks off to recharge her physical and mental batteries.

Radio City Music Hall was a wonderful Art Deco venue decorated in golden hues with marble and Bakelite accents; the acoustics were incredible thanks to the fact that the stage in the auditorium had a wonderful curved canopy designed to resemble a sunrise and even though the ceiling was a massive eighty-plus feet above the seating it felt quite intimate compared to some of the places they usually headlined. In fact, the evening promised to be a little more relaxed and perhaps subdued than their usual energetic performances. They were to be in a fixed place on a candlelit stage which would be a huge change from stomping around it. Although she wasn't sure she could stomp in her dress even if she had wanted to.

There was another knock on her dressing room door and when Meghan opened it this time it was Heath and Josh.

'Well, look at you boys,' Angelia said, grinning at the two suited men who looked about as comfortable as she felt.

'I feel trussed up like a bloody Christmas turkey,' Josh said, tugging at the collar of his shirt and grimacing. The tattoos that covered his entire upper body were only just visible, peeping out from where his hands emerged from his suit jacket sleeves.

'Aye, we're going to melt out there under the lights in this get-up,' Heath said with a huff. 'I don't get it, they've paid to see Angel and the Fallen, not the New York Philharmonic, so I don't get why we have to dress like this. Everyone knows what we usually wear for our shows.'

'Oh, stop moaning and lighten up, you two,' Meghan said. 'It's for charity, remember. And at least you can breathe. Take a moment to think about your lead singer.' She gestured towards Angelia. 'She's been pretty much poured into that dress.'

Josh cringed as he looked her up and down. 'Aye, it is tight, Angel.'

Heath whacked his arm and, without turning to face him, said to Angelia, 'You look great though.'

Josh scowled and rubbed his arm. 'I didn't say she *didn't* look great, did I?'

'For goodness' sake, it's like being in the room with my little brothers,' Meghan said with a deep sigh and a shake of her head as Angelia watched the whole thing unfolding with amusement. Meghan was like a mum chastising her children; a usual state of affairs.

Bear poked his head around the door, but his eyes were covered by his hand. 'Are you decent?'

'Have we ever been?' Josh asked with a chuckle.

Bear removed his hand from his eyes and stepped into the room. 'Oh, you guys are in here. I was just coming to ask Angel if she'd seen yous. Anyway, The Errant Brothers went down a storm. They're done now, so we're up.'

'Right, folks, let's get this road on the show,' Heath said; he said it before every gig as if it was a lucky talisman of a phrase.

* * *

They walked out onto the stage to a loud applause, but it was much tamer than they were used to; no whistles or screams of 'Dom! I want to have your babies!'

The band looked smart, if a little odd with their shaggy hair, stubbled chins and tattoos poking out from their sleeves and collars of their evening suits. Anouk wore a flowing black gown akin to something Stevie Nicks would wear, and Angelia quietly wondered, with no little envy, why the stylist had not put her in something similar.

She perched on the stool, as much as the tight fitting gown would allow, in the centre of the stage as the other band members either sat or stood around her and the spotlight shone down on her as the guys began to play their first song.

The start of the night went well, the audience were responsive and clearly having a great time, and soon the band appeared to have forgotten that they weren't happy with their attire as they vibed along with each other, smiling and seemingly enjoying themselves. But as the night wore on, Angelia's legs began to feel like lead and her eyelids were doing their best to close but she put it down to the bright lights overhead and the myriad late nights she'd had in recent months.

Determined not to let the audience down, she rallied as she looked out at the sea of people swaying in time with their number-one hit ballad that she had co-written called 'Without You', and she smiled. It was always surreal hearing her own lyrics being sung back to her and she loved it so much. She took a deep breath and aimed for the G5 in the finale but much to her concern she found the note, that she usually sang with ease, completely out of reach. It shocked her, and more than a little panicked, she turned to face Heath, who frowned briefly, clearly surprised too. He gave an infinitesimal head shake and smiled, clearly trying to ease her fear and encourage her to carry on. She quickly changed to the octave below and, thanks to the acoustic nature of the set, it sounded okay. Although not as good as Angelia was used to. She was nothing if not a perfectionist.

Worryingly, it happened a couple more times in other songs and she even resorted to holding the microphone towards the crowd for their participation, in the hope of disguising her struggle. Thankfully the audience seemed none the wiser and revelled in this and the band received a standing ovation at the end of the evening.

Once the show was over and the band were backstage, Angelia swiftly retreated to her private dressing room where Meghan helped her out of the dress and into a beautiful Japanese robe she had purchased on the Asian leg of one of their tours.

'You were amazing as always, Angel,' Meghan told her, as she hung the dress back on its hanger. 'The change in "Without You" was unexpected but I liked it.'

Angelia chewed the inside of her cheek. 'Hmm, it wasn't intentional. I just couldn't hit the note tonight.' She shook her head and sighed as she rubbed her hand up and down her neck over her throat. It wasn't particularly sore. 'I'm not sure what's going on. It felt weird… like there was a restriction on my vocal cords.'

'I'm not surprised with how skintight that dress was. It's like I said earlier, it's a wonder you could breathe, let alone sing.'

Angelia sat and stared down at the array of creams and lotions on the desk before her. 'I'm so wiped out, Meghan. It was a struggle to even hold the microphone up. What's that all about?'

'I don't know but maybe…' Meghan fell silent for a few moments, and Angelia turned to face her.

'Maybe what?'

Meghan sighed. 'Look, it's none of my business… but… you've been tired a lot lately and of course the tour has been full on but maybe you should go see a doctor and get checked out. You might be anaemic or something. Or lacking some vitamin or other. I dunno.'

Before Angelia could answer with a protest there was a knock on her dressing-room door. Meghan answered it.

'Hey, Angel, I just wanted to check you're okay,' Heath said as he stepped into the room. Like Josh's accent, Heath's Inverness twang had softened to the point he sounded more American than Scottish these days.

Angelia smiled at his reflection in her dressing table mirror as she wiped the makeup from her skin. 'Yeah, I'm fine, thanks. I think I'm just coming down with a cold, that's all.'

'Aye, no doubt. It'll be the air conditioning on the bus, I reckon. Sean's had the lurgy for a week now. We'll blame him, eh?' He chuckled.

Sean, their driver, was a middle-aged man with at least fifty tattoos, a huge beard, shaved head, and arms like tree trunks. Nothing much fazed him, but he had been coughing and spluttering for a while, so Heath was probably right.

'Yeah, my eyes have been quite heavy, and my arms and legs too. It'll be just my luck to come down with the flu right as we take our break.'

Heath walked over and placed a hand on each of her shoulders. 'Get some vitamin C down you. And get plenty of rest when you get back, yeah?'

Angelia nodded. 'I will, don't worry. What do you and Agda have planned for the break?'

Heath had met his Swedish wife, Agda, when she styled the band for a photo shoot while on their European tour before Angelia joined. She was originally from Uppsala and her parents still lived there. Heath and Agda now had a four-year-old son, Rosco, who was the spitting image of his daddy. Even at his tender age, the boy was bilingual and already learning to play the guitar, professing his desire to be a 'wock star just wike daddy'. He was such a cutie and was at that age where he questioned everything. Heath kept them all amused with updates on his latest enquiries; the most recent being, 'Why do dogs have four legs and can't talk but people only have two legs and can?' Everyone had been amused by his supposed correlation between limbs and the ability to vocalise.

'We're taking Rosco back to Uppsala to see his *mormor* and *morfar*. He can't wait, bless him.'

Heath had often spoken of Agda's parents, so Angelia felt like she knew them. Keeping the smile on her face, she replied, 'Aww, that'll be lovely, make sure to send me plenty of photos.'

'I will.'

'How is Agda doing now?' Angelia asked with genuine concern. Agda was in the midst of her second pregnancy and had been exhausted but refused to stay home, regardless.

'She's much better now. I just wish she'd actually do what the midwife has told her to do and stay home to rest. You women can be so stubborn,' Heath replied with a laugh and a shake of his head. 'I'm hoping she'll at least listen to her parents when we get there. Hey, you could always hop over to Sweden for a few days if you get bored.'

'That's good to hear. But I won't be bored, don't worry. I'm heading to my flat in London to do some online property shopping, and some songwriting too. Might see my doctor and have a bit of a physical while I'm at it. Although I'm sure I'm just run down.' She glanced sideways at Meghan who smiled and gave a single wink.

'More property, eh? You'll own half the world at this rate. Where are you looking to buy this time?'

Angelia had always kept a check on the housing market both in the US and UK and had earmarked a few she was interested in that were coming to auction very soon. 'I've seen a couple on the Isle of Skye that I'm looking into.'

Heath nodded. 'Cool, your first property close to your actual home, eh? And I bet you can't wait to see Scrappy. How is the little dude? I've missed having him around this month.'

'He's great,' Angelia replied as she smiled at the memories of her little salt and pepper miniature schnauzer. 'Getting spoiled rotten by the dog sitter just now from the photos he's been sending me. But you're right, I can't wait to see him.'

The little dog, who had been the smallest of his litter, hence his name, had become the centre of Angelia's world since she adopted him as a nine-week-old puppy. Scrappy's mother, Luna, had been handed in to Battersea Dogs Home while heavily pregnant with him and his two siblings, when her owner couldn't afford her care any more. Angelia had read an article online about the dog and it had been her intention to adopt Luna but thankfully she had found a loving home as her pups reached an age that it was safe to rehome them. And at that point Scrappy had stolen her heart.

'Well, take care and give the little guy a belly rub from me. And the offer stands about visiting if you change your mind. Agda would love you to come and visit so she can take you shopping again.' Agda had a real eye for detail and Angelia loved shopping with her because she made her step out of her comfort zone and try on things she would never even consider if she was by herself. Heath's phone pinged to notify him of a message, and he glanced at the screen. 'Ah, I'd better get going. Agda's feet have swollen and she's tired out.' In Angelia's opinion, the beautiful Swede was glowing, but it was clear this pregnancy hadn't been quite as easy as her first.

'Aww, give her a hug from me. Enjoy your break.'

'You too. Keep in touch and I'll see you in the studio in a few weeks. And don't forget to get your Taylor Swift on and write that revenge song, eh? I can't wait to hear what you come up with.' He grinned, and with that he left.

Angelia had been involved in the songwriting for the band from day one and the guys had all said she had a real talent for capturing raw emotion with her poetry. She wasn't sure she could be bothered wasting her energy on writing revenge songs but she'd had so many lyrics floating around her mind recently as she had reminisced about her feelings for her best friend, Ed, and how she couldn't help thinking they could have been perfect for each other.

4

A few days later, Angelia was at her Hampstead apartment, staring at numbers on her laptop screen as Scrappy slept at her feet. Beside her laptop sat a plate with an unfinished bagel upon it. She had struggled to swallow the bread and had decided it must have been too dry so had abandoned it.

The luxury apartment Angelia inhabited in a gated block on Frognal Rise had been an obvious choice at the time she had purchased it eight years earlier, because at the time the rest of the band had lived close by, too, except for Dom, who had favoured New York to be close to his partner, Rio. Meghan lived in London as well, which was helpful, and it was such a vast city with a dense enough population that Angelia almost had the luxury of wandering around unnoticed. Baseball cap atop her head and sunglasses perched on her nose, she blended in just like all the other celebrities trying to live incognito in 'the Big Smoke'.

As the property auction began live at the venue in Glasgow, Angelia watched and listened from the comfort of her home. Her heart pounded, as it always did on these occasions; they were quite a rush. Her mobile phone was beside her on the table with the speaker turned up to full volume and she chewed on her thumbnail as the auctioneer rambled an almost incoherent string of words, until, at the end, she heard something she understood very clearly.

'Sold! Telephone bidder.'

Her heart skipped a beat as she listened to the gavel hit the auction block and she silently fist-bumped the air when the deep Glaswegian accented voice at the other end of the call informed her, 'The property is yours, Miss MacAuley. Well done. I'll email the paperwork right over.'

'Thank you, Richard. As always, your assistance is appreciated.' She ended the call with her UK-based real estate agent and glanced up to find Josh watching her from his position on the floor in front of her vintage vinyl collection. He had stopped in to visit while Nancy attended a beauty appointment at a salon on Finchley Road. 'What?' she asked with a shake of her head.

He narrowed his eyes. 'So, you've bought another property without seeing it in real life, eh?'

She shrugged. 'I couldn't exactly get there, could I, seeing as I was otherwise occupied entertaining the masses of the US? My dad viewed it for me, though. He said it has loads of potential.'

'Where's this one?' Josh asked as he turned again to flick through the records, pulling out any that caught his interest, to examine them more closely.

'It's in a really pretty little village on Skye called Glentorrin.'

He turned to her again and tilted his head. 'Ah, so not too far from your folks then?'

She smiled and nodded. 'A little less than an hour.'

He placed the vinyl he was holding back into the slot and came to sit beside her at the dining table where she had set up a makeshift office.

'I hope you put that back in the right place, Baron,' she told him with narrowed eyes.

He held up his hands. 'Of course I did. I wouldn't dare mess with the system; you know where I live and I'm not risking you letting the air out of my tyres.' He chuckled.

Aside from Scrappy, Angelia's record collection was her pride and joy. She had albums dating back to when the first LPs were introduced in the forties and took great care of them, some would say to the point of obsession.

'I don't get it,' Josh said. 'Why do you keep buying houses you're not going to live in?'

She smiled and nudged him with her shoulder. 'Same reason you buy sports cars you never drive.'

He feigned hurt. 'They're an investment, I'll have you know.'

She raised her eyebrows. 'Exactly!'

Josh was ten years her senior and had been with The Fallen Angels, as they were first known, from day one as an original founding member. All these years later, the band had seen no let-up in popularity. In fact, Angelia had pretty much been on tour since she'd signed her name on the dotted line following *Scotland Rocks* a whole ten years earlier. She had never looked back. But she was her father's daughter; any money she made she invested and what better way than to buy up abandoned and derelict properties and bring them back to life?

'So have you got a family or organisation in mind for this house already like you usually do?' Josh asked as he bent to scratch Scrappy behind his ears. Since joining the band and making her first considerable amount of money, Angelia had worked with charities for the homeless, and had purchased a string of properties to refurbish that would act as temporary housing for families in difficult situations or support centres where homeless people could seek medical help and a warm meal. And while she was able to afford to do so she had no intention of giving this up. She was often talked about in the press for her philanthropy, but it wasn't always positive. She had been accused of doing things for clout, even though she had never sought publicity for her acts of kindness, quite the opposite in fact.

Pondering Josh's question, she paused for a moment. This property wasn't like the others, however. It was a shop with a two-storey apartment over the top and was situated two doors down from a little bakery on the inlet of Loch Alsh. It was the tallest of the properties situated around the inlet and had been empty for a number of years due to an absent owner whose identity was a bit of a mystery, so it was in need of repair and plenty of TLC.

She remembered visiting Glentorrin with her parents when they were either leaving or returning to the island via the Skye Bridge and knew it was a picturesque old fishing village that comprised pretty little white-painted houses that surrounded an inlet of water. She remembered the small museum there that was housed in an old lifeboat station that was perched on the end of a row by the old slipway. There was a general store, a church and a pub, and a newly built village hall too. She knew this because her good friend, famous actress, Ruby Locke, lived there with her husband, Mitch, and their daughter, Rosie, and when she wasn't filming Ruby held dance classes in the hall. It seemed like the kind of place you could settle down and be happy. Maybe even live peacefully in spite of your notoriety; well, that is if Ruby's life was anything to go by. Angelia had done an online virtual walk around the village an hour before the auction had begun and the place looked just as she had remembered it. Scenic, beautiful, peaceful.

Realising she hadn't responded to Josh, she shook her head. 'Sorry, no family nor plans yet. Not at the moment. It needs a fair bit of work first.'

He stood and walked over to the window. 'Why don't you just spend your money on you? Buy yourself a bigger place in the London suburbs? You love this city and it's where you spend most of your time when we're having a break from shows. You could get a place with a huge garden for Scrappy.'

On hearing his name, the two-year-old salt-and-pepper miniature schnauzer lifted his head for a moment, huffed out a seemingly disgruntled sigh when no treats nor belly rubs were forthcoming, then trotted across to the couch, jumped up and went back to his favourite pastime, sleeping on his back with his legs in the air.

Glancing around her plush North West London apartment, only a stone's throw from Hampstead Heath, Angelia could understand why Josh had asked the question, but London wasn't, and never would be, *home*. It was exciting and vibrant, of course, convenient even, but secretly she missed the times when life was simpler, when she could walk down a street and not be hounded by people. When she could walk into a department store and select clothes for herself instead of relying on a stylist. A time when she could just see her friends for drinks at a bar in Glasgow or Edinburgh and not have to plan every get-together with the precision of a royal state visit. And a time when she didn't need a bodyguard to accompany her when she simply wanted to go out for fresh air with Scrappy. London did allow her a certain amount of anonymity but it felt impersonal for that reason too.

'I don't want or *need* a bigger place here, Josh. Unlike you I'm single and this place already has two bedrooms I don't use.'

'Yeah, but what about Scrappy? He'd love a big garden to play around in, wouldn't you, buddy? One he didn't have to share with that monstrous little chihuahua from the flat below. There are some pretty amazing detached houses with great outdoor space on the outskirts of the city.' Scrappy gave a couple of disinterested wags of his tail but didn't bother to open his eyes this time.

Angelia already felt guilty about the times she'd had to leave her four-legged bestie and had taken to having the dog accompany her on tour every time it was possible. When it wasn't, either her assistant, Meghan, looked after him or he stayed with a professional dog sitter named Billy whose father was a millionaire movie producer. Scrappy did love his walks on Hampstead Heath and Angelia was plagued with guilt that she couldn't walk him there as often as she would like.

There was a buzz on the intercom and Angelia walked over to answer it.

'It's only me, Angel,' came Meghan's voice over the speaker. 'I have something I think you need to see. Is Josh with you?'

Angelia glanced over to where her friend sat, now listening with apparent intrigue. 'He is, why? What's wrong?'

'Buzz me in, please, and I'll tell you everything.'

Angelia did as requested, and within moments Meghan arrived holding a pile of newspapers and wearing a worried frown. 'Something needs to be done about this. It's getting ridiculous,' Meghan insisted. 'Why do reporters think that just because people work closely together they're sleeping together too? It's like they're trying to recreate the Fleetwood Mac drama in every single band, all over again.'

She slammed one of the papers, *The Headliner*, which specialised in gossip relating to pop and rock stars, down on the dining table and jabbed a finger at the headline.

HAS ANGEL FINALLY FALLEN… FOR HER DRUMMER?

This was accompanied by a photo of Josh and Angelia hugging by the tour bus and a caption that read:

Angel and the Fallen's lead vocalist Angel MacAuley and drummer Josh Baron get cosy while on tour, sparking new rumours as to the reasons for Dane Bakker split.

The photo had been snapped from a distance and had been taken completely out of context. Meghan went on to read the article aloud.

A source close to the band told *The Headliner* that the pair have always had a 'strong connection' and that it was only a matter of time before the inevitable happened. They also confirmed that MacAuley and Baron have been spending time alone together at her Hampstead apartment. Meanwhile Miss MacAuley's jilted lover Dane Bakker, who has recently been spotted out with actress Lucille Delgado, has declined to comment, stating he wishes 'to keep his private life private'. Another close contact who wished to remain anonymous claimed that Josh's long-time girlfriend Nancy Carey is in the process of moving out of the home she shared with the drummer in West London.

Angelia pulled her lips into a line and shook her head. 'Why do these people insist on lying like this when they know full well it could cause irreparable damage?'

There had been speculation, not too long after Angelia had joined the band, that she was having an affair with Heath. It had, of course, been completely unfounded, and Den and the management team had done everything they could to stop the rumour mill from turning. Then a new batch of gossip had spread that Angelia was secretly having an affair with Dom, this was the most ridiculous rumour as Dom was very much gay and out publicly, but the rumours claimed that his relationship with a professional male tour dancer for Taylor Swift, Rio Morales, was a cover-up for the affair with Angelia. The band had laughed these things off and everything had gone quiet for a few years, until a year earlier when Josh and Angelia had been under the microscope. Every photo of them together had been accompanied by speculation and regardless of the fact that the whole band had denied these false claims, they had got to the point where the tabloids were using versions of the Queen Gertrude line from Hamlet: 'The lady doth protest too much, methinks.' The band had, therefore, given up reacting.

Angelia had found it exhausting. She had confessed to Fiona and Ed that she was worried Nancy, Agda and Rio must think of her as a serial man chaser.

'I mean you know what they say about smoke and fire,' she had said on one of their regular video calls.

'Angelia, we know you better than anyone and we know you're not that kind of person, honey. It's just rumours,' Fiona had assured her.

'Yeah, and if they weren't blabbering about you it'd be someone else. They must be having a slow news day. Load of bollocks and they know it,' Ed had added.

Thankfully, when she approached each of the partners in question, backstage at one of the shows, they had all shrugged off the rumours as crazy and had reassured her they were used to such nonsense and simply ignored anything printed in the tabloids.

'I hope Nancy hasn't seen all these,' Meghan stated, pointing at the papers with a scrunched nose as if they were emitting some foul odour.

Josh sighed deeply, rubbed his hands over his hair and then picked up his phone. 'I'll message her. Although I know what she'll say.'

'What will she say this time?' Meghan asked, a hint of exasperation to her voice. 'The more it happens, the more suspicious she must get.'

Josh smiled and shook his head. 'Nah, she knows me and Angel are good friends. She knows we've never even come *remotely* close to crossing any lines.'

Angelia felt her face warming. She knew it was only a matter of years ago that her crush on Josh was still raging beneath her skin. It had been a sort of distraction from the devastatingly unrequited feelings she'd had for Ed. 'I've always seen Josh as the big brother I never had,' Angelia said, hoping she sounded convincing, even though she knew there was a time she would've done anything to just kiss him.

Meghan huffed. 'Well, I still think we need to get Den onto *The Headliner* and get them to retract this article. They need to publish an apology. And what does Dane think he's doing, "declining to comment"?' She made inverted commas in the air. 'He could've put this rumour to bed with one sentence. He bloody dumped you for Lucille Delgado, for goodness' sake.'

Angelia gasped. 'He did? I thought he had got together with her after.'

Meghan's face coloured cerise and her eyes widened. 'Shit. I mean—' She closed her eyes briefly. 'Oh God, you were going to find out at some point, but I didn't mean for this to be the way.' She chewed her lip as Angelia stared at her, waiting for an explanation. 'I was chatting with his PR assistant last week and she told me he started seeing the actress behind your back while you were on the Canadian leg of the tour. I'm so sorry, Angel. I really didn't mean to blurt it out like that.' She flopped onto the couch and Scrappy jumped into her lap. 'Don't cuddle me, Scrappy, I'm a traitor.' She huffed and lowered her head.

The truth stung but Angelia knew it wasn't the messenger's fault. 'It's fine, Meghan, honestly. I'm actually surprised I hadn't heard sooner. And yes, in that case he could've helped stop the rumour, but why would he do that? This way he not only gets sympathy but a mention in *The Headliner*. All publicity is good publicity as far as he's concerned.'

She turned to face Josh. 'Put yourself in Nancy's shoes though, Josh. She sees all these articles questioning our relationship. How must that make her feel? She must be sick of it by now.'

He lifted his hands and let them drop heavily back to his sides. 'What can I say to convince you that you really don't need to worry, Angel? Nancy knows how close we are, and she understands. And we've done nothing wrong. You and I have never even had a drunken kiss, let alone slept together. It's not like we're actually *having* the affair the media is constantly accusing us of having.'

Angelia closed her eyes briefly. 'No, but... maybe we should keep our distance for a while. Just until they've moved onto someone else.'

Anger crumpled Josh's brow and he stood. 'Why should we do that? It just makes us look guilty, don't you think so, Meghan?'

Meghan sighed. 'Honestly, I have no clue what to even suggest at the moment. I'll speak to Den this afternoon.'

Josh turned to Angelia again. 'Like I said, you're my best friend.' Pain was evident in his strained tone and downturned expression. 'I need you in my life, not just as my bandmate. I don't see why we should let people stomp all over our relationship and dictate what we do.'

She walked back across the room to where he sat. 'But you love Nancy. You're *in love* with her and regardless of what she says it must be a strain on her to keep listening to people speculate about how faithful you are. In her shoes, I know I'd certainly wonder.'

'So, you're saying we shouldn't be friends now? Just because of some dick-head reporter who's got nothing better to do with his time?' Josh asked with a scoff of disbelief.

'I'm not saying that at all. But I'd hate to be part of the reason she gave up on you. And maybe this whole situation isn't helping me either. I've been dumped more times than I'd like to admit, and I do wonder, after this latest revelation, if perhaps I need to have some time away. If the men I've had in my life can't get past the bond you and I have then I'm never going to find someone, am I? And I would so love to find someone for myself, Josh. Someone who'd actually stick around for the right reasons.' Ed's face sprang to mind and she shook her head to dislodge the unhelpful image.

Josh remained silent and Meghan looked like she might cry. 'I'm so sorry, guys, I can't help feeling I've opened a ginormous can of worms.'

'No, Meghan, this isn't your fault. It's not even yours or mine, Josh. But we have to stop the rumour mill. It's not fair on anyone, least of all Nancy. We need to have some distance. Maybe it would be better if you stopped coming here alone. Maybe we need some time apart... Like properly apart, you know? Some real time and distance. Maybe that would help.'

He laughed lightly. 'You're talking like you're thinking of quitting the band or something.' When she didn't reply, the colour drained from his face and he swallowed hard. 'You're *not*...' He turned to Meghan and gestured towards Angelia. 'She's not leaving the band...' He turned to Angelia again. '*Are* you? I mean, I know you've been having some vocal issues, but you just need rest. We're not playing again until next month so...'

She smiled, picked up the cloth napkin that sat beside her unfinished bagel and whacked him with it. 'You can't get rid of me that easily.'

He heaved a sigh, and she watched the pinkish hue rapidly return to his cheeks as he ran his hands back through his dark brown shaggy hair. 'Don't scare me like that again.' He glanced at his phone. 'Look, I'd better get going, Austin's messaged to say he's waiting with Nancy.' Austin, the band's personal driver in the UK, was a huge wall of a man. He had served in the navy and feared nothing. Except wasps. Angelia recalled a time they were backstage at Wembley Stadium and Austin had come along with his daughter who was a fan of the band, and a rogue yellowjacket had found its way in, somehow, and made a beeline (pardon the pun) for Austin. He had squealed like a total wuss and run around, frantically waving his hands, screaming, 'Get it away from me! Get it away from *me*!' his deep London accent sounding rather high-pitched and completely out of character with his imposing frame. Angelia smiled at the memory.

'Oh, and just to put your mind at ease,' Josh added, 'Nancy has messaged to say she's seen the latest articles at the salon and has told the people who she overheard talking about it that it's a load of bullshit. But she's finished at the salon now and has a dress to pick up for the film premiere tonight.'

Angelia tried to smile. 'That's good to know. Anyway, which premiere are you going to again?'

'It's the new Florence Pugh one. I can't believe you're not going too. She's a huge fan of the band. She'll be gutted if you're not there.'

She scrunched her nose. 'Nah, like you said, I need to rest. And anyway, I might take the opportunity to get some work done on that song I'm writing for the new album.'

He smiled. 'The revenge one? Brilliant.' He bent to scratch Scrappy's belly. 'Bye-bye, fuzzy butt. I'll see you soon.'

Angelia laughed. 'I hope you weren't referring to *me* as fuzzy butt.'

He winked. 'You may never know.' He grabbed his jacket from the cream leather couch and walked over to where she stood. He pulled her into a hug and said, 'Take care of you.'

She nodded. 'Likewise.'

Josh turned to Meghan. 'Bye, Meghan. Let me know what Den says about the article.'

Meghan nodded. 'Will do. I'll walk down with you.' She hugged Angelia. 'I'm really sorry, Angel,' she said again.

And with that, Angelia watched her assistant and Josh, his tall frame clad in his signature black, exit the apartment.

* * *

In the silence that now surrounded her, she walked across the open-plan living area with its white walls, adorned with modern art chosen by her former interior designer – extortionately expensive artwork she now hated – to her grand piano, and sat. She played the first few bars of the song she was writing, not the revenge song about Dane, however, instead this was a song no one would ever hear because it was about her first love, Ed. She sang the first two lines: 'I look to the stars and wonder if you're wishing on them, too, although it hurts so much to know I can never be with you...' She shook her head and rolled her eyes. She turned in her seat and called over to Scrappy, 'I definitely need to meet someone, Scraps. I'm turning into a reincarnated Emily Dickinson with my sad lyrics, and that won't do at all.'

She huffed and stood again. 'I suppose I should clean up, eh?' The dog sat and, with a tilted head, watched her retrieve the plate with the unfinished bagel on from the dining table, and he gave a single bark. 'Oh, you want this?' she asked, pointing at the plate with a wry smile. 'It's pastrami, I'm not sure you like it.' The dog barked again. Pastrami was his absolute favourite. She giggled. 'Oh, you'll eat it, anyway? Just to help me out?' Another bark, his tail now wagging frantically. She placed a hand over her heart. 'Okay then, I appreciate your sacrifice.' She pulled the meat from the bread and tore it into small pieces before feeding it to her four-legged companion who relished every bite.

She thought back to when it had been freshly made, and she had attempted to eat it. She recalled that, in addition to struggling to swallow, she had found chewing quite difficult too. It had been strange. Disconcerting even. But she told herself it was merely exhaustion. Touring was gruelling, after all.

5

After a couple of incidents involving Angelia stumbling while out walking Scrappy, Meghan had nagged over and over, insisting that she should contact her doctor to arrange an urgent appointment, and Angelia had eventually capitulated, simply to stop her assistant from badgering her constantly. An appointment had been made for the following Monday to rule out anything sinister, but Angelia presumed she would be prescribed some vitamins and iron tablets and be sent on her way. She felt a little like a fraud as when she rested, the symptoms eased drastically.

She wouldn't have admitted it to Meghan, but after going over the recent strange symptoms she had experienced, Angelia's mind was full of worry and 'what ifs', so in order to distract herself she contacted Ruby, who was home on Skye, to ask her to set up a date with the handsome actor she had mentioned.

Ezra Harwood was a six-foot-five blond English man with vivid blue eyes around five years Angelia's senior. He was the epitome of what a superhero looked like: muscular, handsome, wholesome. He had a reputation for being a nice guy, too; there had been plenty of clips of him visiting children's hospitals to give out Christmas gifts the previous festive season. But he wasn't Angelia's type traditionally; he was quite the antithesis of the green-eyed, dark-haired orchestra musician she had loved from afar for years.

'Yay! I can't believe I get to set you up. You'll adore Ezra, I think. He's so sweet. Perfect husband material.' Ruby's excitement was evident in her high-pitched voice at the other end of the call.

Angelia laughed rather loudly. 'Steady on, Rubes. It's a first date, don't go buying a hat yet.'

'Sorry, I know, I'm just a bit giddy. He's in London this week on set so I'll give him a call. He might be free tomorrow night.'

Angelia widened her eyes and tried not to retract her admission of availability. 'Oooohkay, that's fast.'

'They're heading off to New York early next week and I know he won't want to miss an opportunity to take you out.'

Angelia rubbed her eyes and nodded, even though Ruby couldn't see her. 'Okay. Okay, go for it. Anyway, enough of that, what are you up to today? And what's the weather like?' It was a sunny mid-April Friday in London, but Angelia knew it could appear to be a totally different season up north.

'It's a bit overcast just now but we're hoping it burns off. You know what this place is like though. Four seasons in a day. I've got a dance class to teach at eleven and then we've got community cinema tonight at the hall. Me and the girls have been keen to get the Ralph Fiennes version of *Wuthering Heights* shown on the big screen and thanks to Jules and Morag doing some research we've finally got the licence.'

Ruby spoke of her group of female friends in Glentorrin as if they were family and Angelia couldn't help wishing she was a part of their ensemble. She had never met these women but could tell from what she had gleaned from chats with Ruby that she would love them all. Jules ran the Lifeboat House Museum, and her husband, Reid, was an artist; Caitlin was the village baker, and her husband owned an outdoor clothing shop and campsite; Morag ran the shop with her husband, Kenneth; Millie had her own marketing company and her husband was a mechanic; Stella owned the pub with her partner, Joren; and Bella was an interior designer, and her husband was the local police inspector. All down-to-earth women living fulfilling, normal lives. Angelia had almost forgotten what that was like.

'That's exciting. I think that has to be my favourite version,' Angelia replied.

'Mine too. Well, sorry to cut and run, lovely, but I'd better get going. I need to drop Rosie Posie off with Caitlin. Her daughter, Grace, is babysitting for me seeing as it's the Easter break. Rosie adores her and Jules's son, Evin.'

'Aww, so sweet. Well, I hope the weather picks up. I'll wait to hear from you about Ezra.'

* * *

On Saturday morning, Angelia awoke to a message from Ruby:

RUBY

Hey, honey. I'm so excited you agreed to go on the date with Ezra. He's looking forward to meeting you. Table booked for 7.30 at The Ivy in the West End tonight. Let me know how it goes!

Feeling a little unsure, she hadn't responded at first, instead she had dressed and taken Scrappy for a walk on the heath at 7 a.m., and had been star spotting as she always did. She had seen a couple of actors and a pretty, petite blonde female pop singer who had smiled sweetly as she jogged by pushing a stroller. Angelia had to do a double take because as she got level to the stroller a little head popped up, but instead of a baby there was an ugly scrunchy-faced dog that barked at Scrappy and almost made her jump out of her skin.

She had gone out with the intention of clearing her head and pondering on what the evening might bring. But above all she needed to think about why she was, in fact, apparently unable to sustain a long-term relationship when her friends could. What was it about her, she wondered, that made men get so tired of her. It was turning into a pity party for one and as she walked back to her apartment, baseball cap pulled low over her face and hair tucked up inside it by way of remaining incognito, she realised she had made no progress at all.

An hour later, Angelia was sitting on her sofa in her yoga pants and a T-shirt after an attempted workout at the gym in her building. She had struggled to lift the weights she normally managed with ease and was once again concerned but told herself she maybe just needed to persevere, build stamina, eat better. She had given up and made her way back to her apartment and even though it was only just after 9 a.m. she already felt like heading back to bed.

She walked into her dressing room and stood in front of racks of clothes, staring blankly. It hadn't been that long since she had been out for dates with Dane but for some reason, she was in a massive fluster about what to wear for the impending date with Ezra. The Ivy was a much-loved celebrity haunt that she had been to a few times with the band, but those occasions were relaxed and casual, a gathering of friends who she had no need to try and impress. She had no clue what to wear for this evening.

She decided to video call Fiona for some moral support and perhaps to ask her advice. Fiona was in a long-term relationship with a high-school maths teacher called Marcus who she had met at a conference, and the pair had seemed to fall instantly in love. They now shared an apartment on the outskirts of Edinburgh, and a cat called Biffy after Marcus's favourite band Biffy Clyro.

'So, are you going to tell me who your date is with or is it top secret? You know I won't contact TMZ, don't you?' Fiona giggled. 'I wouldn't even know how to contact BBC Scotland, for that matter. I'm just so glad you're getting out there. I want you to find someone as wonderful as Marcus,' she said dreamily. 'And Dane Bakker definitely wasn't it.'

Angelia sighed. 'You and Marcus are the perfect couple. I'm so jealous. I want to find myself a Marcus too.'

'And this guy might just be the one, you never know. *And* it will take your mind off worrying about the Josh rumours. I so want you to be swept off your feet. So come on, spill it.' Fiona had known about Angelia's crush on the drummer since long before she was signed to the band. And she was very much aware of the pining that her friend had initially endured. What she didn't know, however, was that the man Angelia actually wanted was Ed. She had never been able to admit this one tiny fact for fear of ruining the dynamic of their wee trio of a friendship. In addition to this, saying it out loud would mean it was real, and so was the fact that she would never be with him.

Angelia was suddenly nervous at the prospect of divulging the details. She cleared her throat. 'Erm... Okay, so...' She cringed and closed her eyes for a moment. 'I can't believe I'm saying this but... I'm going on a date with Ezra Harwood.' She held her breath and waited for her best friend's response.

Fiona gasped. 'You're kidding! The hunky actor? The guy who was in *All the Heroes*?' Her words came out in a giddy rush. 'The guy who's built like a tank and could pick you up and fling you over his shoulder one handed?'

Angelia opened her eyes and felt the heat of embarrassment rising in her cheeks. 'The very same.'

'I can see that you're blushing! Does that mean you really fancy him? I hope so!' She clapped her hands together. 'It's funny, though, I didn't really put him as your type. I mean he's the total opposite of Dane... and he's nothing like Josh either. How did this all happen?'

Angelia told her friend, 'Ruby set us up. Apparently, he's a huge fan of the band and has wanted to meet me for a while now, so she and I have messaged back and forth, and she's told me bits and bobs about him and in the end, I thought why not? I've heard from Meghan that Dane cheated on me with Lucille Delgado and they're now an item. He didn't mess around so why should I?'

'Damn right, honey. You deserve to be happy. And if that's with a tall, well-built, sexy actor then so be it. It's tough but someone has to do it.' Fiona winked into the camera. 'What are you wearing? Where is he taking you?' She frowned and tilted her head. 'Are you having to take security along too? How does that even work? Do you have to feed your security guard if they come with you? Do they sit at the table with you?'

Angelia laughed. 'Good grief, Fee, all you need is a bright light to shine in my face.' She held up her hands in surrender. 'Okay, okay, I'll tell you everything!'

Fiona joined in her mirth. 'Shit, sorry, that did sound a bit like an interrogation, didn't it? But go on. I'm all ears.' There was a noise in the background and Fiona turned and called over her shoulder. 'Hey, sexy, I'm in the kitchen talking to Angel.' She turned to face her phone again. 'Marcus has been at the footy while I did some marking.' A hand appeared in front of Fiona; it was holding a bunch of roses. Fiona looked up and smiled warmly, her eyes sparkling with adoration. 'Aww, thank you, they're lovely.'

Next a face appeared and kissed Fiona's head before turning to the camera. 'Hi, Angel. How are you doing?'

Angelia smiled. 'I'm good, thanks, Marcus, you?'

'I'm good, too, thanks. I'll leave you ladies to chat, bye for now.' He shook his head. 'I still can't believe I get to chat to the lead singer of Angel and the Fallen like it's a normal thing to do.' And with that he disappeared.

Angelia giggled. 'I feel the same way about talking to you, Marcus!' she called after him. He said that exact thing almost every time he spoke to her.

By now she was sure he was taking the mickey, but she still found him funny.

'So, you were about to tell me everything?' Fiona said, clutching her bunch of flowers as Biffy the cat jumped onto the table to investigate, his little grey ears back as he sniffed suspiciously at the pink petals. 'Hey, Biffy Aloysius Clyro, you're not allowed up here. Go on... shoo!' Biffy gave a meow of protest and disappeared again. Fiona glared at the screen expectantly.

Angelia laughed out loud. 'The cat has a middle name? And it's *Aloysius*?'

Fiona shrugged. 'You're telling me Scrappy doesn't have one?'

'No, but I think he needs one now! Perhaps Theodore?'

Fiona grinned. 'Come on, MacAuley, you're using avoidance tactics. Spill it, where is the giant specimen of a man taking you?'

'Okay, so, no, I'm not taking security. And we're going to The Ivy. They're used to well-known people dining there so there'll no doubt be someone more famous than us for people to get excited about.'

'The one in the West End?' Fiona asked and Angelia nodded. 'Ooh, I've seen it on TikTok. You're right, all the stars love that place. I've heard it's Madonna's favourite restaurant, if you bump into her you have to get a selfie.' She winced. 'Sorry. Go on...'

'Anyway, I have no clue what to wear. Hence the real reason for my call.'

'I'd go jeans and a nice top. Maybe a sexy top. But don't get too dressed up, because from what I've seen online it's a fairly casual place. I like that teal short-sleeved Nina Picarro one. I've always been jealous of that top. It's gorgeous. And I think your black velvet jeans, so you're sort of dressy but in a casual way. Oh, and of course strappy heels.'

Angelia knew she had made the right decision in contacting her best friend. She could envisage the outfit, and it was perfect. 'Thanks, Fee, that'll work really well. Hey, just a thought, have you heard from Ed lately?'

Fiona nodded. 'Aye, he's touring with the New York Philharmonic for a short time, didn't he tell you?'

'Wow!' Angelia shook her head as a wave of sadness washed over her. 'And no, I haven't heard from him in a few weeks. I'm not sure why.' Ed had originally landed his dream job playing for the Scottish Chamber Orchestra, but this latest snippet of news had passed her by. 'I'm happy for him though. He must be over the moon.'

'Aye, it's only a temporary gig but he was dead happy about it. And don't take it personally, hon, he's just really busy. He never talks for long when I call him. And his replies to my messages are usually very short.'

'At least he messages you back,' Angelia replied, wondering what, if anything, she had done wrong.

'I don't think he gets much down time, to be honest. He's dating someone new though. Her name's Ava and she's a cellist. She's Australian.'

'Aw... that's nice.' Angelia's heart sank. She was a little disappointed to have heard it second hand too. 'I'll message again and pester him until he replies.'

Fiona giggled. 'Good plan. Persistence is key! Anyway, let me know how the date goes. I'm excited for you.'

Angelia smiled. 'Thanks. I will. I'm so nervous.'

'Aww, don't be. Just be yourself and he will adore you like the rest of us.'

* * *

After checking her appearance one last time in the mirror and applying a little more nude gloss to her lips, Angelia ran her fingers through her long chestnut waves and huffed.

'I'll have to do, Scrappy,' she told the little canine who watched her every move with apparent intrigue. 'Be a good boy and Mummy will be back soon, okay?' She kissed the top of his head and made her way down to the foyer where she was greeted by the concierge, a middle-aged man called Malcolm. He informed her that her driver was waiting just outside.

'Evening, Miss MacAuley,' Austin said as she climbed into the back seat.

'Hi, Austin. Thank you for picking me up but I could've got a tube or a cab. I'm sure you have better things to be doing with your Saturday evening.'

'Nah, you're fine, miss,' he replied in his London drawl. 'Den insisted you had a chauffeur in case there are any paparazzi around. I'm to collect Meghan before I come to pick you up later. Again, just in case...'

Angelia silently rolled her eyes but kept her opinions to herself.

Ezra stood as she approached the table at the back of the restaurant. He towered over her as he bent to kiss her on both cheeks. He smelled incredible; fresh, clean and very expensive. 'Wow, you look beautiful,' he said as he pulled out her chair.

'Thanks, you look lovely too,' Angelia said as her stomach flipped. He really was very handsome in the flesh. As she scooted her chair in, she knocked into the table leg and a bottle of water on the table wobbled over but Ezra caught it before it could hit the tiled floor. *Impressive*, she thought.

A waiter came to hand them menus and take an order for drinks. Ezra was the perfect gentleman.

'What would you like to drink, Angelia? I'm happy to have whatever you like.'

'I'm afraid I'm not that daring so a glass of Sauvignon Blanc will be fine for me.'

Ezra looked up at the waiter. 'Make it a bottle with two glasses, thanks.'

The waiter left them, and they both pored over their menus. 'Everything sounds so good,' Angelia said as her stomach rumbled a little too loudly for her liking. She glanced up but thankfully Ezra hadn't noticed. She had been too anxious to eat during the day, so she was just about ready to eat a horse – but only if it was made of tofu considering she was vegetarian.

'It does. But then again, I love the food at this place,' Ezra replied. 'Well, I think it has to be the pan-fried seabass for me. I hear theirs is one of the best.'

'Hmm, I think I'll go with the wild mushroom carnaroli. I've had that here once before and it was incredible.'

The waiter returned with their wine and took their orders for food. Once he had left again Ezra said, 'Thanks for agreeing to a date with me.' His cheeks flushed pink. 'I've been a fan of your music for a long time now but… I suppose I've been a fan of yours since you joined the band.'

Angelia felt her face warming. 'Th-thank you.' She wasn't sure what else to say.

'Sorry, I didn't mean to embarrass you,' he said with a chuckle. 'Me and my big mouth. So, what do you do when you're not singing?' he asked.

'I love to read but my main passion is always music. Playing it, listening to it, collecting vinyl…'

'Oh, so you collect records as well as making them? Cool. Who's your favourite band? And you're not allowed to say Angel and the Fallen because that's cheating.' He smiled.

'I have so many favourites. I have quite eclectic taste really.'

'Okay, so give me some examples.'

She nodded and thought for a moment. 'I love The Darkness, Pearl Jam, Evanescence… but I also love Taylor Swift and Lewis Capaldi. And I have a soft spot for old Scottish music too. Eddi Reader is my hero, and I love to hear her sing things like "Wild Mountain Thyme" and "Charlie Is Ma Darlin". You?'

His smile widened. 'You weren't joking about having eclectic taste. I'm more of a Harry Styles fan myself,' he said with a chuckle of what appeared to be embarrassment. 'But I also love Fleetwood Mac and eighties rock bands like Bon Jovi and Def Leppard. I saw Taylor Swift on her Eras tour and she was amazing. Tons of energy. So what's your most prized vinyl album?'

Angelia paused to think for a moment. 'Well, now, there's a tricky one to answer. Hmm... Probably my 1968 original pressing of Aretha Franklin's *Aretha in Paris* with the red and plum label. It's not the most valuable record I own but it's one of my favourites because it's hard to come by and I found it in at a record fair in New York.'

'Oh, I love Aretha Franklin. "Respect" is one of my all-time favourite songs,' Ezra said with a wide smile.

'Same!' Angelia replied, matching his enthusiasm.

They chatted easily for the rest of the evening and had little in common but enough to talk about, nonetheless. Angelia was surprised at how relaxed she felt in Ezra's company, but something was missing and she couldn't put her finger on what that was. He was attractive, intelligent, funny... She decided she was putting too much pressure on herself, because on the face of it he really should have been her ideal man. *Maybe it's because I'm still too in my head about what happened with Dane*, she thought. *Maybe I just need to give it time.*

6

During the evening Angelia had heard all about Ezra's family and how his younger sister, of whom he was clearly very proud, had studied medicine at Oxford and was currently doing a residency at a hospital in London. His mum was a retired opera singer and his father a theatre actor. They seemed like such a wonderful family – very close-knit and they sounded like people she would enjoy getting to know. To top it off they had been left alone all night, no starstruck waiting staff – something that didn't tend to happen at The Ivy anyway – no autograph- or selfie-hungry diners. So, all in all, it had been a lovely date.

At the end of the evening, they made their way outside and stood around the corner from the entrance to the triangular-shaped building waiting for their respective drivers. It was a reasonably warm April evening, and the sky overhead was a deep royal blue dotted with tiny specks of silvery white.

'I've had such a great time tonight, thank you,' Ezra said, smiling warmly.

Angelia nodded. 'Me too. Thank you for inviting me.'

'Maybe we should do it again soon?' he asked, hope evident in his bright expression.

She smiled, thinking that perhaps that might be a good idea because there was nothing wrong with this man so far, so the issue was no doubt all in her head. 'That'd be lovely,' she replied.

Two black cars with tinted windows drew up to the kerb simultaneously which made a few passersby stop and take note. Angelia couldn't ignore the sinking feeling that accompanied occasions like this where she just wanted to blend into the background and be 'normal'.

Ezra paused for a moment and then glanced around, clearly feeling something similar, judging by the serious expression that had replaced his smile.

He leaned in a little and whispered, 'I'd really like to kiss you. Is that okay?'

Angelia wasn't sure how to react but wondered if maybe it might help to make her feel more intensely for him, and she really wanted to feel something because on paper he was perfect for her, so she simply nodded.

Her eyes fluttered closed as he lowered his face and paused before his lips touched hers. And for the first time in ages, she felt absolutely... *nothing? Seriously? What the heck?*

After a brief moment, he pulled away and their eyes met.

'Oh,' he said and guilt flooded her as she noted disappointment cross his features. What was he going to say? That it was like kissing a mannequin? Because that's sort of how she had behaved. He cleared his throat. 'Erm... Sorry but... Was that as awkward for you as it was for me?' he asked with a crease between his brows.

She gasped and pursed her lips. 'I'm sorry? What did you say?' For a split second she was rather affronted by his bluntness.

Camera flashes illuminated them out of nowhere. Austin appeared and was joined by another suited man, presumably Ezra's driver, who walked over from the direction of the other car, the pair then did their best to block the path of the intruders.

Ezra closed his eyes briefly, stepped away and held up his hands. 'Shit, Angelia, I'm so sorry,' he said. 'I'm a total prat. I sincerely apologise for what I just said. I didn't mean to be so blunt. You're beautiful and I've had this crush on you for so long that I just thought...'

Realisation hit Angelia and she burst out laughing as relief flooded her veins.

He raised his eyebrows and shook his head, a half-smile on his face as if he was unsure what to make of her reaction. 'I'm funny to you?'

Angelia pulled her bottom lip between her teeth for a second and released it with a cringe. 'Oh God, I'm so sorry to laugh. But if I'm honest it's relief. Because... I felt...'

He tilted his head and narrowed his eyes. 'The same?'

She nodded. 'Exactly. I feel absolutely horrible admitting it because we seem—'

'Like the perfect couple!' he said, holding out his hands.

'Yes! Exactly!'

He covered his mouth with his hand for a moment and his brow creased again, only this time in disbelief. 'Yeah, I felt like I was kissing my cousin or something. Ruby's going to be so disappointed.'

Angelia nodded. 'I know. I feel bad about that too.'

He smiled. 'We had such a fun night, and we do have stuff in common. And for the record I think you are so beautiful. I just... there was no—'

'Spark!' she blurted. 'I know! It's absolutely crazy to me because you're handsome, funny, you have a close-knit family like I do. You're creative and you understand the whole fame thing...' She sighed. 'It really makes no sense whatsoever.'

He sighed. 'So, what do we do now?' he asked, genuine concern in his eyes.

She held out her hand. 'Friends?'

He took it and a wide smile spread across his face and his eyes crinkled at the corners. 'Friends.'

More camera flashes ensued and Ezra stepped in front of her to shield her from the paparazzi that had appeared like stealthy spies at their location. This time there were shouts of, 'Angelia, is this your new boyfriend? What about your affair with Josh?' And, 'Ezra, what's like dating one of the world's most well-known rock stars?' And, 'Are you two getting married then?'

They both ignored the barrage of questions and kept their attention focused on each other.

Angelia smiled up at him. 'Look, I know this hasn't worked out how it was supposed to but... I really would like to keep in touch. I've had a lovely night. Would that be weird?'

His eyes lit up. 'I'd love that. We definitely have a great friendship blossoming here. I'd love to stay in touch.' He held out the crook of his arm. 'Shall we?'

She linked her arm through his and they made their way towards their awaiting cars as Austin and Ezra's driver stepped in to obstruct their photo opportunities.

A few more opportunistic paparazzi had arrived now, no doubt attracted by the growing crowd. More photos were snapped as they approached their vehicles, the flashes a stark contrast to the hitherto otherwise dark night lit only by the stars and the fairy lights around the restaurant's exterior.

'Come on, Miss MacAuley!' one of the photographers shouted out in a strong East London accent. 'Throw us a few crumbs, eh? Will we be seeing more of you together? Can we have an exclusive?'

Angelia glanced up at Ezra and they both smiled but said nothing in reply.

Austin opened the door of Angelia's car and Meghan sprang out of the back seat. 'Hey boss! How did it g—' She stopped abruptly and clamped her lips together when she realised Ezra was still beside Angelia. 'Shit,' she mumbled and then smiled dreamily. 'Good evening, Mr Harwood, I trust you had a delightful meal.'

Angelia couldn't help laughing at the sudden loss of the Welsh accent that had been replaced by upper-class English. 'Crikey, Meghan, are we suddenly in an episode of *Downton Abbey*?' She turned to Ezra who had remained silent up to this point and realised he was staring at Meghan. 'Ezra, this is my... *friend* Meghan Parry. Meghan, this is Ezra Harwood.'

Meghan held out her hand, her face flushed cerise now and she did a little curtsey on the pavement. 'Lovely to meet you, Mr Harwood.'

He took her hand and almost whispered, 'Please, call me Ezra. And it's... it's lovely to meet you, too, Meghan.' He swallowed and his face also tinged pink.

Angelia giggled. 'Erm... I think we need to make some more arrangements for a date,' she said.

As if suddenly snapped out of a trance, Meghan snatched her hand away and turned to face Angelia, eyes wide and face sapped of colour. 'Oh yes, you should totally arrange your next date. I'll wait in the car. Please don't fire me.' She turned to climb back in the vehicle, but Angelia grabbed her arm.

'I meant for you two!' She glanced up at Ezra who was now only missing the background track of that old seventies song 'Dream Weaver' with the way he was making doe eyes at Meghan.

Keeping his focus on Meghan, Ezra nodded. 'I'd like that very much,' he said absently before turning to Angelia. 'Shit, would that be really weird for you and me?'

Angelia shook her head. 'Not in the slightest. What do you say, Meghan? Fancy a date with Ezra?'

Meghan glanced at Angelia with raised eyebrows and a distinct air of shock. Then, as if realising Angelia was serious, she nodded emphatically. 'Yes, yes, that would be... yes! I mean thank you, boss, erm, Angelia.'

Angelia grinned. 'Okay, I'll make sure he gets your number. Now, can we get home? I need my beauty sleep, and I want to cuddle my dog.'

'Sure, of course. Bye, Angelia,' Ezra said. 'Bye, Meghan.' He said her name as if it was the best word he had ever uttered.

* * *

On Monday morning, Meghan arrived to pick her up for the doctor's appointment, even though Angelia had insisted she was capable of getting there by herself.

'It's quicker if I drive you. And anyway, I can tell you all about yesterday with Ezra,' Meghan had replied. 'Oh, and did you see the news this morning?'

Angelia rolled her eyes. 'The photo of Ezra and me kissing? Yeah, I did. Sorry about that.'

'Pfft, don't be sorry, the vultures will always make mountains out of molehills.'

Angelia arrived at the private clinic on the outskirts of London for her doctor's appointment without much fuss, only recognised by a couple of passersby as they climbed out of Meghan's bright sunshine-yellow Mini Cooper and her assistant ushered her quickly into the building. When it was time for Angelia to be seen, Meghan stood with her and hugged her tight.

'I'm right outside if you need me.'

'Okay, thanks, but I'm fine, *honestly*,' she replied with a smile before turning and entering the consultation room.

'I appreciate you seeing me on such short notice, Doctor,' Angelia told Dr Violet Latimer, someone she had known for the eight years she had been living mostly in London. She glanced nervously around the brightly lit room, her heart thumping at her chest and her palms a little clammy. Posters on the walls showed diagrams of the body and listed various symptoms and the ailments they could indicate. 'I'm sorry about Meghan forcing the issue though. I'm sure it's nothing.'

'Oh, no, don't worry, Angelia, Miss Parry was right to encourage you to be seen, she clearly cares a great deal for you. And I can't have you out of action for recording your next album. I'm so looking forward to hearing it. So, what brings you here today?' the grey-haired, well-spoken woman asked with a tilt of her head and a genuine smile. Angelia guessed she was in her late fifties and was full of admiration that she hadn't succumbed to the Botox craze.

Angelia went on to describe the bizarre list of symptoms and watched for clues as the doctor sat, elbows resting on her desk, fingers steepled and a crease of concentration between her brows. The doctor then asked a series of questions including some around when the symptoms were at their worst, and if repetition of certain activities exacerbated things, and when Angelia answered she made copious notes on the file before her.

When she was done talking, Dr Latimer examined her, testing her grip and ability to raise her arms and legs against resistance. Once she had finished, she sent Angelia along to the nurse who drew some vials of blood. Angelia hated blood tests and was glad when she was back in the doctor's room. Dr Latimer sat behind her desk, her expression a mask of stoic professionalism. 'Okay, Angelia, I'm going to refer you to a friend of mine. Dr Novak is a neurologist on Harley Street and he specialises in autoimmune conditions. The blood results may take a while, but I have a feeling I know what could be going on so I'd like to get his opinion.'

Angelia felt the colour drain from her face and she swallowed through the tightness closing her throat. 'A neurologist? Autoimmune conditions?' She shook her head and gave a nervous laugh. 'That... that sounds serious. I presumed I needed iron tablets... or... or just rest. W-what exactly do you think is wrong?' She could hear buzzing in her ears now and the bright white room seemed brighter still.

Dr Latimer smiled in what Angelia presumed was supposed to be a reassuring manner. 'Try not to worry. I'd just like to get him to run you through some specific tests so we can ascertain what's going on here. There are a couple of things we could be looking at but I'd rather get his expertise on things before I go telling you something that may not be accurate. Most people take a partial diagnosis and suddenly become qualified doctors after Internet searches. Next thing you know they're giving away all their worldly possessions, or buying motorcycles, or taking up paragliding. I would rather you just wait, and we'll see when Harry can fit you in. I know we shouldn't make exceptions for people, but I've known you a long time and I'm very much aware of your schedule and the effect this is having on your ability to work. I also know you'll want answers pretty fast, and we'll aim to make that happen, but you will have to bear with me. Can you do that?'

Angelia stared blankly for a few moments, every possible horrendous scenario hurtling around her head. Realising she hadn't answered, she swallowed and nodded. 'Erm... yes... yes, of course.'

'You've gone very pale, Angelia. Would you like a glass of water?'

Without speaking, Angelia nodded again and Dr Latimer stood and walked over to the water dispenser at the opposite end of the room. She returned a moment later and handed Angelia a small disposable cup. With a shaking hand, she took the drink and sipped it while trying to process what had, and hadn't, been said.

* * *

When they were back in Meghan's car and on their way to Angelia's apartment, Meghan huffed. 'That's a bit shitty, that is. You can't go saying things about autoimmune conditions and then not say anything else. Was she trying to make you panic?' Meghan's Welsh accent thickened when she was cross. 'I think you should ring her back, I do. Make her tell you what she suspects.'

Angelia watched the streets of London pass by the car window; people were going about their business, walking their dogs, shopping, eating takeout sandwiches, chatting on mobile phones; all seeming to do so without a care in the world. 'I'm not even sure I want to know at this point, Meghan.'

'Is there anyone you'd like me to call for you? Maybe you shouldn't be alone right now?'

Angelia made an unladylike snorting noise. 'Oh, no! No, don't be daft. I'm fine on my own. There's no point panicking until I know there's something to panic about. And don't say anything to the guys either, please. I don't need them all fussing over me.'

'Fine. I'm staying with you then,' Meghan informed her. 'And I can ring your mum and dad if you—'

'No!' Angelia's heart leapt. 'No, please don't do that. There's nothing to tell them at this point and if you call them, they'll drop everything and come down to London which is silly. Honestly, I'm fine on my own and I'm sure you have other things to be doing. I think it's just the talk of neurologists that's scared me a bit. But I'm okay.'

Meghan sighed. 'You're so stubborn,' she said with a good-natured smile.

'I know. I think I just need a distraction. So, come on, tell me about what's happening with Ezra.'

A wide smile spread across Meghan's face. 'We chatted on video call yesterday. He's so lovely and we totally lost track of time. So, then he said he was starving and asked if I fancied meeting him at a pub close to his hotel. We sat in this cosy little nook and ate pie and chips and talked loads more. I feel like I've known him ages, Angel.' She sighed dreamily. 'He said the same about me.'

'That's so sweet. I'm just sorry again about the photos of me and him kissing in the paper this morning.'

'Like I said, you don't need to apologise. Who'd have thought it, eh? Me sitting in a pub eating steak and kidney pie and chips with a gorgeous, famous actor? I can't believe it. I never expected him to be so down-to-earth. He sounds like he'd be into oysters and foie gras.' She giggled. 'I can't believe it's actually happening.'

'Well, it certainly is. The way he looked at you, Meghan,' Angelia said with a shake of her head. 'I think he's besotted.'

Meghan jiggled in her seat. 'I think I am too.'

7

For the rest of the afternoon, Angelia sat on the sofa with Scrappy who couldn't seem to get close enough to her. He clearly sensed something was amiss. He was such a sensitive wee soul. With one hand she stroked his fur while the other was clutching one of her many copies of *Wuthering Heights*, her go-to book when she needed a distraction, her favourite book *ever*, a book she had over one hundred different versions of – it was more than a book to her. She tried to immerse herself in the chaotic relationship within the pages, the angst and turmoil that was Cathy and Heathcliff, but her mind kept wandering off until she eventually gave up and decided to nap. Scrappy snuggled into her, his head resting just under her chin, and they both fell asleep.

She was woken by her phone vibrating itself towards the edge of the coffee table. Scrappy leapt up and barked as she reached and rescued the handset just before it collided with the oak flooring. The lamps in the room that were fitted with timers had illuminated now, casting a warm glow across the space, and Angelia was surprised that it was pitch-dark outside. She hadn't expected to sleep for so long.

Glancing at the screen, she read the time as 10 p.m. and hit the answer call button in a panic when she saw who was calling. 'Hello?' she asked in a strained voice, rubbing at her eyes and worrying why on earth the surgery could possibly be calling at this time of night.

'Angelia? It's Violet Latimer. Sorry to bother you so late in the day. But I have good news, I've been waiting on a reply from Harry Novak. He's been at an awards dinner and has just replied. He can see you tomorrow. You need to be there at ten thirty. Wear something comfortable like leggings and a T-shirt, okay?'

Angelia straightened up and put her feet down until they touched the floor. 'Oh... oh right, okay. Sure. Thanks, Dr Latimer. I'll be there.' She wondered what kind of doctor's appointment warranted such comfortable clothes, and what she could possibly be letting herself in for.

'And I know it's easy for me to say this but try not to worry. Stress will only make things worse.'

The call ended and Angelia stared at the screen as it faded to black. She turned to the little dog who sat, his gaze fixed on her as if he knew exactly what was going on. 'Well, Scrappy, it looks like I may be getting answers sooner than anticipated.'

She messaged the group chat for the band and let them know what was happening. Luckily Heath and Agda hadn't left for Sweden just yet and the only person not in London was Dom. They agreed to meet at Angelia's apartment during the evening after her appointment. They were all concerned, which she had expected, but she was still grateful.

* * *

On Tuesday morning, Meghan insisted on accompanying Angelia to the Harley Street clinic, and on arrival Angelia was surprised to discover that Mr Harold Novak was a fellow Scot. He had grey hair, and she guessed he was in his mid-sixties. He had kind blue eyes and wore dark-rimmed glasses and a white coat with his name embroidered on the left breast pocket. A lanyard around his neck showed a photo of him from around ten years earlier and beside the photograph it said:

Clinical Neurologist

'Good to meet you, Miss MacAuley. Please have a seat. My grandchildren are huge fans of your music. I'm more of a Schubert man myself. Now, I've heard from Violet Latimer about your symptoms, and I think it sounds fairly straightforward. There are a number of tests we'll need to do to ascertain the level of your weakness but there's nothing to worry about. Nothing too invasive.'

A morning of tests ensued, some of them a little strange in her opinion, involving what appeared similar to acupuncture needles, and electric currents, but Angelia now understood why Dr Latimer had recommended comfortable clothing. Just over an hour later, Angelia sat before the consultant again but this time he had graph printouts laid on his desk before him. Meghan had joined her for moral support and a second pair of ears. Mr Novak had been talking for a few minutes, but nothing was really sinking in for Angelia.

'So, to clarify, the electromyography tested the amount of electrical activity in your muscles. It gave a good indication that there is an issue with messages reaching your muscles via the nerve pathways. This, along with your other symptoms, including the weakness in your vocal cords, and the information Dr Latimer passed over to me, has confirmed my suspicion that you have a condition known as generalised myasthenia gravis.'

Angelia's thoughts whirred around her brain at a hundred miles an hour and she struggled to form anything cohesive from them. 'I'm sorry— myas— *what*?'

The consultant smiled patiently. 'Myasthenia gravis is an autoimmune condition, Miss MacAuley. It's not hereditary, nor is it contagious. Scientists have yet to discover what triggers it, but when it occurs in women it tends to be around your age that it happens, whereas in men it tends to be later in life. To put it in layperson's terms, and I don't mean that to sound patronising but it's important you understand what you're dealing with, it's when antibodies attack particular receptors in your body as if they are the enemy, and this results in fewer signals making it through, ultimately manifesting in muscle fatigue or weakness. And, unlike some conditions where exercise can strengthen and improve the condition, myasthenia symptoms are worsened with increased, repetitious activity, hence the reason for your vocal and chewing issues. It's a kind of interruption of the signals, if you will. It tends to affect the muscles over which you have voluntary control, such as arms, legs, voice, eyes, etcetera.'

Angelia nodded slowly but didn't really understand any of what he'd just said. One horrific thought fought for dominance. 'Am I... am I...' She struggled to get the words out, partly due to shock and partly because she didn't want to ask the question aloud, lest she bring about some kind of negative manifestation.

The doctor smiled kindly now and tilted his head. 'Are you going to die? Is that what you were trying to ask?'

She nodded again as her eyes welled with tears, and she chewed the inside of her cheek until she could taste the metallic tang of blood. Meghan reached across and took her hand, giving it a squeeze.

'Well, we're all going to die someday but I highly doubt you will die of the condition, Miss MacAuley. In days gone by, I will admit the mortality rate was definitely higher. But now that we know more, there are a variety of treatments available, and these are increasing all the time as more and more research is carried out. We just need to work out which treatment is best for your particular case, but rest assured that with careful monitoring most people with this condition go on to live full lives, if a little changed.' He flicked through the papers on his desk and pulled out a chart. 'I was able to expedite your blood results, and they confirm you have the rarer, seronegative – or antibody negative – strain which means certain treatments are not appropriate because the antibodies that most patients have are not found in your blood. We will therefore try some medication. Tablet form. It may take a while to get the dosage just right, but we will get there.' He paused for a moment, placed down the document and intertwined his fingers, resting them on the desk and fixing Angelia with a stern gaze. 'My main concern, however, is your gruelling schedule as a touring musician. As I mentioned before, repetitious movement of the affected muscles exacerbates the condition, but so does stress. And your voice is one of the main things affected. Along with the medication, the only surefire way to deal with this is frequent rest, no more touring, or a complete change of career, I'm afraid. But I am certain that continuing as you are currently will only worsen your symptoms, rendering you unable to tour anyway.'

Angelia widened her eyes as her heart thumped almost painfully at her chest. 'But... no... I love my job. If you're trying to say I need to quit, I can't. I can't let the band down. It's not just my career we're talking about here, Mr Novak; I have a responsibility... a... a contract.'

Meghan squeezed her hand again. 'I'm sure if we talk to Den and the band we can—'

'No. This is my life, Meg. My dream. I don't know who I am without the band. Surely there's something else I can do to make it go away.' Tears spilled over onto her cheeks, and she swiped them away. 'So how do we cure it? Is there a surgery? And how long do I need to rest for? A week, two? A month?' Her words came out in a rush, and she suddenly wanted her mum and dad as she had whenever she was ill as a child.

He sighed. 'I'm afraid it's not something that can be cured, Miss MacAuley, not yet anyway. There is a great deal of research being carried out but we could be years away from a cure. A thymectomy is the only surgery available but it isn't always necessary or recommended because it doesn't work for all cases. Myasthenia gravis is a chronic lifelong condition that requires lifestyle changes. It's more about *managing* your symptoms than curing them and that's where the medication comes in, but it can only do so much, and if you continue how you have been working the medication will give some relief but not enough to sustain that lifestyle. You will most likely need to drastically reduce your performances, or, as I said before, consider a complete change. You do run the risk of worsening your condition otherwise. Myasthenic crisis is the worst-case scenario, which can result in hospitalisation and that's something we want to avoid at all costs. I'm not trying to scare you; I just want you to understand the full implications and severity of the condition.'

Angelia's heart plummeted in her chest, and she exhaled as if she had been punched. 'But... the band... What will I tell them? I can't let them down. And the fans—'

'Miss MacAuley, you will be doing yourself a serious disservice if you don't heed your body's warnings. You've already had several. You cannot sustain a life of touring and singing for protracted lengths of time and expect to be well. That's the reality of it. And I know that's blunt, but you are an intelligent person, and I would be doing you no favours if I sugar-coated this. It doesn't have to be life threatening, but you must make the necessary changes to your lifestyle in order to live as normally as possible.'

* * *

Angelia stared out of the window on the journey home, watching as the rain-soaked London streets passed by in a blur, and the tears were persistent. Her future with Angel and the Fallen seemed to be up in the air and she wasn't sure how to process that. She couldn't reconcile how it would be possible to carry on and deal with this condition simultaneously. What would the guys say? Would they be angry? Disappointed? Meghan periodically reached across and gave her arm a reassuring squeeze. Angelia had tried to talk through her diagnosis in the hope it would make things clearer in her mind but had struggled to do so without her emotions getting the better of her, and in the end, she had instead resorted to silent contemplation and worry. Meghan had clearly been upset but trying not to show it. She had discreetly wiped at her eyes on a couple of occasions and Angelia had felt bad that she couldn't ease her sadness when she was swamped by her own.

When they arrived back at the apartment, Meghan was the picture of positivity. 'You're going to get through this, you know.' She hugged her tightly. 'I'm just at the end of the phone if you need me. I can be here in a flash.'

Angelia nodded. 'Thank you, Meg. I know.'

Meghan sighed. 'I'd much rather stay with you. I don't like the idea of you being alone with this news. I'm worried about you.'

'I'm fine, honestly. It'll take a while for it to sink in, I guess, but I think I just need some time alone to process it, that's all.'

Meghan had reluctantly left and after Angelia had had a good cry, she video-called her parents. It was 2 p.m. and the rain hadn't let up all day, it was if she had brought it on herself with her current mood. She gave them as much information as she could remember and tried her best not to cry but her voice wobbled on several occasions.

'That's it, we're coming down,' Angelia's dad said into the camera. He stood from the dining table where they had set up the laptop so he and her mum could be present on the call. 'I'll contact head office right away and let them know.' It had been the reaction she had anticipated.

'Dad, it's fine, you don't need to rush down here. I'm going to be fine. I'll get the tablets and follow the doc's instructions, and I'll be fine.'

Her mum leaned towards the camera. 'Sweetheart, you're our baby; we want to be with you. This is a huge thing you're going through.'

Angelia nodded. 'Yes, I know, but—'

'I won't take no for an answer, Angelia. You need us. You might not think you do but...' Her dad's expression was filled with worry and her mum's eyes were glassy with tears. If she was honest with herself, all she wanted in that moment was a hug from her parents.

'Look, why don't I come home instead?' she asked.

Her mum straightened her back. 'To Skye? Can you do that?'

Angelia shrugged. 'I'd like to. I mean, I could do with coming to see the property I've just bought in Glentorrin, so you know, two birds, one stone...'

Her dad sat again beside his wife. 'But what about your safety? Fans finding out you're here? You know what happened last time.' He was right to be worried. Last time she had visited home, hordes of fans had camped outside her parents' house and she had ended up having to leave under cover of darkness and relocate to a secret location on the mainland just outside the village of Gairloch. The secret location had been the home of Nick Dacre, lead singer of Sonic Idols, the other band managed by Den.

Angelia huffed. 'That's the only obstacle really. I'll speak to Den, I'm sure something can be done. I'm seeing him and the rest of the band later today to let them know what's going on anyway. We're having a break for a few weeks now the tour is over, so the timing is good at least.'

'What if Den says no? He might think you coming here is too risky.'

Den was a Yorkshireman, an overly tanned one with a dirty laugh. But as a manager he was top notch. Sonic Idols were another huge band, and they had only ever had good things to say about his abilities; what he didn't know about looking after artists wasn't worth considering.

'Let me talk to him and see. He only wants what's best for us all, so I trust his advice.'

'Okay, love. Well, it will be good to see you regardless of whether you come here, or we come to you. I'm going to do some research into this myasthenia thing. I'd like to know what we're up against.' This was typical of her father; he wanted to know all the facts and for them to face every hurdle as a team. It wasn't just Angelia with the condition, they would *all* deal with it, as a family. And he was a great one for approaching things in a pragmatic way; research was always the key. He looked into everything before making any major decisions, whether it be a new car, a new computer or even a new breakfast cereal.

'Thanks, Dad.' Angelia tried not to allow the emotions churning her insides to appear on her face. But her mother knew her all too well.

'Sweetie, don't try to put a brave face on this. You must be so scared. But we'll get through this, okay? You're not going to face this alone.'

Angelia cleared her throat and nodded. 'I know, Mum. And I appreciate you both so much.'

Her mum's chin trembled. 'We know you do, love.'

'Look, I'd better go. I have the guys and Den coming round for pizza so I can tell them. Meghan will be here too because she probably took more in at the appointment than I did.'

'Okay, darlin', we're here any time of night or day. Just drop us a message or give us a call, okay?'

She forced a smile. 'Okay. Bye for now. Love you.'

Her mum smiled through her tears. 'Love you, too, sweetie.'

'Aye, love you, darlin', and remember, *any* time,' her dad added.

She ended the call as the doorbell chimed the arrival of the band.

8

'Jeez-oh, Angel, I've never even heard of it,' Heath said as the band sat in the lounge area of her apartment. 'But you'll get through it, and we'll help all we can.' The crease between his brows betrayed him.

Anouk, who was seated beside Angelia, reached out and squeezed her arm. 'I have actually heard of it,' she said, 'but I've never met anyone who has it. I'm so sorry, Angel, you must be worried sick.'

Josh stood at the window, staring out at the garden below, hands in his pockets, unmoving and silent. It was dark out now and the strings of fairy lights were illuminated, giving the trees a magical appearance.

'And you think going home to Skye for a while is going to help, do you, love?' Den asked.

Angelia nodded. 'I mean, it won't cure me, nothing will, but I'd really like to see my mum and dad. I know I'm an adult and that probably sounds a bit daft but it's how I feel.'

Dom, who was on video call on Angelia's laptop, leaned forward and rested his elbows on his knees. Staring directly into the camera, he said, 'Aye, I totally get that. Don't you, Den? Put yourself in her shoes, mate. The lass needs her mum and dad at a time like this.'

Den held up his hands. 'I didn't say it was a bad idea. I'm just getting my head around it all. There'll have to be planning. We need to figure out the logistics. She can't just turn up at home without us planning the visit, look what happened last time. Her folks were overrun with teenagers wanting autographs. I'm sure they don't want that again.'

'I'm sure it'll be fine, Den. We all go home without issue most of the time,' Heath added with a smile in Angelia's direction.

Bear stood from his seat and walked over to Angelia. He scooped her up in his arms and held her. 'If I could take it off you I would, Angel. This is just shitty. I mean totally and utterly shitty.' He placed her down again and returned to his seat, shaking his head. 'Shitty,' he said one last time. He was a gentle giant, so caring and thoughtful.

'We'll get you the best care there is, babe, won't we, lads?' Dom said with a waver to his voice. 'You just take all the time you need.'

'Aye, we'll get you back on your feet and right as rain, ready to knock your fans' socks off on the next tour,' Den added, glancing around for the agreement of everyone else.

'Don't stress her out about tours, Den,' Anouk snapped. 'She needs to take this one day at a time. You heard what she said about the things that can make symptoms worse. We need to avoid that at all costs.'

Den nodded and his cheeks tinged with pink. 'Oh, yes, of course, sorry, I didn't mean to... I was just trying to be positive. I'll tell you what, I'll contact the studio and push things back indefinitely.'

Guilt niggled at Angelia when she saw the worry in Anouk's eyes and the remorse in Den's. 'Guys, I'm sorry to drop this on you. I know it must be hard after what happened with Lorelie.'

Heath huffed. 'Hey, don't you be feeling bad for something that's not your fault. And don't worry about us. We're big enough and ugly enough to look after ourselves. Our main concern right now is you and your health. There's nothing more important than that right now. We're a family.' He turned his head to peer over his shoulder at Josh. 'Right, Josh?'

As if coming out of a trance, Josh turned. Angelia could see his eyes were red rimmed and bloodshot. 'Sorry, what?'

Heath sighed and spoke through clenched teeth. 'I was just saying that Angel shouldn't be worried about how *we're* feeling just now. She should be thinking about herself. *Right*?'

Josh cleared his throat. 'Oh... aye... aye, right. Excuse me for a minute, I need some air.' He walked through the apartment and into Angelia's study that had a private balcony, closing the door behind himself.

Heath glared after him. 'I'm... erm... just gonna nip to the little boys' room.' He stood and stormed across the apartment in the same direction his bandmate had gone. It was obvious he wasn't going to the loo.

Angelia stood. 'Heath, let me go—'

Heath held up a hand, frowned and shook his head. 'It's okay, Angel.' He disappeared through the same door as Josh and closed it behind himself.

'Please eat, guys, the pizza's going cold,' Angelia said as she stood and walked over to the dining table. 'I'll go grab some more wine.'

As the others finally tucked into the pizza, Angelia sneaked over to the door of her study and opened it a tiny fraction.

'— and I get that it's hit you hard, but Angel needs our support right now. So put her first instead of yourself, will you, you self-centred arse.'

'Hey, I know, I know she does, all right? I get it. I do. But... It hurts too much, man. I love that girl so much and it kills me to know I can't do anything to help her. I feel so damn useless, Heath.'

Heath's voice softened. 'I know, mate, I do. But you need to stop thinking like this, because that won't help her at all. It's a shock but it's not life threatening, it can be managed, changes need to be made, yes, but we'll deal with them together, as and when they're necessary. And to be honest, we were all in need of a break anyway. This just means we get longer, that's all.'

Josh lowered his voice almost to a whisper and Angelia had to strain to hear over the chatter of the others. 'The thing is, Heath... I think... I think I love her.'

Angelia's heart skipped in her chest, and she held her breath as she listened.

'Love her like we all do, or, like *love* her, love her?' Heath asked, a hint of incredulity to his voice.

Silence.

Heath spoke again. 'Come on, Josh, what about Nancy? You talked about proposing to her. You've been with her forever, mate. Are you going to throw that away?'

'Of course I'm not,' Josh hissed. 'I could never be with Angelia. We'd never work because of my deep love for Nancy. But I've been sitting on these feelings for years now and tonight kind of... confirmed it, I suppose. I felt like I'd been gut punched when she told us about this MG thing. I couldn't handle it. I just wanted to scoop her up and tell her everything would be fine and that I would sort it all out, but I can't and that does my head in.' His voice broke and he cleared his throat. 'And the thing is, I know she feels something for me, too, or at least she used to. I could see it in her eyes, Heath. Can you be in love with two people at once?' His voice was strained and filled with pain.

Heath sighed deeply. 'How should I know? I've only ever loved Agda. I've never even been remotely interested in anyone else, so you're asking the wrong person. But my guess is that if you're capable of loving someone else when you're with Nancy there must be something not right there. I mean, you say your love for her is deep but you've been together since high school and you're not even engaged after all this time.'

'I've been going to propose to Nancy so many times,' Josh said, almost pleadingly. 'I've even got the ring. But… something always stops me. She said recently that if I can't commit to her 100 per cent she'll leave. I can't let that happen, Heath. She's the one I'm *meant* to be with but… Angelia came along and… I felt this instant spark. This connection. Like we're soulmates or something crazy like that. She calls our bond an invisible string. She's right except that for me it's something more than just a friendship bond. But I can't act on my feelings. Because I *do* love Nancy. And I need to commit to *her*. So, I need to let this thing with Angelia go. So maybe her going home for a while isn't such a bad idea.'

There was a silent pause and Angelia wished she could see their faces. Her heart hammered and she felt a little lightheaded with shock.

Heath broke the silence after a few moments. 'Yeah… yeah, I think it might be a good thing to get some distance between you because Angel has been messed around enough by dickheads and I won't let you be another one. She's like my kid sister. And yes, I think she had a crush on you when she joined the band, but she had the sense to let that go years ago. You're wasting your time. Just let it go and move on, Josh. She doesn't need this and Nancy doesn't deserve it. In fact, I love you like a brother, Josh, but you don't deserve either of them, in my opinion. Just bloody grow a pair and be a friend to Angel, for feck's sake.'

'Angel, are you going to come and eat before Bear finishes off all the pizza?' Den shouted and Angelia jumped, feeling a little like a kid caught with their hand in the cookie jar.

She felt heat rising in her face and hoped to goodness Heath and Josh hadn't realised she was outside the door, listening in on their very personal conversation, because nothing good had come from it. She ran on her tiptoes towards the kitchen and when she had created enough distance between her and the study she called out, 'Just getting some wine, be there in a sec.'

Her head was spinning, her mind reeling from what she had heard. So, he did feel something for her after all. Although it was useless to have this little snippet of knowledge as she had heard from Josh's own lips that he would never be with her. He might feel a connection to her but his connection to Nancy was evidently stronger. And that was fine really because she couldn't be the one to break them up. Nancy was such a lovely person and didn't deserve any of this. No, it was time to well and truly let this crush go. And her mind was made up.

She was going home.

* * *

The following day, Angelia managed to get hold of both Ed and Fiona and arranged a video call with them at 4 p.m. GMT, meaning it was 11 a.m. in New York where Ed was, to update them on what had happened. Ed sat there, shirtless, in bed, his hair all scruffy and flat at one side. Angelia couldn't help smiling and for a split second imagined what it would be like to wake up next to him. She shook her head and made a joke about his appearance and him being dragged through a hedge backwards.

'Yeah, sorry about the state of me. Late night with The Phil. Then an after party. Absolutely knackered,' he explained through a yawn.

Angelia had gone on to explain the diagnosis she had been given the day before. Fiona was on her Easter break and had been full of positivity and optimism, as always, but Ed had seemed a little shellshocked.

'And they're sure there's no cure?' he asked, his brow furrowed as he stared into the camera.

Angelia nodded. 'They're sure. But they're researching all the time, so you never know.' She tried to sound upbeat.

He had huffed the air from his lungs through puffed cheeks and rubbed his hand over his face. 'Jeez… I don't know what to say, Angel. Are you okay? Shit, that's such a stupid question.' He shook his head. 'I wish I could hug you.'

Angelia had kept it together up to that point but his words and the sentiment behind them made her eyes sting. 'Me too.'

'And are the meds working?' Fiona asked.

'Meghan only collected them today, so I've only taken one. But the doc said they should kick in pretty quickly.'

'Well, I'm coming to see you as soon as I can,' Fiona declared. 'You need your besties at a time like this. But you'll beat it, Angelia MacAuley. I have faith in you.'

'I'll come over as soon as I can too,' Ed added. 'Fee's right. And I... I miss you... both of you.' His eyes appeared glassy and it was a little out of character for him.

'Is everything okay, Ed?' Fiona asked, beating her to it.

He nodded as he rubbed his thumb across each eye in turn. 'Yeah! Oh God, yeah, I'm fine. Just sore eyes. Like I said, knackered.' He yawned again as if to exaggerate his earlier point.

In order to lighten the mood, Fiona told them all about the conversations she had overheard when she had accompanied some of her high-school students to play a concert at a local primary school. The little kids were all seated on the floor in rows and waiting for the concert to begin and it was clear they were excited about the upcoming visit from the Easter bunny, and some of them had been talking about the fact.

'I heard one of the wee ones say to his friend, "If the Easter bunny lays eggs doesn't that make him a chicken?" and the friend replied with, "Nah, don't be daft, Connor, he doesn't *lay* the eggs. My dad says he buys them from the Cash and Carry near Ikea. That's where the farmers drop them off." Then, after pondering this for a minute, the first boy said, "I wonder why they only come out made of chocolate when it's Easter. The ones I have for my breakfast are never made of chocolate." And the other boy gave a deep sigh of exasperation and shook his head before telling him, "Connor, you're a wee dafty, they feed the chickens on special stuff in the lead up to Easter to make them chocolate. Don't your mummy and daddy tell you anything?" It was hilarious... and a little worrying.' The three friends laughed at her stories and the call ended on a decidedly lighter note than it had begun on.

* * *

On Good Friday, later that week, Angelia and Scrappy headed north with Meghan in the little yellow Mini. Angelia had tried to insist that she would make the journey alone, but Meghan wouldn't hear of it.

'Look, Angelia, I think of you as a friend, not just my boss. I would like to come with you, not only to keep you company but if I'm there and there are any issues with rogue fans, or anything else, your mum and dad have an extra person to help out.'

'But what about Ezra? You and he were just getting to know each other.'

Meghan smiled. 'You've heard of WhatsApp and video calling, haven't you?' she said with a nudge to her shoulder. 'And anyway, I don't want to be one of those women who sits around pining. It's just not me. Ezra is away filming in New York, and he calls me when he gets the time but I'm not hanging on the back of the door like some lovesick— whatever lovesick thing hangs on the back of doors,' Meghan said with a giggle. So, Angelia had accepted the offer of a lift rather than flying and having to hire a car.

Meghan had collected her prescription for the next few weeks, and made a Spotify playlist for them to listen to as they travelled. They made a few toilet stops for the wee dog and eventually arrived at Gretna Hall Hotel – just along the road from the famous Gretna Green Blacksmith's Shop wedding venue – where they would spend the night. Meghan had ensured everything was booked ahead of time, so Angelia didn't need to worry, and she had even got special dispensation for Scrappy to stay with them in their twin room.

That night, however, Angelia couldn't seem to switch her mind off and she tossed and turned in bed until she eventually gave up. She put on the complimentary fluffy white robe and sat by the window looking out at the stars overhead, with Scrappy snuggled in her lap. She replayed what she had overheard between Heath and Josh in her mind and then thought about Ed and his reaction to her news. She was evidently in her self-torture era.

The following morning, Meghan ordered room service for them, but Angelia didn't have much of an appetite.

'Why don't you go get some fresh air while I call and let Den know how the journey's going?' Meghan suggested after she had showered and tied her hair up in a ponytail. 'I know you didn't sleep that well so some fresh air might help.'

It sounded like a good plan, so Angelia donned her signature baseball cap and tucked her hair up into it, clipped Scrappy's lead to his collar and set off. The sky overhead was powder-blue and scattered with cotton-wool-ball clouds. It wasn't exactly warm, but it was dry. They walked along the road to the Blacksmith's Shop, the world-famous wedding venue, where a happy couple and their friends were getting ready for the first wedding of the day. The bride wore a stunning long-sleeved ivory lace dress, and the groom a green and blue tartan suit. Angelia stood just out of sight and watched as they snapped group photos with beaming smiles on their faces. She couldn't help the twinge of envy she felt at their happiness. She had always expected to be in a long-term relationship by the time she reached her current age, but alas, it wasn't to be. She turned around and walked back to the hotel where Meghan had packed their things and loaded the car.

As they drove the six remaining hours of their journey to Portree on Skye, Angelia gave up fighting sleep and dozed, waking up for brief intervals as they passed through Glencoe with its dramatic mountain backdrop and then as they passed Eilean Donan Castle where it sat proudly on its spit of land that stretched out into Loch Duich, against a cornflower-blue sky.

It was good to be back in her home country, surrounded by space and every possible shade of green. She felt her shoulders relax as the familiar scenery passed by the windows in a blur as she drifted off to sleep once more.

* * *

By dinnertime that Saturday evening, Angelia was standing in the kitchen of her family home, sandwiched between her mum and dad as her mum sobbed. Scrappy jumped up at Angelia's legs, evidently wanting to be included in the group hug too.

'I'm fine, Mum, honestly.'

Her mum pulled away and held her at arm's length. 'I know, sweetie, I'm sorry, I'm just so happy to see you.' She turned to face the woman standing by the microwave, smiling. 'Thank you for bringing her home, Meghan. And for staying with her.' She walked over and hugged her.

Meghan returned the hug, patting her on the back. 'It's okay, Mrs M. I'm happy to help.'

'We're so grateful to have our girl home for a wee while,' Angelia's dad said as he shook Meghan's hand rather officially, making Angelia smirk. He turned back to face Angelia. 'Sit down, I'll make a pot of tea. You too, Meghan.' Angelia sat at the kitchen table and Meghan followed suit.

'So, this medication that Dr Novak has prescribed,' her mum said. 'What does it do?'

'It's something that reduces this particular chemical in my blood which means the signals can get through so my muscles don't fatigue as quickly.'

'Gosh, that sounds very involved. And how are you feeling?'

Angelia shrugged. 'I'm fine so far but I've only just started taking it. It seems to be helping which is the main thing.'

Her mum smiled but it was tinged with concern. 'Well, that's good. And how were the band about it all when you told them? I hope they handled it okay. I know Josh must have been worried. I think he looks on you as a younger sister,' she said with a fond smile.

If only you knew the truth, Mum, Angelia thought and she sighed as she remembered Josh's face as he'd left her apartment with the others. His eyes had been filled with something she had never really seen before. Possibly regret. Definitely pain. Although they had all left together, he had been the last to walk out and he had hugged her so tightly that it felt like goodbye and she had cried herself to sleep that night. She shook her head lightly to dislodge the memory.

She cleared her throat. 'They were worried about me but so supportive. I was very concerned about telling them about my diagnosis after what happened with Lorelie, but they were great. Told me to take whatever time I need.'

'Did the doc say anything about you going back on tour?' her dad asked.

'He said that touring would be counterproductive right now. Which means the European tour in six months' time is on thin ice. Den has been great though. It can't be easy doing his job.'

Her dad huffed. 'I'll bet he's paid well enough so don't be worrying about him. And he *should* be great about your situation. It's not like you've asked for any of this,' he said as he placed a tray on the table complete with teapot, milk jug and sugar bowl. He usually just made tea straight in the mugs, forgoing the teapot, so he was clearly on his best behaviour seeing as they had a guest. Angelia was relieved that he hadn't fished out Nanna's china teacups from the back of the cupboard too. He chewed his lip for a moment.

'What about the new album? Aren't you supposed to be in the studio in a few weeks?'

Angelia nodded. 'We are but Den's put a hold on it. He's given everyone an extra month off.'

'Well, that's nice. I'm sure Heath and the others are grateful for more time with their families. Heath's wee boy is such a sweetheart from the photos you sent,' her mum said as she reached for the teapot.

Angelia smiled. 'Oh, aye, Rosco's a real character. Just like his dad.'

'What will happen long term though?' her dad asked as he took a seat opposite her at the table. 'You can't put things on hold indefinitely, surely? And you signed contracts.'

Angelia shrugged. 'Honestly, I don't know. I have a lot of thinking to do, I suppose. Although I assume there's a clause in the contract somewhere for when things like this happen.' She fell silent for a moment and tried to imagine life without Angel and the Fallen. 'Music is all I've ever known and this band has been my life for ten years. I've loved every second of it but...' She sighed and her chin trembled; she had no clue what could or should follow those words.

As if sensing her sadness, her mum said, 'Look, let's change the subject, eh? You don't have to make any decisions this evening. Now, Dad tells me the property you've bought in Glentorrin has lots of potential. Have you any idea what you might want to do with it?'

Her mum poured the tea and Angelia picked up her mug; a Snoopy one she'd had for years and had managed to keep it completely intact, much to her surprise and joy. She shrugged. 'I'm not really sure, to be honest. I'll have a look around and see what ideas spring to mind, I suppose.'

'Why don't we go tomorrow and have a look?' her dad asked brightly.

'Don't you have work to do? You usually end up working on something even on Sundays,' Angelia said with a teasing smile.

He sipped his tea and shook his head. 'Nope. I'm off for the week. Decided I was going to spend some quality time with my girls.' He glanced up and met Meghan's gaze. 'Oh... and... and you too, Meghan.' Then he turned his attention to Scrappy who had jumped up and placed his paws on his leg as if he too wanted to be a part of it all. 'And of course you as well, wee Scrappy.' There was a silent pause before Angelia, her mum and Meghan burst into laughter. He frowned and smiled simultaneously. 'What? I just wanted to include everyone.'

9

Early on Sunday morning, Angelia was accompanied by Meghan and her dad on a visit to Glentorrin to view her latest property acquisition. Her dad parked the car outside of the newly purchased building and Meghan climbed out first, glancing around herself and smiling.

'This place is beautiful,' Meghan said. 'I don't think I'd ever want to leave if I was you.'

With her hair tucked up inside her signature disguise of a baseball cap, Angelia climbed out of the car and inhaled lungs full of the fresh Scottish sea air. She had missed this island and hadn't realised just how much until now. The sunglasses she usually wore in London as part of her attempt to be incognito were essential attire on this occasion as the sun hung high in the sky, casting a bright golden hue over the pretty village. There was a chatter of birdsong in the air, and a rippling of water lapping at the sea wall, and the place had such a calm, idyllic feel about it. The one thing missing, much to Angelia's delight, was traffic noise.

The white-painted building she now owned stood at the end of a row of others facing the inlet of water. At the opposite side of the inlet was the Lifeboat House Museum, a place Angelia was keen to visit after hearing stories of the place from Ruby.

'It's a far cry from the smog of London, eh? So much fresh air,' Meghan said as she stood, hands on hips, scanning the location with intrigue. 'It reminds me of a model village me and my mam visited when I was little. So quaint.' She shook her head and smiled.

'It's a lovely setting for sure,' Angelia said as she too gazed across the stretch of water where shards of light were dancing around on its surface. She had always loved the sound of water; it was always so soothing to her, and she often used rain and river soundtracks to help her sleep. A small blue and white fishing boat bobbed up and down at its mooring and a couple of seagulls sat on the water just floating, seemingly without a care in the world.

As she turned to her left, Angelia could see the beautiful, grand old house up on the small hill that she recognised from photos as that belonging to Ruby Locke and her husband, Mitch, and below that was a tree-lined village green and what looked to be the new hall Ruby had mentioned. Along from this was a pretty stone-built church that she could just make out behind its verdant barrier of green, leafy trees and bushes. A little further up the road she could see a pub called the Coxswain and a little village shop too. It was picture-postcard perfect, and she could understand completely, aside from the obvious fact that she had fallen for an island resident, why Ruby had decided to make this place her home and respite from her busy film career. Although these days her film work was kept to a minimum and she in fact ran a dance class in the previously mentioned village hall. *The best of both worlds*, Angelia mused.

Angelia had missed the peaceful nature of village life while ensconced in the big city she had been calling her temporary home. This little place, however, had serenity and peace in spades. *What was there not to love?* She felt her shoulders relaxing and, as she exhaled, she felt some of the anxiety she had been holding onto since her diagnosis leaving her body.

Over by the village shop, a teenage boy with a mop of dark hair and girl with long red curls were holding hands as they walked their respective dogs; one tiny and one huge in comparison. They greeted an older woman with neat grey hair who was standing in the shop doorway leaning against the jamb, and they chatted animatedly for a while, laughing as the woman petted the dogs; the larger of the two clearly very excitable. Scrappy would've loved to go over and say hello if she hadn't left him at home with her mum, she thought. He loved to play with other dogs.

'Well, here we are,' her dad said, holding out his hands in a kind of 'tadaaaa!' gesture, drawing her attention to their real reason for being in

Glentorrin. He unlocked the outer set of narrow double doors to reveal another, partially glazed entrance door.

Before she stepped inside, Angelia took another moment to assess the surrounding shops and houses. Her double-fronted shop was similar in stature to the bakery further along the road, at first glance, only the bakery had one single window to the retail space. Both had living accommodation to the rear that extended above.

She turned her attention to the frontage of her property once more. The sign above the door had been painted over, many years before, hiding the visible clues to its origins. Although, in its last iteration, Angelia had discovered, the building had functioned as an antique shop and before that an ironmongers, but those businesses had existed many years before. It had lain empty since then and it was clear by a simple inspection through the pretty arched windows and through a gap in the shutters that the interior was covered in a layer of dust so thick you could write in it.

'Angel!' came a voice from across the village and she turned to see Ruby jogging towards her from the village hall.

Angelia turned and walked quickly towards her. 'Hey! It's good to see you!' The pair hugged. 'Dad, Meghan, you remember Ruby?'

'Aye, of course. Lovely to see you, Ruby,' her dad said.

Meghan blushed bright red. 'Erm... hi, Ruby.'

Ruby narrowed her eyes. 'Hmm, I've got a bone to pick with you, Meghan Parry.'

Meghan's eyes widened. 'Oh?'

Ruby laughed. 'I'm messing with you! But Ezra can't stop bloody talking about you and he's driving me mad. He's like a besotted puppy dog.'

Meghan beamed. 'Ah, okay. And sorry, not sorry.'

'I take it things are going well for you two?' Ruby asked with a tilt of her head.

Meghan nodded. 'Oh, yes. He's wonderful,' she replied dreamily.

Ruby turned her attention back to Angelia. 'I can't stay; I've got an older ladies' dance class starting soon but I wanted to come over and welcome you. How are you doing?' Ruby asked with evident concern etched on her face. 'Are you okay? Are the meds helping?'

Angelia had sent a long message to Ruby after her diagnosis and told her she was coming home for a while. She nodded. 'I'm getting there, thank you. And it's early days with the meds but so far, so good.'

'I'm so glad to hear that, honey. So, this is your first visit to the shop since you bought it, are you ready to see what you've let yourself in for? I don't think anyone's been in there for over a decade.'

Angelia chewed her lip. 'Hmm. I'm nervous. And I'm a bit baffled as to what to do with it, to be honest.'

Ruby waved a dismissive hand. 'You'll think of something. And I can tell you right now, the villagers are just happy it's not going to be derelict any more. The thing with Glentorrin is it's a versatile little place and we get lots of tourists passing through in summer so whatever you choose I think it'll be buzzing. I bet it's good to be home, even if it's a short-term thing,' Ruby said with a wide smile.

Angelia turned to look at the houses and shops overlooking the inlet of water. 'It is. I do love this island. It's always so hard to leave.'

Ruby leaned in and kissed her cheek. 'Well... maybe you don't actually have to this time.' She gave a wink. 'Right, I'd better be going. I've a date with some tap shoes and a bit of Cliff Richard.' She giggled, turned and jogged off towards the hall once more, waving over her shoulder. 'Bye for now!'

'Shall we go inside?' her dad asked, putting an arm around her shoulder. 'As you'll see, it'll need a good clean up before you'll really get to see its full potential,' he said as she followed him through the doors. 'I took the liberty of getting the power switched on, although from the survey it's clear some rewiring will be necessary before you trust the electrics.'

Once inside, her dad fully opened the shutters and stood in the middle of the shop floor area, arms folded across his chest as he assessed the place and nodded. 'Aye, I had to use my imagination on your behalf when I came to look at it the first time. But you see the potential, eh?'

For a few moments, Angelia stood, wide-eyed, gawping, open-mouthed as she watched the dust motes dancing in the light breeze they had brought in with them through the door. She wondered if she had perhaps bitten off more than she could chew. It looked so much worse than the photos in the online auction brochure. It was now clear why no locals had been prepared to bid on it. She wondered if it was going to be a major money pit and if she should seriously consider just selling it straight on to some other willing lunatic. As it was, it was a completely different prospect to the houses she had bought previously. They had been solely residential, or empty and newer commercial buildings, and most had only needed updating and a lick of paint before a family or service provider could move in, whereas, this place needed a complete overhaul.

She inhaled the musty smell of damp and her nose tickled. *It'll probably need fumigating*, she thought as a feeling of dread crept over her when she spotted what appeared to be rodent droppings on the floor.

'Don't just stand there, Angelia, have a good look around. Get a feel for the place. Get your imagination working,' her dad insisted. He had a point.

She began to wander around, and her dad flicked on some lights that did little to illuminate the space. Shelves partially lined the walls at one side, and a few old rickety tables were dotted around with boxes of goodness knows what sitting untouched and likely to remain so. The wall sconces held flickering candle-style bulbs that gave out about as much light as the thing they mimicked. No good for this day and age. Maybe that had been quite fitting when the place had been filled with antiques and curios, but they were enough to ruin your eyesight. At the back of the shop floor was a door and when Angelia poked her head through, she saw that it led out to a kitchen and toilet, so at least it had the important facilities. She decided to investigate those later but, surprisingly, the more she wandered around the more she could see past the grime and abandonment.

The old cash desk was dark wood and quite ornately carved on the front like something out of a Victorian film set. Even better was the old register with its brass buttons and prices in pounds, shillings and pence. *How has that not been taken and put into a museum?* she pondered. She was grateful, however, that it hadn't as it was a beautiful old antique. She decided she would have to incorporate it into whatever design she decided to choose for the place. Ruby had informed her that one of her friends was a top-class interior designer and lived in the village, which was going to be very handy indeed.

'You know what I think would be so cool in here?' Meghan blurted and both Angelia and her dad turned to look at her, at which point her cheeks flamed and she winced. 'Whoops, sorry, did I say that out loud? My bad.' She held up her hands.

'No, no, Meg, what were you going to say?' Angelia asked with intrigue because her own mind was drawing a blank.

Meghan's eyes lit up. 'You know how you're utterly obsessed with records? And how vinyl is making a major comeback right now?'

'Aye, although they never went out of fashion in my opinion,' Angelia's dad said and it was true. Like Angelia's, her dad's record collection was his most prized possession, and it was played regularly on the old stacker system in the living room.

'Go on, Meg,' Angelia said.

'Okay, so...' Meghan began to walk around the shop gesturing. 'Imagine listening booths here like they had in the 1960s and 70s. Then over here racks of vinyl, old, new, vintage, you name it. You could source them from all over the world. This counter is perfect for that retro feel. You could bag yourself some memorabilia from all the cool decades and hang them on the walls or use these old shelves. People love that kind of stuff. Posters on the walls, too, of all the past and present music stars. I think someone would snatch your hand off to rent a space like that so you could make a real good passive income.' She shrugged as if it was obvious.

A wide smile spread across Angelia's face. 'Oh, my word, you're right. That would be so ridiculously cool!' she said as her heart skipped and she began to envisage Meghan's idea. 'But this is Glentorrin, not Edinburgh or Glasgow, would anyone realistically come here for records?' she said rhetorically to no one in particular.

Meghan scoffed. 'Can I just point out that Skye is one of *the* most popular tourist destinations in Scotland and people from all over the world come to visit? The business owner could offer a mail home service, so people didn't have to carry their purchases with them on their travels. And if they stock some rare things people would come from miles around to buy from here. Record collectors are serious people.'

'Do you really think they would?' Angelia asked. 'I mean, do you think someone would want to rent somewhere like that that's already specifically set up as a record store?'

'I think Meghan has a point,' Angelia's dad said. 'It would give the place a real purpose. And if you do it just right, it could be amazing. There's plenty of parking in the main village so that wouldn't be an issue. Add to it that this is the first village you come to when you cross the Skye Bridge, and the last one as you leave, and I think you could be onto a winner. People love to support independent shops. It could be really good. And like Meghan says, the passive income you'd get from the rent would be great for when you're back touring again, seeing as you choose not to profit from your other properties.'

She was happy that everyone seemed to be confident she would be back out on tour again soon, but she was still unsure as to when that might actually be. But another income that she could make good use of for charity work would be welcomed. Not to mention the fact that if she wasn't able to go back on tour again the income would be needed, eventually, to live once the royalties slowed down or even stopped.

'I think I'll contact the interior designer Ruby mentioned and have a wee chat with her.' Angelia was excited for the first time in a few weeks and could hardly wait to find out what could be done with the old shop.

10

Back at home later that morning, Angelia was lounging on the sofa looking at images of vintage record shops on her phone and creating a Pinterest mood board with her favourites, while Scrappy lay fast asleep and snuggled into her side. Why hadn't she thought of it herself? It was such an obvious suggestion now she thought about it. She had been obsessed with records since she was wee, and she knew that record collecting was a popular thing to do these days. In her opinion you just couldn't beat the sound quality of vinyl. It wasn't the crispest sound but there was something so comforting about it. The nostalgia produced by the scratch of a needle on the vinyl was immense.

Meanwhile her mum and her dad were out tidying the back garden, which Angelia knew to be code for *talking things through*. They were still coming to terms with the fact that their daughter was facing a future filled with many changes that they couldn't really help with, and it had been hard for them both. They weren't overbearing at all, but they did like to problem solve. The fact that this was a problem with little to no absolute solution was vexing for them.

Angelia glanced around the room at the family photos dotted here and there; photos she could remember being taken and the emotions that went along with them. And the paintings of local scenes on Skye that she adored. The rocky, otherworldly images of the Quiraing and the Cuillin; the dramatic palette of colours of the sky at sunrise and the cerulean blue of summer all held a special place in her heart. It was comforting to be back in the little detached bothy conversion she'd shared with her parents while growing up. Things felt normal here.

Her luxury apartment in North West London had been the first thing she had purchased when her finances had allowed, she was certainly her father's daughter, and while 'the big smoke' had become her second home it wasn't quite the same as her *real* home. For the last decade she had spent most of her time flitting between her place in London and hotels in New York when she was recording and not on tour with the band, with only short visits back to Skye. Often, in the past, she'd flown her parents out to stay with her in the USA or Europe, and they'd explored the vibrant city locations together until she'd become too famous to leave the hotel in those places without some kind of security. Skye offered her a reminder of the life she'd had growing up and it was a welcome change. Far less complicated.

Her phone rang and Ed's name flashed up on the screen. Angelia sat up straight as her heart skipped and she immediately hit the button to accept his call.

'Hey, Angelia, how are you?' he asked, his voice croaky with sleep.

'Hi, Ed, I'm okay, I think. How come you're phoning so early? It must be 6.30 a.m. in New York?'

'Yeah, I'm going to be heading out soon and I wanted to give you a call before I set off. Fiona messaged to say she's coming to visit you today. I wish I could come too. I'm missing you guys like mad.'

Angelia swallowed the lump that lodged in her throat on hearing the sadness in his voice. 'Missing you too,' she replied.

'How's the medication going?' he asked.

She nodded, even though he couldn't see her. 'Yeah, good so far. The symptoms are definitely less although not completely gone. I think it'll be trial and error for a while.'

'But at least it's starting to work which is positive. I'm going to come and see you as soon as I can, I promise.'

'Don't worry, Ed. I know what it's like to be busy with touring,' she said with a smile. 'How is it going? Still enjoying The Phil?'

There was a pause. 'It's... erm... hard work.'

She sensed he was about to say something else. 'But you're loving it, right? It's been your dream for ages so that must make it worthwhile, surely?'

'Yeah, yeah, it's great.' There was little to no sincerity in his voice, and she was about to press him on the fact, but he continued. 'Look, I'd better go. I'll call again soon to let you know when I'm coming to see you. Love you.'

Her heart ached a little on hearing those words when she understood the friendly meaning behind them all too well. 'Love you, too, Ed. Good to hear from you. Bye.'

The line went dead and she placed her phone face down on the arm of the sofa, wondering what it was that he hadn't said about his work with the New York Philharmonic.

The doorbell sounded and Meghan, who had been reading at the kitchen table, insisted on answering it, old habits and all that. Angelia knew who it was going to be, so she followed her assistant to the hallway. Meghan opened the door and immediately recognised the visitor.

'Oh, hi, Fiona. Lovely to see you again. Come on in.'

As soon as she was inside, Angelia grappled Fiona into a bear hug.

'I've missed you so much!' Fiona said, her voice wavering with emotion. She pulled away and held Angelia at arm's length. 'Are you okay? I can't believe what's happened, Angelia. I wish I could do something.'

'I'm okay. It's just been such a weird and stressful time. But I'm so happy to see you. Thank you for coming over.' Fiona had set off from her home in Edinburgh at five in the morning. It was now half eleven.

'No thanks needed, honey. You're my best friend. I'm just glad I've been able to get out of the in-service day tomorrow so I can stay over.'

'It's such a long way to come to stay one night though. You've driven for over five hours, Fee.'

Fiona shrugged. 'Like I said, you're my best friend.'

Angelia's eyes stung and her chin trembled. 'I do love you, and I'm so grateful.'

Meghan left them to chat in the kitchen while she went to 'take a nap' which Angelia now understood to mean she would be having a conversation with Ezra, and without her assistant or parents in the room she finally felt able to open up about the way she was really feeling, something she had avoided doing with her parents up to now, until they had accepted, and got used to, the news she had imparted.

'The consultant I saw pretty much told me I should rethink my whole career. But what would I do without the band though, Fee? Without this life I've worked so hard for. Who the hell would I even be?' Angelia stared into the ruby-red liquid as a berry-scented fragrance drifted up with the steam from the fruit tea in her mug, infiltrating her senses but doing nothing to ease her aching heart.

Angelia was still reeling from the discovery that she had a life-altering condition. Dr Novak had been in regular contact to ensure the side effects of her new medication weren't too bad, and he had continually insisted that she not overdo things until the dosage was just right. And even then, he had said she needed to reconsider her busy schedule, and he had reiterated that she should seriously contemplate whether her life as a rock star was something she should think about amending. He'd also warned Angelia that if she went back to the level, and frequency, of performing that she had sustained for the last decade, she ran the risk of something called a myasthenic crisis which could be life threatening, so was something she wanted to avoid at all costs.

She sighed. 'If I give it all up now it will be like the last ten years of my life are wiped out. As if they never happened,' she whispered, the realisation of what she faced sinking in. 'Singing is all I've ever really known and I'm not sure I'm ready for it to be gone.' Her heart sank further than she ever thought possible and the ache in her chest deepened. 'I'm almost thirty-one, I didn't even finish my music degree, so I literally have *nothing* else.' Her stomach knotted at the sound of her speaking voice which was so much weaker today thanks to the emotional stress she found herself under. She lifted her head as tears spilled over, and she met the concerned gaze of her best friend. 'I know everyone will probably think that I have plenty of money and don't need to work but I do, for my own sanity. I can't sit around and be idle, Fee. It's just not in my nature.'

Fiona was eight years into a career that she absolutely loved, as a high-school music teacher in Edinburgh. From the way she talked about her job, it was clear the kids adored her, and she was very well respected.

Ever the stalwart optimist, Fiona reached out and squeezed her hand. 'Come on, Angelia, you'll get back there. This isn't the end. It can't be. Just rest up for a few more months now you're on your meds, and the old pipes will be back to normal. Good as new.' It was clear that regardless of her facial expression Fiona was in denial, too, which wasn't really helping.

'I wish I believed that, Fee, but Dr Novak is an expert on this condition and he says there's no cure. The medication manages the myasthenia but doesn't take it away. Perhaps I just have to resign myself to the fact that my voice is never going to be as strong as it was. I just don't know what else I can do. I could still record with plenty of breaks, but I can't expect the band to accept that because studios charge by the hour. And if I can't tour, maybe I should step aside so they can find someone else. Live music is what they're all about. What they love. It'd be selfish of me to expect them to accept anything less than 100 per cent from me. And from myself for that matter.'

Guilt had eaten away at her since the talk with Dr Novak. What would the band do after losing yet another vocalist if she did have to resign? Would they disband? Go on to other projects? Or would they try to find a replacement? She couldn't, after all, expect them to continually put their livelihoods on hold and wait for her to feel ready again. What if her condition worsened? It was a possibility. And they deserved to be given the opportunity to move on with their own careers because continually touring and recording had clearly begun to put a strain on her that she knew she couldn't realistically cope with long term.

Since the filming of *Scotland Rocks*, Angel and the Fallen had been number one in the Billboard charts on numerous occasions and in later years the band had been consistently listed in the most streamed songs on Spotify. Angelia had co-written many of the songs that had charted too which was another dream come true.

The decade following the TV show had been filled with fun and friendship and had taken her all around the world to places she could only have dreamed of visiting had she not been chosen. Spending months on the road with five complete strangers had been a daunting scenario before she had embarked upon her new career, but she had fit right in and for the first six months she'd had to pinch herself every time she awoke. Especially on mornings where she'd found herself in a swish hotel room ready for recording at New York's world-renowned Electric Lady Studios.

She often sat and daydreamed about the first time she'd stood, eyes closed and heart pounding, at the microphone in the recording booth. She'd not quite been able to believe she was standing where legends like Taylor Swift, Stevie Wonder, Led Zeppelin – to name only a few – had all recorded.

The most distinct memory about that first time, however, was opening her eyes to see the other five members of the band beaming at her through the transparent partition. Josh had held up a sign that simply read:

GO ANGEL!

Her new and affectionately bestowed nickname had been the catalyst for the band's sudden and unexpected name change. And at that point, all the worry, all the feelings of inadequacy and the imposter syndrome that had taken up residence in her mind, had dissipated.

* * *

'Has Josh been in touch since you overheard him talking to Heath?' Fiona asked without making eye contact as she pulled at a non-existent thread on her jeans. Angelia had confided in Fiona just after it had happened and her friend hadn't seemed surprised, just concerned.

Angelia knew the question had been hanging around at the back of Fiona's mind and had been waiting for her to ask it. 'Not since that night. Although I wasn't expecting him to contact me considering how he freaked out about the myasthenia thing. It really pissed me off because the others were great and he just sort of... shut down.'

Fiona nodded and lifted her chin and a crumple of concern furrowed her brow. 'I know he told Heath that he loves you but... You know he'll never leave Nancy, don't you, honey?'

Angelia sighed. 'I know and I wouldn't want him to. It was a shock, admittedly, and there was a time I would've been desperate to act on it but Nancy doesn't deserve that. They've been together for so long and she's stuck by him regardless of the rumours in the tabloids about him and me. She's been loyal to him for all these years and I wouldn't want to be responsible for ruining that.'

'Even though you know how he feels about you? You adored him for so long, does that just go away, or are you being brave? Wasn't it tempting to say something?'

Angelia closed her eyes for a moment, knowing that the person she really wanted was Ed but that she couldn't admit that even to her best friend because it was a line she couldn't cross. 'Honestly? No. I'm over that crush. You don't need to worry.'

Fiona shook her head and reached out to squeeze her arm again, clearly misunderstanding her reaction. 'Hey, you will meet someone, you know? There's someone out there just waiting to sweep you off your feet. And you can't help who you fall for, I get that. I just don't want you to get hurt. You deserve someone who loves you back and is free to do so.'

Angelia nodded. 'I know.' She thought in silence for a few moments before speaking again. 'You and Marcus are so perfect together and you met in such a *normal* way. I'm scared I'll never meet someone who'll love me like that. I've had so many failed relationships I'm scared to even try. And especially now I have this diagnosis that could be about to take my career away.'

Fiona leaned closer. 'Hey, stop that right now. There is someone out there waiting for you, I just know there is. And this condition isn't going to put the right person off. Why would it? It's not like you've grown an extra head, for goodness' sake, Angel. You need to stop thinking like that.'

Fiona was right. But Angelia had no clue how she *would* even meet someone. Almost everyone on the planet knew who she was, which made it difficult to meet a man who would just love her for *her* and not be affected by the fame thing.

* * *

That night Angelia's dad made a huge vat of his famous chilli, and they all sat around the dining table like the old days when Fiona used to come home to Angelia's on weekends when they were at university. Angelia and her dad told her mum all about the shop and Meghan's idea that it would make an excellent record shop.

'It would make a really awesome bookshop, too, but I suppose you don't want to be competing with your mum,' Meghan said with a mischievous grin.

Her mum had rolled her eyes. 'Oh, hell, no. One bookshop in the family is plenty, thank you. It's hard enough getting people to buy full-priced paperbacks as it is. I definitely don't need competition.' She turned to Angelia and with a crumple of concern to her brow she said, 'And if I'm honest, love, I'm not sure that making the space into a record shop is the best idea either.

Surely, it would be best to leave it flexible so someone can rent it and make whatever they want from it? Just my opinion,' she said, holding up her hands.

Fiona nodded. 'Sorry, but I'm with your mum. If you make the place too niche it may make it tricky to rent it out.'

A sinking feeling tugged at Angelia's insides. She had loved the idea of a record shop and could not see past that now. 'We'll see. I'm going to think about it and speak to the interior designer Ruby has recommended, and I'll take it from there.'

11

The following morning, Angelia stood on the doorstep, ready to say an emotional goodbye to Fiona after a pep talk in which Angelia was reminded 'who the heck she was and how tough she could be'. Fiona had clung to her and with a wavering voice had said, 'You may not be able to beat this thing completely, Angelia, but it sure as hell won't beat you, okay? We won't let it.'

Angelia had nodded through the fog of tears. 'Thank you again for coming all this way. I do appreciate it.'

Fiona's chin had trembled. 'Stop thanking me, you wee dafty. I'll come up again before you leave and Ed has said he'll come and see you too.'

'I don't want you to all go out of your way, though. It's not like I'm on my last legs or anything,' Angelia had said, forcing a giggle.

'Hey, it's what besties do. Now you take care and keep me posted of any changes.'

'I will. Drive safe and let me know when you get home.'

Fiona climbed in her car and drove away, Angelia standing at the door until she could no longer see her best friend's little blue car.

After dinner that evening, her mum and dad were introducing Meghan to the delights of their favourite reality TV show, *Dance Yourself Dizzy*, in which non-dancing famous people paired up with members of the public and were sent to a sort of dance bootcamp where they learned specific dances and then performed in front of a panel of judges. It was like a more chaotic version of

Strictly Come Dancing, and according to Angelia's mum and dad it was totally addictive.

Angelia went through to the garden room and picked up one of the guitars from its stand. She began to pluck the strings and reminisce about the songwriting sessions she had enjoyed with the lads from the band. But in the back of her mind, the whole time, were the plans for the shop she had bought. What else could she do with it if Meghan's suggestion wasn't viable? Her phone pinged with a WhatsApp message. It was from Ruby.

RUBY

Hey, lovely lady! I'm just teaching a class but wondered if you fancied meeting me at the Coxswain for a drink after? It would be great to catch up. R xx

She checked her watch and saw that it was only six o'clock. Maybe she could sneak out and head down to Glentorrin by herself? Maybe she could chat with Ruby and get her opinion on the shop. She hit reply.

ANGEL

Hi, Rubes! Would love to! Will be driving so no alcohol for me but that doesn't stop you from partaking! Will head down now and visit the shop while I wait for you. Angel xx

She tiptoed through to the door of the living room and could hear Meghan and her parents talking about an actress from some daytime sitcom show who had just danced the *bossa nova* with a butcher from Epping Forest, and how she was too wooden and he really did look like Bambi on ice, and that they were sure they were going to be kicked off the show. Hearing them engrossed so deeply in what they were doing, Angelia decided to risk driving herself down to the little coastal village without letting them talk her out of it. No one knew she was here, after all, and the chances of anyone coming all the way to Skye to find her on a whim were pretty non-existent. She scribbled a brief note explaining she had gone to Glentorrin to meet Ruby and wouldn't be too late back, grabbed the shop keys from the kitchen counter and her mum's car keys from the rack by the front door. It had been a while since she had driven but she always kept her insurance up to date in case she needed to drive. And technically it wasn't car theft because after she had passed her test her mum had bought her the car she now used as her own; no point it standing unused on the driveway while she was on tour.

She carefully opened the front door and held her breath as it creaked, waiting for Meghan, with her superhuman hearing, to come rushing out. But when nothing happened, she made a dash for it.

Driving south on the island was a journey she had made often when she had first found the freedom that came with passing her driving test, aged seventeen. The sky overhead was still bright and even though the temperature had dropped slightly she wound down the window a little to breathe in the fresh Scottish air. As she listened to Queen's *A Day at the Races*, the CD her mum had clearly been listening to the last time she had driven the car, the road wound its way past familiar, pretty little villages and fields filled with crops; she saw people sitting in their gardens making the most of the pleasant early-evening weather, dog walkers, children playing, and was reminded why she loved her home so much. And why London would never replace it in her heart.

The road that extended south from Portree eventually skirted the coast and a glance to the left out of the passenger window gave the spectacular vista of the evening sun glinting on the water of Loch na Cairidh. The view was clear right across to the peaceful, uninhabited Isle of Scalpay and its sunny carpet of yellow gorse and pink sea thrift. Spring had very much sprung and the air smelled fresh with salt, and she knew this view would only get more and more beautiful on the approach to summer – the time of year the island was at its most picturesque in Angelia's opinion. An eagle was flying just off the coast as if purposefully keeping up with the car and Angelia smiled as it glided to a stop on a tree by the side of the road. Once again, the sense of home washed over her as she drove and enjoyed the stunning scenery that surrounded her.

Around fifty minutes after she had set off from home she pulled into Glentorrin and parked in the spaces adjacent to the village hall, beside a minibus that had a college logo emblazoned on its side panel. When she climbed out of her car, she could hear music coming from inside and over the top of that she heard Ruby's Yorkshire accent as she shouted instructions to her class of dance students.

'And one, two, three, four, pow, pow, step, step, that's it, guys! Brilliant! The audience at the summer concert are going to love this!'

A few teenagers were gathered at the museum side of the inlet taking selfies as a man with a clipboard chatted to his female companion close by. Angelia guessed they were the people from the minibus and that they were on a school trip. She walked across the road to stand at the railing that surrounded the inlet in front of her newly acquired building and admired the view for a few moments. The bakery was closed but the sweet aroma of fresh baking still travelled through the air to tantalise her senses. The lights were on, and Angelia could imagine the baker in there preparing bread and cakes for the following day's trade. The pub seemed to be busy with locals wandering in and out, chatting and laughing.

Angelia had been completely oblivious to the fact that people were watching her so when she felt a tap on her arm her heart leapt and she almost jumped out of her skin. She turned to find herself surrounded by another small group of older teens and guessed they must have been the remainder of the school party.

'Excuse me. Sorry to bother you but aren't you Angel from Angel and the Fallen?' a female member of the group asked. She was wearing a T-shirt that had been on sale as the band's merchandise a couple of years earlier. Angelia hadn't anticipated meeting anyone who would recognise her at this time on an Easter Monday evening, and certainly not in this location, so was a little thrown. She considered lying and saying something along the lines of, 'Sorry, I get that a lot but I'm not her, just a lookalike,' but immediately felt guilty. It was people like this girl who bought their records and supported the band by buying concert tickets, so she couldn't, in good conscience at least, lie to them. It wouldn't be right.

Angelia opened her mouth to speak but then another of the group pointed at her and talked about her as if she couldn't hear him. 'Yeah, it's her. I told you it was her. You *wouldnae* listen when I said but I'm telling yous, it's definitely her.'

'Are you her?' the first girl asked. 'I'm a really big fan.' She was wide-eyed and her eyes appeared glassy with tears.

Angelia had hoped to remain undiscovered for a little while longer but evidently that hope had been dashed. She inhaled a deep breath and smiled. 'Yes, yes, I'm Angel. Nice to meet you.' She held out her hand.

A collective gasp travelled through the group, and was followed by excited mutterings as they closed in on her. The first girl covered her mouth with her hand for a moment before grasping Angelia's offered one and saying, 'I knew it was you! I love your music. I think I might be your biggest fan. You're the best singer in the world and I'm so happy to meet you. I can't believe this is happening. Please can I have a selfie?' Her words came out in an emotional rush.

Angelia noticed that the rest of the group from the other side of the inlet had now joined them and their teachers had walked across to see what was going on. She smiled and nodded. 'Sure, a selfie is fine.'

For the next ten minutes, Angelia posed and smiled at phone cameras, signed arms, T-shirts and bits of paper and chatted to the teenagers and their teachers who, it transpired, were also fans of the band. She discovered that there were fourteen of them plus the two adults, and they were indeed on a college geology trip. They were from a campus near Inverness and were travelling north on Skye to a camping pod site near the Quiraing, planning to study the rock formation of the landslip.

Eventually one of the teachers shouted to get their attention. 'Come on, everyone, let's leave Miss MacAuley to go about her business, shall we? We need to get to the campsite before it gets too dark.' The male teacher then turned to Angelia and shook her hand. 'Thank you so much for taking the time to speak with us all. I'm sure this wasn't on your agenda for the day, but I can see that you've made these kids very happy indeed.'

Angelia laughed nervously. 'That's okay. They're a nice bunch.'

One by one the group shook her hand and reluctantly left her to go back to the minibus. Once they had all gone, she spotted Ruby leaning against the wall of the hall, smiling and shaking her head, so she went across to join her.

When she reached her friend, they hugged. 'Hey, you. Do you ever stop working?' Ruby asked with a laugh.

Angelia smiled. 'Apparently not. They were a nice group of kids, though. But I may be all over Instagram by the end of the evening,' she said with a wince. 'Not really what I hoped would happen.'

Ruby pursed her lips and linked her arm through Angelia's and they set off over to the pub. 'Hmm, not conducive to a quiet visit home, eh?'

'Not really but it's an occupational hazard for both of us, I suppose.'

Ruby laughed. 'You got that right.'

The pub was busy with locals, many of whom Ruby seemed to know, although no one made a fuss. Angelia went with Ruby to order their coffees from the bar.

'Evening, Ruby,' said the large bearded man behind the bar. He looked like he belonged in the cast of *Vikings* and had very smiley eyes. 'How are you?' His accent reminded her of Agda's.

'Evening, Joren. I'm good, thanks. Yourself, and Stella?'

He nodded. 'Can't complain. She's in the back working her magic with haggis and neeps,' he said with a deep chuckle that seemed to vibrate up from his feet. 'Who is your friend?' he asked, smiling at Angelia, and then leaned forward to whisper, 'I already know who you are, of course, but I don't want to be a fan girl,' he said with a wink.

Angelia couldn't help giggling. She liked him immediately and held out her hand. 'Good to meet you, Joren, I'm Angelia.'

He shook her hand. 'Angelia, what a beautiful name. Like the Richard Marx song,' he said with a nod. 'Unusual. And very cool. What can I get you ladies to drink?'

'We're just on coffee tonight, thanks.'

Joren gasped, feigning shock. 'You must have serious stuff to discuss. Coming right up.'

'Thanks, Joren. You're a star,' Ruby replied.

He laughed, clicked his fingers and pointed at her. 'I could *literally* say the same!'

They took a seat at a table by the fireplace and Angelia looked around, taking in her surroundings. She was surprised at how relaxed she felt in the place. A couple of people glanced over, and she saw a spark of recognition, but they didn't approach the table, and she was grateful for that. The pub was quite traditional with tankards hanging above the bar and a shelf of old whisky bottles that ran around the main room. The walls appeared freshly painted in a cosy shade of deep red and the furniture was all dark oak. It was the epitome of the quintessential Scottish pub and Angelia liked the place immediately.

'So have you had any ideas for the old antiques shop yet?' Ruby asked when she walked back over and placed two mugs of fresh coffee on the table before them and took a seat across from Angelia.

'Funnily enough, Meghan came up with an idea. I'm just not sure it's viable.'

Ruby took a sip of her coffee and raised her eyebrows. 'Ooh, tell me more.'

'Well, you know how I'm pretty obsessed with vinyl?'

'You? Obsessed? Surely not,' she teased. 'I mean, I barely remember that time we were in Glasgow during the *Scotland Rocks* shoot and you dragged me into every single record shop we came across… *twice*!' She smiled.

Angelia laughed. 'I can't help myself. It's an addiction. Anyway, Meghan suggested—'

'A record shop? It's a no brainer, really,' Ruby said with a chuckle.

'Hmm. But is it a viable business for a place like this? Will people come to Glentorrin to buy records?'

Ruby placed her cup down and leaned her elbows on the table. 'The thing is, people don't necessarily come to Glentorrin to buy anything in particular. But that said, if there's a good record shop here, I don't see why people wouldn't buy from it. The village gets so many visitors passing through each year that I think it would actually work. And once people knew it was here, I reckon people would travel. And it's something you're crazy passionate about. Although, who would run it for you?'

Angelia stared into her mug. 'I'll probably just hire someone and be a silent owner.' She shrugged.

Ruby straightened up. 'Wouldn't you want to be a noisy owner?' Ruby asked, grinning. 'I know what you're like with your records, Angel. I think you'd find it hard to not be directly involved. Although I suppose it would be hard with the band and travelling.'

Angelia shrugged. 'I'm trying to be realistic about my future. I know there's a good chance that touring isn't going to be possible for me any more, and the band may want to replace me.'

'I doubt that they would want to do that, honey. They adore you. They wouldn't ditch you like that.'

Angelia lifted her chin. 'No, they maybe wouldn't make that decision themselves but… maybe I could make it for them.'

Ruby's eyes widened. 'But why?'

'Because it's not fair for me to keep them hanging on when they could go on without me, Ruby.'

'I really think you should hold off from making rash decisions. You're still getting used to your diagnosis. Please give it plenty of thought, won't you?'

Angelia nodded and rapidly changed the subject.

* * *

Angelia arrived home around 11.30 p.m. to find her mum waiting for her at the kitchen table.

'Aw, Mum, you didn't have to wait up for me,' she said as she leaned on the door jamb.

'I know, love. I just wanted to make sure you got home okay. I worry about you getting accosted by fans or something but then I remember we're on Skye,' her mum said with a light laugh. 'It's lovely to have you home but I wish you'd take Meghan with you if you go out. Otherwise, what's the point of her being here?'

'To be honest, I wasn't the one who wanted her to come with me. That was Den's insistence. But I'm fine going out by myself here. It's home.'

Her mum sighed. 'You could still get kidnapped or something, though, love.'

Angelia laughed. 'Not really likely but I promise to be careful. It's nice to go out without worrying about the same stuff I have to worry about in London. More people means more chance of being recognised. I'm just making the most of it.'

Her mum stood from the table and walked over to kiss her forehead. 'You're stubborn just like your dad,' she said with a small smile. 'Did you go to the shop?'

Angelia thought back to the group of teenagers but chose not to mention them in light of her mum's worries. 'No, I was just at the pub with Ruby drinking coffee and catching up. It was lovely actually. The Coxswain is so cosy.'

'That's nice. I'm off to bed anyway. Love you.'

Her mum walked away and Angelia called after her. 'You don't need to worry, Mum, honestly. Love you too.'

12

A couple of uneventful weeks passed in which Angelia had frequent Zoom calls with Mr Novak, the consultant, and she was introduced, on one such call, to Lydia, a nurse from Inverness who specialised in working with myasthenia patients, with the instruction that if she had any problems Lydia would be a good point of contact. Fiona had been in regular contact by video call and Ed by WhatsApp.

Heath, Bear, Dom, Den and Anouk had taken it in turns to contact her individually, so as not to overwhelm her or pressure her into feeling she had to return to them. And, of course, there had been the usual messages with silly memes in the band's group chat. Josh, however, had been strangely silent.

Angelia and Meghan had spent time at the shop cleaning and preparing for meeting the interior designer Ruby had mentioned and the place was looking a little more shipshape. The village residents had been so friendly and welcoming. While people had known who she was, no one had made her feel like an outsider. She had been treated like any visitor, welcomed and with warmth.

A daily visit to Caitlin's bakery became part of their routine, although Meghan commented frequently that she should definitely stop eating cake or she might not fit through the door of her Mini any more. Suffice it to say the visits to the bakery continued.

'Ooh, no, eat the cake I say,' Caitlin had said. 'Life's too short to worry about what size you are.'

Meghan had laughed. 'You would say that, you're the one selling the dangerously addictive little demons.'

They had a lunchtime visit to the Lifeboat House Museum where they met Jules and learned about the old lifeboat and the lives saved by the crew. Jules seemed sweet and very friendly.

'You'll have to join us for our book club if you decide to stay on the island,' Jules had said. 'Although I have to admit it's usually about drinking wine and gossiping rather than the book we've read,' she'd added with a giggle.

'That sounds good to me!' Angelia had replied, feeling a strange sense of belonging thanks to local women she had encountered.

Now that the medication was taking more of an effect, Angelia was champing at the bit to get out in the fresh air, so on a sunny Tuesday, after May had arrived in an array of vivid colours, the hedgerows around the bothy were vital with new life and there were a few extra hours of sunshine, Angelia directed Meghan on a drive around some of her favourite Skye beauty spots. Whilst she drove, Meghan gushed about how stunning the island was as Scrappy sat happily in his car seat in the back of the Mini, with his front paws on the base of the window. It was as far as his seatbelt would allow but he was clearly enjoying the view of the birds he could see. Every so often he gave a little growl and a single bark.

Following Angelia's instructions, Meghan pulled her Mini into the car park at the base of the Old Man of Storr and they climbed out. Scrappy's tail began wagging frantically and he sniffed the ground in one place, and then another, and another; his senses overwhelmed.

'It's funny but when I was a kid I didn't appreciate the beauty of Wales. I grew up in Cardiff so I'm a city girl at heart, and I used to think views were a bit shit. My mum used to take me places on the train and go, "Look at the view out there," pointing out the window and I'd be like, "Yeah, whatever," and go back to reading my book. But I tell you what, this place is spectacular,' Meghan said. 'I mean, these views are anything but shit.' She laughed.

With Scrappy leading the way, Meghan and Angelia set out, the latter determined to at least try to walk the gravel path that led to the summit, but her legs weakened rapidly and with tears in her eyes she had to sit and rest.

She took a book and a bottle of water out of her rucksack and insisted that Meghan make the journey without her while she waited with Scrappy, sitting on the flat rock she had found. She sat, face tilted towards the sky, enjoying the warm heat of the spring sunshine as Scrappy greeted every person that passed them by.

After only half an hour, her assistant returned, rosy-cheeked and smiling. 'I didn't go all the way to the top because I hated the thought of you sitting here by yourself.'

'I'm not by myself. I've got Scrappy, haven't I, buddy?' Angelia said, scratching the little dog behind his ears.

'Aww, did you look after Angel wike a good wittle boy?' Meghan asked him in a babyish voice that he clearly appreciated. He tilted his head as if fully understanding every word. 'I tell you what, the views from up there are stunning. It's made me want to go back home and visit the Brecon Beacons so I can look at the place through fresh eyes.'

They ate a picnic in the shadow of the Old Man of Storr with a bright blue sky overhead and once again Angelia marvelled at the place she called home and tried not to dwell on the fact she couldn't make the climb she had once loved. She explained to Meghan that from the top there was a panoramic view that took in the Sound of Raasay right across to the island itself and then a little further north to Rona. And that on a clear day, you could see right across to the Scottish mainland. From their viewpoint, only part of the way up, the sea appeared almost glasslike, calm and reflecting the rays of the sun that danced on the surface as if they had a life of their own.

'It's even more beautiful in the summer,' Angelia said. 'But having said that, you should see it when the place is covered in a blanket of snow. It's like something from a painting.'

'I'll have to come back with you in the winter,' Meghan said with a sigh. They sat in silence for a while and just admired the view until Meghan said, 'If it's okay with you, I think I might spend some time video calling with Ezra this evening.'

Angelia nodded. 'Absolutely. You being here with me isn't really conducive to a fledgling relationship, is it? I really don't mind if you want to go back to London, you know. I've bumped into fans a few times in Glentorrin now and it's been fine. I haven't felt threatened or unsafe.'

Meghan nudged her with her shoulder. 'You trying to get rid of me?'

Angelia gave a small laugh. 'Not at all. You're my friend as well as my assistant and it's always fun being with you, I just think you could be doing something a bit less boring with your time than babysitting an adult.'

Meghan continued to gaze at the land spread out before them. 'I think Den was worried about you being hounded by crazed fans. Or maybe it's that he doesn't want you to get used to being back at home too much, and if I'm here you have a constant reminder of where you belong. But I don't really think you *need* me here, do you?'

Angelia shook her head slowly, worried about offending her. 'Need? No, probably not. I think what I do need is time to adjust to things and to think about what I can do going forward. I used to walk this path so easily when I was younger and it breaks my heart knowing how much I struggled today, but I just need to work out what my limits are, that's all. And I *will* figure things out. I've been reading up on the MGUK website about people with this condition, and what they've achieved in spite of it, and it's given me renewed hope. It's not all negative, doom and gloom like it felt at the beginning and that's progress. I'm feeling so much more positive in general. Today was probably a bit ambitious but we've had fun and some amazing fresh Skye air.'

'And the views from here are incredible,' Meghan added. 'Come on, let's get back to the car and you can take me to see your mum's bookshop, eh?'

* * *

That evening, after dinner, Meghan disappeared to her room to call Ezra and Angelia decided she would like to go back to Glentorrin to visit the shop again. She hadn't made a habit of venturing out on her own since she had met the group of college kids the other day, but she saw no reason why she shouldn't. Her mum and dad were not so sure. They were concerned about something happening with her condition while she was alone, even though she had explained, in detail, that it was unlikely. She couldn't be upset with them, however, they simply cared about their daughter.

'I'll come with you,' her dad, said reaching for his car keys. 'We can have a chat about things on the way.'

Angelia held up her hand. 'No, Dad. It's okay. You stay here. I think I'd like to just go by myself. Scrappy can come too and I'll take my phone and call you if I need you, but Ruby's in the village if I do need anything. I just want to go and have a really good look around and see what plans I can come up with.'

Her dad glanced at her mum and then back to Angelia. 'But—'

'I'll be fine, Dad. You don't need to worry.'

Her mum nudged him. 'See, stubborn just like her father.'

Angelia put on her baseball cap and tucked her hair up into it, pulled on her jacket and within minutes, Scrappy was clipped into his car seat.

Just under an hour later she parked her car by the village hall, which was all in darkness this evening. The sky overhead was now a little overcast, and the temperature had dropped but it was by no means cold. She lifted Scrappy out of the car, and as they began to walk across to the shop, she spotted two men standing by the inlet. As she got level with them, she noticed they both had cameras and presumed they had been photographing the wildlife or the pretty location. But one turned and spotted her and hit the other on the arm and in her periphery, she saw him nod towards her. They began to follow her, which caused Scrappy's ears to prick up. He kept looking behind himself and giving low growls.

'Hey! Hey, love, are you going to pose for us?' one of them asked in a Glaswegian accent. Angelia didn't reply. The other began to type on his phone and within only a few moments two more men came out of the pub and made their way across to the others.

'Are you going to stop for a chat, Angel?'

Angelia stopped and turned to face the men. 'I'm sorry, *who*?'

'You're that Angel lassie, the singer from the band. We saw yous on the Instagram here with some kids a few weeks ago and we've been coming over ever since to try and catch you. We've come over special from Glasgow to see if we can get some good shots. Don't leave us disappointed, eh?'

Angelia scrunched her nose. 'Nah, I think you're mixing me up with someone. I'm a shop owner, not a singer, pal.'

'I told you it *wasnae* her,' one of the newcomers said with a huff. 'We've wasted weeks coming back and forth here on a bloody wild moose chase. You should never just believe what you see on Instagram, Davey. AI is everywhere now. You're too gullible.'

'I think you mean wild *goose* chase,' the fourth one said.

'Goose, moose, what's the difference? Neither of them is here, you numpty. And neither is the Angel lassie.'

'Aye, she is. It *is* her,' the first man, presumably called Davey, said. 'She's the same height and every'hin'.'

Angelia turned, tugged on Scrappy's lead and began to walk briskly away. She safely made it a few hundred yards, and the group continued to argue amongst themselves with raised voices. 'I told you she was going to be here. Apparently, her mum and dad stay up by Portree. It's definitely her.'

They hadn't even noticed that she had walked away which amused her no end. It was like listening to something out of a *Monty Python* sketch and Angelia was tempted to stay and watch it all play out.

'I think it's her too. Come on, let's get some shots and then we can get back to the pub. We can make a decent amount on shots of her *fae* the tabloids, I'm telling yous,' Angelia heard the first one say just as she ducked out of sight behind a leafy spruce tree in the churchyard. She glanced down at Scrappy and whispered, 'Shhh.' The dog gave a wag of his tail and turned to make sure they hadn't followed.

'Don't forget I'm bloody driving, Boaby, and I'm no driving yous all home pissed *oot yer heids*, I can tell yous that for nohin'.'

As their contradictory conversation ensued, Angelia paused behind the tree as she watched them look around, confused. She finally managed to lose the group of so-called paparazzi by sneaking in through the unlocked door of the church.

13

Churches had always been a bone of contention to Angelia. She had always been spiritual but never religious. She was uncomfortable with organised worship and a God who somehow – according to doctrine, at least – keeps tabs on people's attendance at a purpose-built structure with fancy windows and opulent outfits. She had felt out of place at every church wedding and christening she had ever attended. Add to this the fact she was a singer in a rock band called Angel and the Fallen, which could potentially be seen as blasphemous, and she was grateful that she hadn't burst into flames when she had crossed the threshold.

A group of people stood at the front of the church but had, thankfully, not noticed her entering. They were too deep in an intense conversation so she picked up Scrappy and slipped into a pew at the back where she would be hidden by a pillar if anyone were to look around in her direction.

A petite elderly woman with, bizarrely, purple hair was standing, arms folded across her chest and shaking her head. 'So not only has Geraldine broken both her wrists falling off rollerblades – I mean what was she thinking at her age – but now you're telling us Amelia has chicken pox?' she said with a huff. 'All we need now is for one of those steroids to hit the earth and we've a complete set.' She harrumphed sulkily as Angelia stifled a giggle.

'Come on, Granny, it's not as bad as that,' a blonde woman told her with a small laugh as she slipped an arm around the older lady's shoulder. 'And I think you mean *asteroid*.'

The purple-haired woman glared up at the blonde. 'Aye, Arabella, that's what a said.' She then added, 'We've lost our organist and our choir manager less than a month before the summer concert, so I'd say it's pretty bloomin' castratory.'

The woman named Arabella grimaced. '*Catastrophic*, Granny.' And Angelia chuckled. She liked the purple-haired lady already.

'Hi, can I help you?'

On hearing the soft familiar Scottish accent spoken by people from around the Edinburgh area, Angelia almost jumped out of her skin. She turned to see a very handsome, clean-cut man in a navy button-down shirt and jeans, looking down at her from beside the pew.

'Oh, erm, no, I'm fine, thanks.' She turned quickly in the opposite direction and glanced nervously over her shoulder towards the door, wondering who else was about to enter.

'It's okay, I told them you'd got in a car and left the island,' he said with a smile.

Angelia's face flushed with heat. 'Oh... thanks. But... erm... Look, if you're a reporter, too, I'm just not—'

She made to stand up but he held up a halting hand and laughed. 'Well, I've never been accused of *that* before but no, you're safe. I only report to him upstairs, not the world.' Her crumpled and confused expression and the way she glanced towards the ceiling looking for an upper floor must have been a huge giveaway. He held out his hand, smiling. 'Ferris Blaikie, curate extraordinaire,' he said.

'Oh!' was all she could manage to say as she pointed to the ceiling, the fact he meant *God* dawning on her.

He reached out to stroke Scrappy's head, and the little dog seemed to relish the attention. 'Please, you're welcome to stay as long as you like, Miss MacAuley.'

'You do know who I am then?'

He grinned and nodded. 'I certainly do. Ruby said you were buying the old antique shop across the way and that we might see you around the village a wee bit.' He glanced around a little conspiratorially before whispering, 'But I'm also partial to a bit of rock music too.'

He must have been in his early thirties, with neat brown hair and smiling eyes to match. He was tall, good-looking and broad shouldered and didn't look how she expected a curate to look. Although what that was *exactly*, she wasn't sure.

'Are you allowed to listen to that sort of stuff?' she asked in surprise.

He chuckled. 'Yes, of course we are. It's not the Dark Ages, you know. And to my knowledge you're not a group of devil worshippers who bite the heads off animals.'

She felt a little foolish and her face warmed with the heat of embarrassment. 'No, I suppose not. Well, thank you for hiding me, anyway,' she said, smiling. 'I appreciate it.'

'No bother at all. I heard you were coming home to Skye for some peace and quiet and to escape all that stuff so...'

'Right...' she said.

'Aye, I was saying to Ruby it seems the stars just love this wee village.'

Angelia nodded. 'So it would appear.' He turned to walk away. 'So, you're a curate? What does that mean? Are you a kind of trainee vicar?'

He smiled to reveal a row of slightly crooked but healthy-looking sparkling white teeth. They gave his face character, she thought, and then wondered why on earth she was giving him a dental assessment.

He grinned. 'I suppose you could say that. I'm ordained but I'm working here to assist Father McAllen until I'm assigned my own parish.'

Angelia nodded. 'Right, cool.'

'Are you a churchgoer, Miss MacAuley?' Ferris asked with a tilt of his head.

She cringed. 'Please call me Angelia. And no, not really. I'm not exactly a religious type, to be honest. Sorry.'

He shook his head. 'No apology needed. You're welcome to stay until you're comfortable to leave. But like I say, they've gone now.' He paused and then slipped into the pew in front of her. 'I'm intrigued as to why you chose this as your hiding place, though.'

Angelia felt that warmth in her face again. 'In all honesty it was the first place I came across while I was running away from those paps. I tried the door, and it opened so... here I am.' She held out her free hand to exaggerate her point.

He raised his eyebrows and nodded. 'God does work in mysterious ways.' And then added, 'If you believe in that kind of stuff, of course.'

'Which I don't, I'm afraid,' she replied.

'Noted. And who's this cute little chap?' he asked, reaching out to stroke Scrappy again.

'This is my best friend, Scrappy. He's not a big talker but he's quite the listener,' she said with a grin. 'You don't look like a priest,' she said without meaning to and clapped her hand over her mouth. 'Ooh, sorry, I meant to just *think* that rather than say it aloud.'

He laughed. 'Ah, well, you see, you came in before proper nightfall. At that point I grow a bushy beard and most of my hair falls out before thick-rimmed specs appear on my face and I start asking people for cups of tea.'

Angelia laughed along, wagging a finger. 'Ah, that explains it. It's the timing.'

'Aye. It usually is. So—' Before he could say anything further the chatter between the group at the front of the church became heated and loud.

'I'm just saying there's no point carrying on if we don't have anyone to lead us,' a woman aged around sixty, with badly dyed, *very* dark brown hair and wearing a flowery dress, said.

'Well, you can *away 'n boil yer heid*, Gertrude McHugh,' the purple-haired, rather feisty, woman told her, as the elderly men in the group stood by silently, seemingly a little gobsmacked.

'Granny! That's plenty!' the blonde-haired woman – Arabella, was it? – said.

'Sorry but she's been a negative Nelly from day one. Am I the only one who remembers the Christmas concert rehearsals? It was all, "I don't want to sing anything by Michael Bubbles, he's no Frank Sinatra,"' the purple-haired woman mimicked the McHugh woman. 'And "Isla Guthrie, it's round yon virgin, not Round John Bergin." Honestly, you make one mistake,' she chuntered and shook her head while patting her perfectly styled lavender hairdo.

'That's it! I've had enough. I'm going to go back to knitting club in Broadford,' the McHugh woman said with a stamp of her foot. She wagged an index finger in the face of Lavender Haze. 'And for the record, Isla Guthrie, the lyrics in "Dancing Queen" aren't anything to do with feeding beef on a tangerine, nor is there *any* ABBA lyric that says "*take your teeth out, tell me what's wrong*."' She grabbed her jacket. 'I knew this was a waste of time, right from the get-go.'

'Aye, well, you go and get gone then,' the purple-haired granny said, and Angelia almost choked on a laugh that escaped.

'Excuse me,' Ferris, the curate, said as he stood. 'I think they may be in need of a referee.' He grimaced and turned to walk away but stopped. 'Look, if you need to talk to someone while you're here, I'm a great listener. I'm not quite as cute as your current confidante, admittedly, but unlike him I've been known to give out some pretty sound advice too. And I'm here most days.' He smiled and then turned again to head hurriedly towards the chancel. 'Ladies! Gentlemen! What seems to be the issue?'

Angelia watched as Ferris calmed the frayed tempers of those involved in the dispute.

When they had, not particularly quietly, explained their predicament, he said, 'Well, I would be happy to play the music for you, temporarily, if that helps?'

As Ferris took a seat at the keyboard, which was situated off to the side, Angelia decided it was a good time to take her leave. Ferris played the opening bars to Katrina and the Waves' 'Love Shine a Light' and as she reached the door, Angelia glanced back over her shoulder to see the keyboard-playing, friendly, rather handsome, curate nodding along with the sheet music as the group of people rearranged themselves now their number had decreased by one.

* * *

As Ferris had said, the coast was most definitely clear so Angelia and Scrappy wandered over to the shop. Once through the door, she flicked on the lights. They would definitely be the first order of business, she decided as she squinted around the space in the meagre amount of illumination they offered, as the sun had begun its descent. Now that she had recovered from the shock of the initial viewing of the place, and it had been cleaned up and cleared of the detritus, she felt better able to view it as a blank canvas, with an open mind. It was going to take some serious work, but she could see someone really making a go of a business here. She released Scrappy from his lead and the curious canine headed off, sniffing at every spot within his reach as he always did when they brought him.

As she stood in the same area she had only a couple of days earlier, armed on that occasion with a sweeping brush, she could now envisage racks of albums against the walls and in the centre. She could imagine music playing over a fancy sound system that would obviously be needed for such an establishment, and she could visualise people queueing up at the old cash register to pay for their unique finds. A smile spread across her face as she daydreamed about the place all decked out for Christmas too with fairy lights strewn from the ceiling and perhaps a tree in the corner with old CDs fashioned into ornaments.

Her heart skipped at the thought of creating something wonderfully different. Something no one would expect from either her, or from the little coastal village of Glentorrin. She understood what her mum and Fiona had said about making the place viable for a variety of business possibilities, but Meghan's idea of a record shop just *felt* right. It was exciting and, of course, appealed to her passion for music and record collecting. All she had to do now was kit the place out and hope that someone would love her vision and Meghan's idea.

14

After she had looked around the retail area of the ground floor, Angelia made her way up the stairs to the living accommodation, closely followed by her canine companion. It was quite a decent size and consisted of two bedrooms, a kitchen, a living room and a bathroom straight out of the 1970s. It was devoid of taste, unless of course orange and brown were your kind of thing, and it was clear this part of the building hadn't been touched since the age of flower power and Formica. It was ugly but almost liveable, she decided. Almost.

Her imagination ran riot on what this place could become. Someone would be so happy and at home here. Even in its current state there was something warm and cosy about the place. The whole apartment would fit, easily, into the open-plan living area of her place in London. But that wasn't such a bad thing. Her London pad was vast and too echoey to be deemed cosy or homely. In fact, she had often felt it was far too big for just her and Scrappy.

As she stood there examining the damp patches on the walls that almost looked like part of the wallpaper pattern, her phone rang. She lifted it from her back pocket and saw Ed's name flashing up on the screen.

Her heart skipped a little dance in her chest. 'Hey, Ed. How are you doing?' She hoped her tone wasn't quite as needy to him as it sounded falling from her lips.

'Hi, Angel. Yeah, I'm not too bad. I've been really busy so I'm sorry I've not had a chance to call again until now.' To be fair, he had been messaging regularly to ask how she was. 'I'm glad the meds are taking effect now but I was sorry to read your message about struggling to walk up the Storr earlier. That must have been frustrating. Are you okay now you've rested?'

She was so happy to hear his voice and leaned on the window ledge to give him her full attention. 'I'm fine. It was silly of me to even attempt it knowing what I know of this condition. But I'm okay. I've decided to look at the positives in everything, rather than dwell on the negative.'

'That's the Angel I know and love,' he said with a smile to his voice. She laughed.

'Anyway, how are you *really*?' she asked, happy to change the subject.

'Yeah, honestly, I'm good. Exhausted but good.'

'Fiona tells me you have a new girlfriend.'

There was a brief silence. 'Oh, she told you about Ava.' It was a statement rather than a question.

'She did, ages ago actually. Seeing as you tell me nothing these days.'

'Sorry, yeah, as I said—'

'You're busy?'

'I'm back in a couple of weeks and I thought I might come and visit you if you're still at your mum and dad's.'

Angelia's spirits were suddenly lifted. 'That'd be lovely. I'd really like that. My mum and dad are going on holiday to Canada for a few weeks at the end of May. They tried to tell me they were cancelling it, but I wouldn't hear of it. It's not like I'm incapacitated. I'm perfectly capable of looking after myself. And they've wanted to go to Canada for as long as I can remember. Mum has sorted cover for the bookshop and Dad has special permission from the bank's head office for taking three consecutive weeks off, so it seems silly to cancel it all now. And there's nothing anybody can do. I just have to adjust things in my life and I'll be fine.' She sounded a lot more convincing than she felt.

'That actually lines up with when I'd be coming over. Could I maybe stay for a few days? Keep you company?'

'That'd be great. Although I should warn you, I'm being watched like a hawk by Meghan.'

Ed chuckled. 'They sent her with you then?'

Angelia rolled her eyes. 'They sure did. I mean I've been here… what? Three weeks so far and I've only had two small incidents; one with a group of great kids who I took selfies with and then today there was a group of pretend paparazzi who thought they recognised me.'

'*Thought* they recognised you?'

'Yeah, it was hilarious. I told them they were mistaken and they all set about arguing over whether I was actually me or not, but I managed to lose them by going into the church in Glentorrin.'

'You in a church? You don't do churches.'

Angelia grinned. 'Not normally. I was saved by the curate.'

'Eh?' Ed laughed again.

'The church in Glentorrin has a curate assisting the rector and he managed to get rid of them. He was really sweet about it all.'

'So, *he* recognised you too? A vicar?' Ed asked with a hint of surprise to his tone.

'He did. Apparently, he's partial to a bit of rock music.'

'Are they allowed to listen to that kind of stuff?' he asked, echoing her own words. 'Or is he a rebellious curate?'

Angelia smiled. 'Oh yes, things have changed in the world of religion apparently.'

'And what were you doing in Glentorrin? And where even is that?'

It had slipped her mind that he wasn't familiar with Skye. She'd known him so long she had almost forgotten he was from Hampshire. 'It's the first village you come to as you cross the Skye Bridge. And I'm here because I've bought another property.'

'Oh, cool. Fee said you were looking again. Is it another house?'

'No, this one's a shop and a flat above. I'm trying to decide what to do with it. Meghan suggested a record shop.'

'Oh, now, you're talking! That's so perfect for you. You could set one up with your collection as it is. That would be awesome,' Ed said enthusiastically.

'Except I'm not selling a single one of mine, thank you very much,' she replied with a light-hearted laugh.

'No surprise there. Seriously, though, I think it's the best idea for you. Vinyl records are making a big comeback. Loads of my friends are into vinyl. I've been to some cool record shops in New York. They can be so atmospheric. Oh... hang on a sec...' He fell silent a moment. 'Yeah, Ava, I'm coming,' he said off into the distance with a tinge of annoyance. 'Sorry, Angel, I need to get going.'

Angelia nodded even though he couldn't see her. 'No worries. It's been good to talk to you, Ed.'

'Yeah, you too,' he almost whispered. 'I miss you.' It wasn't like him to be sentimental, but it had happened both times he had spoken to her recently. There was definitely more to it, and she wondered if he was okay. *Perhaps he's just homesick*, she thought.

'I miss you too,' Angelia replied, swallowing down a surprise ball of emotion.

'Bye for now.'

'Bye for now, Ed.'

* * *

As she locked up the shop, her phone buzzed with a message. It was Josh.

JOSH

Hey. I miss you. Sorry I've been so quiet but this thing with your diagnosis has really affected me. I feel so useless and I hate that. I am thinking about you though. All day. Every day. You never know, I may come and visit if your folks are still heading to Canada. Can't wait to see you. J xx

A twinge of annoyance squeezed her insides. Had he really just made this situation about him? After remaining silent for weeks, had he seriously just messaged her to say *he* was having a hard time?

She didn't bother to reply right away for fear she would say exactly what she was feeling about his selfish message and instead drove home with the silver moonlight lighting her way.

* * *

Later that night, after a long chat with her parents about the shop, Angelia lay in bed, exhausted but wide awake. So many things were whizzing around her head, vying for dominance; Josh and his message, what she had overheard him saying to Heath, her feelings for Ed, her future with the band. Sleep evaded her as it had done a fair bit since her diagnosis. So, she lay there, staring at the patterns on the ceiling made by the branches of a tree in the garden as it danced in a breeze, silhouetted by moonlight. She stroked the soft fur of Scrappy's side and listened to the funny noises he made while sleeping. She was so grateful to have him. He was an excellent distraction and had the knack of cheering her up even on days where she felt like everything was going wrong.

Being wide awake in the small hours of the morning rendered her stuck with her own inner dialogue and she eventually got around to the inevitable thoughts on her relationship status. Everyone seemed to have someone these days. Even the young dog-walking teenagers she had seen in Glentorrin weeks before. Fiona was blissfully happy with Marcus and the eternal bachelor, Ed, had met someone too – although she tried not to picture what Ava might look like. She would no doubt be perfect, beautiful, talented. Simply because that's what Ed deserved. Meghan was spending lots of time chatting to Ezra and she regularly oozed swoons and sat there all dreamy-eyed as she talked about her new beau. Yup, it seemed everyone was falling in love except for Angelia.

The handsome curate sprang to her mind with his smiling eyes and kind nature. *Oh, good grief*, she thought, *I must be desperate if I'm thinking about a bloody priest. How the hell would that even work? I'm not religious. I don't go to church unless I have to. And I have been known to swear like a trooper on tour. No, I'm better to just wait and surely my prince will come someday. Won't he?*

Although she knew that in her line of work the men she was likely to meet were either fans, fellow rock band dwellers or actors. She just wanted to meet someone normal, whatever that meant, and down-to-earth. Someone with a regular job who maybe didn't know her as 'Angel from Angel and the Fallen' but as Angelia MacAuley – the… human being? Who was she kidding, though? The band was so well-known she'd have to go to Antarctica to find someone who'd never heard of her. And as much as the cold on Skye didn't faze her too much, Antarctica just didn't appeal. Temperatures of minus eighty-five sounded horrendous and she was sure dating penguins wasn't something she wanted to do, even though *Happy Feet* had been a fabulous film.

She laughed out loud at her train of thought, making Scrappy jump up and give a single bark. How had she gone from feeling lovelorn to dating penguins? She definitely needed a better distraction. She grabbed her phone and typed in the details for the interior designer from Glentorrin that Ruby had told her about into the search engine. Bella Donaldson had some excellent reviews, and the photos of her work were wonderful.

The images showed a stable block conversion at Drumblair Castle near Inverness, where she had created rental apartments that were little homes from home, with stunning fabrics, gorgeous artwork and beautiful touches that gave a feeling of luxury. And speaking of luxury, Bella had also worked on a refurbishment of a hotel in the north of Skye where William Morris prints had been used. Angelia was surprised to see the manager of said hotel was none other than Carlton Somers, former male model. Angelia shivered involuntarily at the mention of his name. She had encountered him when the band had played at a Nina Picarro fashion show some years earlier. He had been quite a slimy character, full of himself and a bit too leery for her liking. She wondered how on earth he had wound up managing a hotel. Although, if the rumours about his treatment of a well-known makeup artist had been true, perhaps he'd been dropped by his agent.

Angelia was certain, after what she had viewed on the website, that Bella Donaldson was the person for the design of her record shop so, deciding to strike while the proverbial iron was hot, she emailed Bella immediately to ask for a meeting.

15

Angelia shook a pill from the bottle she had been given and made her way down the stairs, closely followed by her canine best friend. She arrived, yawning and drained, to find her dad and Meghan sitting at the kitchen table drinking coffee and chatting.

'Oh, there she is. Good morning, love. Did you sleep well?' her dad asked as Scrappy walked over to him for his morning cuddle.

She had tried her best to keep the severity of her insomnia from her parents so as not to worry them further. 'I did, thanks,' she lied as she ran some water into a glass and swallowed the tablet. This time, thankfully, it went down with ease. Swallowing had been an issue again over the past few days.

'Ah, that's good. There's coffee made,' her dad said with a smile as she bent to kiss his head. 'I'm just about to head off for work but wanted to wait 'til you got up to check you were okay.'

'Thanks, Dad.' She poured herself a mug and inhaled the steam with closed eyes, relishing the earthy aroma. Coffee was her rescue remedy. She didn't often eat breakfast but couldn't function without her first mug of coffee, and her lack of sleep meant it was even more necessary and appreciated. 'I emailed Bella Donaldson, the interior designer down in Glentorrin, last night,' she announced. 'I want her to come and have a look at the shop to see what can be done now it's cleared out and cleaner.'

'Great idea,' her dad said as he stood from the table. 'I look forward to hearing what she says.'

Angelia took a seat at the table, opposite Meghan. 'I suppose the decorating is the fun and easy part. What may be trickier is finding someone who wants to either buy or rent the place to run it as a record shop. Maybe I'm being too specific, after all.' Her heart sank a little as she spoke.

'Hmm,' her dad said thoughtfully. 'Maybe, if you're so keen on having it converted into a record shop, you could keep the place and just hire in a manager to run it?' he said with a shrug. 'That way it can be whatever *you* want but you'll own it and simply employ someone. You can choose and source the stock and decide how it's run. It's another thing for your portfolio and it's something that means a lot to you. You've been obsessed with records since you learned how to operate my old turntable. And even though it's a little different for Glentorrin, it's more of a passion project. You could see how it goes and if it doesn't work, you could sell it on.' He shrugged as if it was as easy as all that. But maybe it was. She didn't need the money right now so it was the perfect opportunity to try such a thing out. Her dad continued. 'I actually think people would travel to it from the mainland. Like they do for your mum's bookshop. If you create the right atmosphere and curate a good selection of vinyl, sheet music, maybe band and vintage movie posters, too, I think it could be very successful. You'd maybe need a warehouse as well but we could look into that as and when...'

She loved this about her dad. He was very business-minded and always had the best ideas. A jolt of excitement flipped her stomach. Having her dad's approval was always something she sought, even as an adult; luckily for her she acquired it on most things. And the thought of owning her own retail business was as enticing as it was terrifying.

'Yeah... I actually like the sound of that. I could do that. I could own a record shop,' she said with a nod of affirmation.

'The fact that *you* own the place couldn't hurt with publicity either,' Meghan added.

Her dad wagged a finger at Meghan. 'Very good point. You hear about actors owning restaurants and being flocked with people hoping to spot the celebrities. It must be good for business.'

'Oh, definitely,' Meghan said with enthusiasm. 'Mark Wahlberg has a burger joint; Jon Bon Jovi owns a wine company *and* a community kitchen. So many more famous women have started companies too. I know of a few fashion and beauty brands but none that own a record store. It's good to be the first.'

'The more I think about it, the more excited I get,' Angelia said.

'The fact that you're so excited speaks volumes, love,' her dad said with a smile. 'It's good to see you lighting up like that again.'

Angelia sighed. 'I can't wait to talk to Bella Donaldson now.'

* * *

Once she was showered and dressed, Angelia checked her emails and was delighted to see a reply from the interior designer.

Dear Angelia,

It was lovely to hear from you and to learn about the possibility of a business moving into the old building in Glentorrin. It has such potential. If you're free this afternoon, I can meet you there around 2 p.m. My mobile number is in the signature section of the email so just drop me a text if that's easier.

Hopefully see you this afternoon.

Best wishes,

Bella

Angelia's stomach flipped with giddiness, and she dropped her a text right away to confirm the appointment. She then informed Meghan she would need to take a drive to Glentorrin again. Of course, Meghan jumped at the chance.

The weather was mild but a little overcast as they travelled south on the island in the little yellow Mini Cooper and when they arrived in the village, Bella was waiting outside the shop. Angelia was surprised to discover she was one of the women from the church who had been involved in the dispute over the injured organist and poorly choir manager, or was it the other way around? Anyway, she was the granddaughter of the feisty purple-haired old lady who Angelia had taken an immediate liking to from afar.

Bella smiled brightly as she saw the car coming to a stop. Angelia climbed out and lifted Scrappy to the floor. His tail began to wag excitedly as he saw the potential new friend waiting for them.

'Bella Donaldson?' Angelia asked with a smile.

Bella's face coloured bright pink and she held out her hand. 'Yes, yes, that's me. It's lovely to meet you. I was a little nervous when Ruby mentioned she had given you my details. I'd heard you had connections to Skye but never expected to actually *meet* you,' Bella said, her words coming out in a rush. 'Oh, heck, sorry for rambling, I'm a wee bit starstruck. Me and my husband love your band. We came to see you in Glasgow a few years ago and you were amazing.'

Angelia shook the offered hand and smiled. 'Ah, thank you. And thanks for meeting me at such short notice.'

Bella waved a dismissive hand. 'Oh, it's no bother at all. I'm excited to see inside the old place. It's fascinated me for a while now.'

'Well, all I can say is it's a good thing you're seeing it after we've cleaned up because until now it was a bit grotty,' Angelia said.

'Oh, I've probably seen worse.'

'This is Meghan, my assistant,' Angelia said as she gestured to her and the two women shook hands.

'And who's this little cutie?' Bella asked as she bent to greet the mini schnauzer.

'This wee nugget is Scrappy. And he will no doubt love you forever if you keep giving him pets. He's very friendly.'

Meghan took a hold of Scrappy's lead and Angelia unlocked the wooden outer doors and then the inner ones. She stepped inside followed by Bella, Meghan and, of course, Scrappy.

'Oh, wow. I can see what you mean about the vision that's required,' Bella said with a giggle. 'It's certainly a blank canvas. But honestly, the hotel I worked on was far worse.' She wandered around making notes on an iPad and snapped photos too. 'Such potential,' she whispered as she glanced up at the ceiling and let her attention track the whole room. 'I think this place would make a splendid record shop; it's got bags of character and people love buildings like this with charm for retail spaces. I can definitely imagine it full of customers. Especially at Christmas.'

Angelia widened her eyes and grinned. 'I thought of it at Christmas too. I can really imagine it all decked out with twinkling lights and a tree over there in the corner.'

Bella nodded. 'Oh, absolutely. I'm glad we're on the same page there.'

Angelia added, 'And I'd really like to incorporate the old cash register in the design, if possible.'

Bella turned to face her. 'Well, that goes without saying. It's a fabulous piece of history and it'd be a shame not to include it.'

They eventually made their way upstairs and Bella made notes about the rooms, their layouts, window positions, and she used a laser tape to take some measurements. Angelia was impressed with how thorough she seemed to be.

'Now, what I ask all my clients to do is create a sort of mood board filled with colours they like, styles, etcetera, so I can get a feel of the kind of look you'd like to go for. Will you be living here in the flat when you're not on tour?' Bella asked.

Angelia hadn't really thought about living in the place herself… until now, that is. 'Oh… I'm not really sure. I don't know when I'm going to be touring again, to be honest, because…' She stopped herself from saying anything further. After all, she didn't know Bella and even though she seemed like a nice person, she didn't want to trauma-dump on someone she had only just met.

Bella held up her hand. 'Don't worry, I don't need to know anything further than who I'm decorating the place for. I can aim for neutrals if that makes it easier, then the resident can add their own artwork to make the place theirs.'

Angelia nodded. 'Sounds great, thank you.'

A short while later, Angelia waved goodbye to Bella who walked off along the road that led out of the village and Angelia remembered passing the police station on her way in. *That must be where she lives*, she thought as she recalled Bella's website mentioning her police inspector husband.

As she locked up the shop, she heard Meghan speaking to someone behind her. Her tone was authoritative and a little stern. 'Can I help you, sir?'

A little concerned, Angelia turned to see Ferris, and an off-lead black Labrador, walking in their direction. Today he looked a little more priest-like in black trousers and a black shirt with the sleeves rolled up to his elbows. All that was missing was the slip of white from his throat usually worn by people in his role.

Ferris raised his hand in a wave to Angelia. 'I was just out for a walk with my dog, and I spotted Angelia so I thought I would come and say "hi",' he said, pointing behind Meghan.

She held up her hands in a halting gesture. 'That's very kind of you but *Miss MacAuley* isn't—'

'It's fine, Meghan, this is Ferris. He's the one who helped me at the church.'

Meghan's eyes widened and she raised her eyebrows at Angelia, giving a little wry smile that Angelia understood immediately to mean, *He's rather cute*. 'Ah. Okay. I'll wait in the car with Scrappy.'

'How are you doing?' Ferris asked as Angelia bent to greet his canine companion. 'By the way, this is Judy,' he said, scratching the beautiful dog behind the ears.

'Oh, she's lovely,' Angelia said as she stroked the silky back coat and the dog wagged her tail, her tongue lolling out and her brown eyes bright with evident happiness. 'And I love the name.'

He grinned. 'My mum named her after Judy Garland. She was a huge fan. You know, *Meet Me in St Louis*, *Easter Parade*, the whole lot. She loved them all.'

Angelia peered up at him. 'Loved?'

He smiled and nodded. 'Aye. She passed away around five years ago now. Judy was her dog but now she's mine, aren't you, lass?' The dog gazed up at him and her tail continued to wag.

Angelia stood again. 'I'm sorry to hear about your mum, Ferris.'

'It's fine. But thank you. So, how are you doing? Managing to avoid Scotland's finest paparazzi?'

Angelia laughed. 'So far, yes, and I'm good, thanks. You?'

Ferris narrowed his eyes. 'Aye, not too bad. I'm glad you've had no more trouble. I've been keeping an eye out for strangers hanging around suspiciously,' he said with a wink.

Angelia felt her face flush with heat that rose rapidly from her chest. 'Thank you. It gets quite tiring seeing yourself in the tabloids. I feel like I'm always discovering new and delightful, although mostly untrue, things about myself, so I avoid reporters at all costs when I can. But thank you for asking.'

'I was just about to go to the café for a cuppa and a slice of cake if you're free? It's our favourite spot, eh, Judy?' When Angelia glanced over her shoulder at Meghan where she sat in the driver's seat he added, 'Your bodyguard can come, too, of course.'

Angelia giggled. 'Her name's Meghan and she's actually my assistant, although I wouldn't mess with her. She knows martial arts. Let me ask her.' She wandered over to the car and Meghan opened the door. 'Would you and Scrappy like to come for a coffee with me, Ferris, and Judy?'

Meghan peered at the curate through the windscreen and pursed her lips. 'No thanks, I think I'll leave you and the handsome curate to chat. I'm going to video call Ezra. He's in London. I'll be fine here with Scrappy.'

'Are you sure?' Angelia asked and Meghan nodded.

'Absolutely, I don't want to cramp your style, boss,' she said with a wink.

Angelia rolled her eyes. 'He's a vicar,' she whispered.

'Yeah, but he's not the celibate variety, is he?'

Angelia shook her head. 'Incorrigible,' she replied. 'I'll consider bringing you a cake.'

Meghan beamed. 'Something with chocolate would be awesome. If I see any crazed crowds of fans I'll call you,' she said, teasing.

Angelia smiled. 'Funny. This is Glentorrin, not some bustling metropolis, I think I'll be fine.'

Meghan gave her a knowing look. 'Says the woman who was chased into a church looking for sanctuary from a group of paparazzi only a couple of weeks ago.'

Angelia stuck out her tongue like a petulant toddler and Meghan snorted with laughter.

'Right back at you. Now go and enjoy your coffee date with the hunky priest.'

Angelia crumpled her brow and whispered, 'Erm, it's not a date.'

Meghan grinned. 'Sure thing, boss.'

Angelia turned and walked back to Ferris and Judy. 'Okay, I've got time for a quick coffee,' she said in the hope he would know this *wasn't* a date, in case that's what he was thinking, which she doubted anyway; did vicars even date? And maybe he was already married. She realised she had no clue.

Once in the café, Ferris pointed to a table in the corner. 'Why don't you take Judy and have a seat and I'll order. What would you like?'

'Coffee and a piece of cake would be good, thank you. Any kind is fine.' She sat at the table Ferris had pointed out as he went to the counter. It was a pleasant café close to the bakery, with sage-green panelling halfway up the walls and very pretty artwork that showed local scenes Angelia recognised. They were similar to the ones Bella Donaldson had used in the designs she had seen on her website, and she absently wondered about the artist. The tables were covered with green gingham tablecloths and a healthy potted plant sat in the centre of each with lush, verdant leaves and a variety of coloured flowers. The sweet aroma of cakes and bread emanated from the direction of the kitchen and Angelia remembered she hadn't eaten anything yet today.

Once she was seated and Judy had lain down at her feet, the woman behind the counter glanced over at Angelia and her eyes widened as her mouth formed an 'O' shape. She whispered something to Ferris who also glanced over to where she sat. He said something in a hushed reply and the woman nodded and smiled before making a zipping gesture over her now-closed mouth, and throwing away an invisible key. Angelia gave her a nervous smile.

16

Moments later, Ferris arrived at the table and sat opposite her. 'She'll bring it over when it's ready. I ordered you the carrot cake, I hope that's okay.'

'Sounds lovely,' Angelia replied.

'I think you've got a new friend,' he said as he gestured down to where Judy lay beside her, her head resting on her foot.

'That's fine with me,' she said. 'I mostly prefer dogs to people.'

He sucked air in through his teeth. 'Ooh dear. Things are that bad, are they?' When she didn't reply, he continued, 'When I saw you last, you looked like the weight of the world was on your shoulders. Are things any better now?'

Ah, so this is more of a therapy session, is it? Angelia shrugged. 'I'm fine, really.'

He leaned a little closer. 'Look, I know you don't know me from Adam, pardon the pun, but like I said at the church, I'm a good listener. It sort of comes with the job, I suppose. If you did need to talk to someone not connected to whatever you're going through, I'd be happy to be a sounding board. And I can assure you I'm not the type to sell my story, so Kendric MacKinnon won't be turning up to interview you based on anything I've said.'

Angelia gave a small laugh. 'Kendric MacKinnon? Is he still doing his slot on daytime TV?' she asked. 'I remember him from ages ago when he used to present the weather.'

'He is. He's a sort of roving reporter these days. Still very popular with ladies of a certain age,' he said with a wink and a brief tap of his nose. After a short pause, he tilted his head. 'I'm going to miss this place, you know. When I get my own parish. I haven't been here that long but long enough to know Glentorrin is such a great place to live. The people are so friendly, in spite of what you may have thought when you witnessed the choir debacle,' he said with a smile. 'Isla's a real character, but she lives at Pabay View in Broadford so technically she's not a villager.'

'I actually thought she was brilliant. From the purple hair to the malapropisms and even right up to the feisty attitude.'

He smiled. 'Aye, I agree with you there. I wish she was my granny.'

Angelia laughed. 'Me too.'

'So how is it going with the shop?' he asked as he sipped his tea.

'It's slow going but I've spoken to Bella Donaldson now so hopefully things will start moving faster.'

He eyed her with intrigue for a moment. 'So, why *are* you here really?' he asked.

'That's a bit deep, isn't it? Why are *any* of us here?' she asked with a grin.

'You know what I mean. People in your position don't often come back to their hometown unless something big is happening. Or has already happened.'

She nodded towards her latest acquisition. 'I bought the shop here, that's all.' He didn't speak, instead he kept his gaze fixed on her and a small smile on his face. Her stomach knotted and she felt under the spotlight. 'Why do you want to know anyway?'

He shrugged. 'I can read people. Especially people going through stuff. Call it a sixth sense.'

She scoffed and wiggled her fingers at him. 'Ooooh, do you see dead people too?'

He shook his head. 'You use humour as a defence mechanism.'

She rolled her eyes. 'What's with the tuppenny psychology? You don't know me well enough to make such comments. You may *think* you know me, like plenty of other people do, but you don't have a clue,' she informed him, immediately regretting the way it sounded. But before she could apologise the waitress, or café owner perhaps, placed a tray on their table. Angelia looked up at her and with a wavering voice said, 'Thank you, it looks delicious.'

The woman, a tall, slim brunette, blushed profusely and said, 'Wow, thank you. That means a lot. And thank you for coming.' She hovered for a moment longer as if she wanted to ask for something, perhaps an autograph? But then she turned and hurried away.

Once the woman had left them, Ferris said, 'I'm sorry, Angelia. I've been far too familiar with you, and I apologise for my barrage of personal questions. I can assure you I had the best of intentions but please forgive my intrusiveness.' He gestured to the exit. 'Would you rather I leave? I can ask Meghan to come in and—'

Angelia shook her head. 'No, no, it's me who should be apologising. I shouldn't have snapped like that. I don't know what's gotten into me lately.' Then she added, 'Actually, it's probably a lack of sleep. And maybe worry too. But that's no excuse, just an explanation, I suppose. But whatever, I'm sorry and no, I don't want you to go.'

He nodded. 'Well, I promise to stop asking questions. You didn't come home to be interrogated, that's for certain. I'm sure you get enough of that wherever you go.' His smile was gone now, and Angelia felt a twinge of guilt which manifested as a dull ache in her chest.

She lowered her gaze and stared at the creamy frosting on the huge chunk of carrot cake that had been placed before her. She could smell the vanilla and imagine the delectable crunch of the ground nuts on the outside, but her appetite just wasn't there. She couldn't even bring herself to lift the fork.

As if reading her mind, Ferris said, 'You can always get a to-go box and have it later.'

She lifted her gaze to meet his and her chin trembled and for some bizarre reason, as if a gate had been opened, she began to talk, 'The truth is... I've been diagnosed with something called myasthenia gravis. I think it might have permanently stolen my singing voice. I've been really struggling to hit certain notes for a while now, and I've had issues with swallowing, chewing, walking for long periods, and working out too. And there are times when my eyelids feel so heavy I can barely keep them up. To be honest, I'm terrified of what the future will look like for me now because singing is my passion. It's all I've ever done. But my consultant has recommended a break from touring, and then a drastic reduction in it going forward, hence my return home. I feel like I'm letting the band down and that they would be better off replacing me but if they do that I don't know what I'd do with myself. I feel completely lost. I love singing with all my heart, and I have no idea what else I'm capable of. I've been trying to keep it together because my folks are so worried and I want them to know I'm absolutely fine, but the truth is... I'm *not*.' Her words came out in a rush and once she had finished her monologue, she placed a hand over her mouth, closed her eyes and let tears stream down her face. 'I'm so sorry for dumping all that on you. It's not giving a great impression, is it?'

Ferris reached out and placed a hand on her arm. 'Hey, no apologies needed. You've had a lot of worrying things dumped on you all in one go. Here was I thinking it was the fact that you and Josh had split up. I got that totally wrong. What you're dealing with is huge, Angelia, and you're trying to deal with it alone. There's no wonder you're not sleeping.'

Angelia pulled a napkin out of the dispenser on the table and wiped the moisture from her face. 'Josh and I aren't a couple, we never have been,' was all she could initially manage to say.

'Oh! I got that wrong too. Maybe I don't read people as well as I thought,' he said, crumpling his brow.

Angelia shook her head. 'Everyone thinks we're having an affair. It's always in the tabloids and it's so draining. But he's been in a long-term relationship for years with his childhood sweetheart, Nancy.'

Ferris nodded. 'Right, I see. I'm so sorry for my misinterpretation. I'm just as bad as the papers for misconstruing things.'

She shook her head. 'Don't be sorry. It's fine. And I *did* think I loved him at one point, as it happens. But that crush has been over for a while now. And anyway, he and I would never work.'

'Look, I'm going to do some reading up on your condition. I'd like to understand more about it. And maybe you and I can try to come up with a plan?'

Angelia crumpled her brow and shook her head. 'A plan for what?'

'The future. You may be feeling like a lost cause just now, Angelia, but I can assure you that you are capable of so much more than you think.'

Angelia sighed. 'But you don't really know me, why would you go out of your way to help like this?'

He smiled. 'Because I don't like to be beaten and I sure as heck don't like my friends to be beaten either.'

* * *

Angelia took a piece of Malteser traybake for Meghan and a sausage roll for Scrappy back to the car. Scrappy was so excited his whole body wagged and he drooled all over Meghan's car upholstery, much to Angelia's amusement.

'So, how was your non-date with the vicar?' Meghan asked as they travelled back to the north of the island.

Angelia couldn't help smiling. But it wasn't for the reasons Meghan might've thought. 'Still definitely *not* a date, and it was nice. He's a very kind man.'

'Hot, too, if you like religious guys, which I have to say I kind of do if they all look like him. I wouldn't kick him out of bed for folding his bible pages.' She chuckled at her own joke.

Angelia couldn't help laughing out loud. 'Meghan! You're taken. And he's just a friend. Besides, I couldn't date a vicar.'

Meghan turned her head briefly. 'Why not? He's human, not an angel, unlike you of course.' She winked.

'Because I'm not in the slightest bit religious and I think that's probably a deal breaker. Not that I want to date him anyway.'

Meghan shrugged. 'Nah, if you love someone you can make any scenario work.'

Angelia scoffed. 'Love? I've known him five minutes and we've been for a coffee once. I wouldn't go buying a hat just yet.'

'I think he likes you. And I mean *likes* you, not just likes you in a vicary *because-he-has-to* kind of way. I can see it in his eyes.'

'Oh, stop it, Meghan.' Angelia laughed and rolled her eyes. 'You're reading way too much into this. Anyway, changing the subject, I think you should take tomorrow off. Go explore the isle on your own for a wee bit. I'll be staying home to work on the mood board for Bella, so you won't need to worry about me.'

'Really? That'd be cool. I'd like to go back and see the Old Man of Storr and maybe take in the *Quiraings* this time. On photos I've seen online those mountains look like something out of a sci-fi flick. Dead creepy but in a good way, you know?'

Angelia almost giggled at her bizarrely elongated pronunciation of the name. 'I *do* know. And FYI it's pronounced the "*kuh-rayng*", and it's singular,' Angelia said with a smile. 'You should definitely go. Looking at the weather app, it should be a good day.'

* * *

After dinner that night, Angelia's dad got his guitar out and began to play as her mum sat with a book and Meghan watched him with curiosity, swaying along and smiling.

He sang as he played and for a moment Angelia was taken back in time to the many occasions she would sing along with her parents instead of watching whatever rubbish sitcom was on the telly. Those days would always be special to her, and she was grateful that she'd had the kind of parents who didn't insist she went out and looked for a 'proper' job. Instead, they had always encouraged her to follow her dreams, more concerned with her happiness than any kind of financial wealth. The fact that she'd ended up wealthy had been a bonus. They had always supported her and what she wanted to do rather than guiding her into a steady nine-to-five sort of career.

Angelia's mum poured wine for everyone and soon her book was placed face down on the side table and she had picked up her *bodhrán* and joined in with her husband, tapping out the rhythm on its skin. The evening was filled with magic and wonderful music she hadn't heard in years. It was clear Meghan was enjoying herself too as, encouraged by Angelia's mum, she grabbed a set of bongos and tried her best to keep the beat. She laughed hysterically when she spontaneously decided to play a solo that turned out to be akin to something from a comedy show.

Her dad played the opening bars to one of Angelia's favourites, 'Wild Mountain Thyme', and she couldn't resist joining in. It was the first time she had sung properly in weeks and even though she was filled with trepidation it felt good. She didn't do too much, however, and stopped when she felt her vocal muscles begin to tire.

The fact that she had sung filled her with joy and she went up to her room at bedtime with a smile on her face, reminiscing about some of the fun she'd had with the band. But she didn't want to give herself false hope. Then out of the blue she began to think about the possibilities of the record shop and for the first time imagined herself as the one behind the counter. An unexpected flutter of excitement travelled through her body and she wondered if perhaps there was a good reason she had set her mind on the project.

17

The following morning, Angelia waved Meghan off and then took Scrappy for a short walk down the lane from the bothy. It had rained overnight but now the puddles were drying up as the sun burnt through the clouds. The air had a familiar crispness to it and there was a fresh fragrance of pine trees and petrichor.

Scrappy trotted along by her side, stopping to sniff along the way but never straying too far even though he was off lead. Behind the house, the distant rugged mountains stretched skyward and all around her were bees, butterflies and other insects traipsing from one petal to another. It was such a relaxing place to spend time, unlike London where everything seemed to run at warp speed, and that included vehicles *and* time.

Later, she met Ruby for lunch at a cute place in Broadford where they sat overlooking the water. Angelia was full of admiration as to how a movie star like Ruby could freely move around the island, with such confidence, when she was so easily recognisable. And when she was recognised, she took it in her stride and was always so friendly and open.

During their lunch, a couple, who must have been in their twenties, had been looking over from the next table and whispering. It appeared they were trying to pluck up the courage to come over. Ruby turned and greeted them and then on their way out they came over and asked for autographs and selfies from them both.

They chatted briefly and then went on their way. It was a pleasant interaction and Angelia wondered if that's how her life could be back home on Skye now.

'You make life look so easy,' Angelia said. 'You don't seem fazed by being recognised so close to home.'

Ruby shrugged. 'The way I look at it is if it wasn't for people like that, I wouldn't get to do what I love. You looked quite nervous. Have you had some bad experiences?'

Angelia thought back to some of the interactions she'd had in London. 'Most fans are lovely, but I've had a few unnerving situations where people have been a bit grabby. And I tend to feel a little panicked and claustrophobic when that happens. Den tried to insist I brought a bodyguard with me to Skye.' She rolled her eyes. 'I refused, so Meghan, my assistant, came instead. Although, to be honest, I wouldn't mess with her,' she added with a laugh.

'I've had some tricky situations, too, but they are so few and far between. Less so nowadays. But I'm grateful to have had such an exciting life so far. But it's about to get even more exciting.'

Angelia tilted her head. 'How so? A new project in the offing?'

Ruby smoothed a hand over her tummy. 'You could say that.'

Angelia jumped up from her seat and dashed around to hug her friend. 'That's wonderful news! Congratulations. Rosie will be so excited to be a big sister.'

'She doesn't know yet. But she's been asking for a baby brother so hopefully she won't mind if it's another girl.'

'I'm sure she'll be delighted either way.'

'Speaking of projects, how is it going with the shop? And have you thought any more about what you're going to do now?'

Angelia huffed. 'I've created a mood board and emailed it to Bella so that side of things is progressing but as for me... I'm still not sure, to be honest.'

'You're such an incredible songwriter, Angelia, maybe you should think about writing for films or TV or something. I could really see you writing movie scores. I could put you in touch with people who would help.'

That certainly appealed to her. 'I'd never actually thought about that but it's worth considering.'

'That way you get to be creative without the worry of the touring and stress of performing. You could keep putting your talent to good use. Because if you're anything like me you wouldn't do well at just sitting home doing nothing regardless of how much money you had coming in from royalties.'

Angelia nodded. 'That's the thing I'm most concerned about. I hate to be bored, and I think I will always need something to do.'

'Well, just say the word and I'll make some calls.'

They left the café after a couple of hours of catching up and Angelia headed back to the bothy feeling excited for her friend and optimistic for herself.

On her return home, her phone pinged with a WhatsApp message from Heath.

HEATH

Hey, Angel. I hope you're well. I've invited everyone to have a video call tonight if you're free. Den too. It's important but shouldn't take too long, so I hope you can make it. Just let me know as soon as you can.

H xx

Angelia stared at the screen as if answers would magically appear there. What could they possibly need a video call about? *All* of them? Shit, were they going to fire her? Was this time off she was taking just too much?

There was no point second guessing, she decided, and it could be something simple like an update about recording or the next tour. She would try not to worry and would just wait and see.

She replied to his message and said she was free all day. A further reply from Heath came through fairly quickly to say a Zoom had been arranged for 9 p.m. UK time to ensure everyone could join across the various time zones. Of course, Heath was in Sweden, Bear was in London, Den had taken a trip to California to see a potential new band to add to his portfolio, and Anouk was visiting friends in Quebec. She presumed Josh was in London, too, although she hadn't heard from him, and there was a good chance Dom had gone home to Glasgow to see his mum with his long-term partner, Rio. She was aware that Rio had been touring with Taylor Swift but that he'd been given some time off along with the crew, so things had worked out well there.

The meeting was preying on her mind for most of the day and cabin fever had pretty much set in. She had informed her parents and had messaged

Meghan to let her know that the call would be happening in case she'd known anything about it. Meghan was still out ticking locations off her bucket list but replied quickly, to Angelia's surprise.

MEGHAN

I wonder what that could be about. Den hasn't said anything. Want me to head back? M xx

Angelia hit the reply button.

ANGEL

No, don't be silly. I'm sure it's nothing serious. Just go and enjoy yourself. I'll update you when I know.

Angelia ended the message with a smiling face emoji. A rapid response came from Meghan.

MEGHAN

If you're sure. Are you happy for me to stay out this evening? I've met some Norwegian girls and they've invited me to go for drinks with them. They say there's room in their hostel if I want to stay over. Obviously, I'll come home if you'd prefer.

Angelia couldn't help feeling a little relieved to have a night off from being watched and her every move noted and reported back to their management.

ANGEL

No, Meg, I don't mind at all. It sounds like fun so you should definitely stay out. I will message you after the call.

After that conversation, Angelia could tell she was driving her parents mad with her foot tapping, nail biting and sighing because her dad pulled out a deck of cards and demanded they sit and play poker for a while to give her something else to focus on.

Angelia couldn't concentrate and lost every single game, which was a first. She resorted to pacing again until her mum snapped, 'For goodness' sake, Angelia, you're going to wear a bald patch on my lovely Persian rug!'

At that, Angelia flopped onto the sofa and called Scrappy up to sit on her lap. Cuddling him usually had a calming effect on her. She flicked through the channels on the TV but could find nothing to hold her attention. She went through every possible scenario in her mind that could occur on the call but for some reason each one came around to her losing her role as the front person of the band. She couldn't blame them if they did want to find another vocalist though. What use was a singer who couldn't actually sing? She wondered if they would resort to a similar method of finding her replacement as they'd used to find her. She tried to imagine watching the show from home, knowing how painful that would be. Surely, they wouldn't put her through that, would they? Maybe they were going to demote her to backing singer and Anouk was going to step up. She was quite shy in front of the microphone but confidence could grow, and she could definitely sing. She had a gravelly quality to her sound, probably more fitting, if she was honest.

An hour prior to the call, Angelia went up to her room followed, as always, by Scrappy, and she paced there instead as she chewed on the skin around her thumbnail. As if he was as frustrated by this as everyone else, Scrappy whined every few minutes and Angelia translated this to mean, 'For woofness' sake, give up already.'

She sat on her bed beside him. 'Sorry, my wee pal. I'm just nervous,' she told him with a scratch under his chin. 'What would I do without you, eh?' He wagged his tail and jumped up to try and lick her face.

To kill a little time, she applied some makeup and tidied her hair, knowing she would have her camera on. She didn't want the band to see her looking pale and it made her feel more presentable. She wondered how it would feel seeing them all again after what felt like a long time, even though realistically it hadn't been that long. And she wondered if Josh would be there or if he would make excuses to be absent. When it was almost time for the Zoom call, she sat at the desk in her room and checked the microphone and camera on her laptop.

* * *

Then, as the band and Den appeared, one by one, on the screen before her, her heart thumped at her chest and her palms grew clammy. Josh's face appeared and he looked jittery. He didn't seem to want to look at anyone and that made her sad. She just wanted to go to bed, cuddle up with Scrappy and catch up on sleep; maybe forget the world and recent goings on for a little while too.

'Hey, everyone. It's good to see you,' Heath said, smiling into his camera. 'I hope you're all enjoying the much-needed, and long overdue, break. Thanks for making time to join the call.' If Angelia didn't know better, she'd be forgiven for thinking he looked nervous. He was chewing his lip and kept glancing off to the side where, she presumed, his pregnant wife Agda was sitting with their wee son.

'Before you start, Heath, can I say something?' Josh interjected. He too had been very fidgety since he'd appeared on camera, and Angelia wondered what he could possibly want to say that couldn't wait and that justified his interrupting Heath.

Heath sighed. 'Sure, go on.' He hadn't hidden his annoyance; his flared nostrils were a dead giveaway, that and the fact his lips were pressed together as if he was trying to stop himself from saying something he might regret.

Josh grinned into his camera. 'Cheers, bro. So... I'm excited to tell you all... I'm getting married!' he blurted, and Angelia's heart plummeted to the floor. 'I asked, and Nancy said "yes"! So, we've set a date for a spring wedding next year. Obviously, you're all invited even with... well, you know...'

Even with what? Angelia thought absently. And no, she didn't know. Although she couldn't ask because she was fighting tears. A hard lump of emotion had lodged in her throat, and she had to force a smile and join in the applause that Den had instigated. If Josh considered her such a good friend, why was she finding out like this? And why had he been so absent from her life lately when she needed him the most?

'Ooh, I love a good wedding, me!' Den said in his broad Leeds accent, beaming, his skin a little more orange than normal in the run up to his annual holiday, and the fact he was in California, of course. The band had agreed, long ago, that their manager was addicted to tanning, whether fake or otherwise.

Heath, however, was silent and Angelia felt sure he was looking through his camera and directly into her mind. He closed his eyes briefly and she thought she saw an infinitesimal shake of his head. Evidently, he didn't approve of Josh's delivery of his news. She recalled the conversation she had overheard between Heath and Josh at her London apartment, and how after hearing Josh had feelings for her, Heath had informed Josh that he needed to get his head straight about her and not mess her around. She had been grateful that Heath had cared enough to stand up for her. And clearly now Josh had 'got his head straight' on what he wanted; it wasn't Angelia, after all. She supposed she should be relieved.

Eventually Heath cleared his throat and said, 'Congratulations, Josh and Nancy. Although what she sees in you, I'll never know.' Angelia sensed a barbed undercurrent of truth in his words.

'You know you love me really,' Josh said rather more jovially than if he too had noted the same bitterness. Luckily for him, he was oblivious. 'Anyway,' Josh added, 'I just wanted to share my news. You can crack on with your thing now, H.'

Heath nodded. 'Okay.' He paused for a moment, and Angelia watched as he inhaled a long, deep breath and released it. 'Now this hasn't been an easy decision to make and I'm not sure how to tell you all other than to just...' He shrugged. 'Say it... So... I'm quitting the band.'

There were a couple of gasps and then a heavy, stunned silence descended on the call. Angelia felt the tears she had been fighting spill over and tried, surreptitiously, to swipe them quickly away. So, it was over after all; just not in the way she had anticipated.

Apparently sensing the shock, Heath added, 'Look, guys, I'm sorry to be so blunt about it but... I have a family now and the touring's just too much. As you all know, Agda is pregnant with our second baby, and I want to be around this time. We've just found out we're having a girl.' He smiled and his eyes sparkled with tears of joy. 'I hope you can all understand.'

'Shit, Heath, I thought you were going to tell everyone the tour was cancelled but not this!' Josh said, running his hands back through his hair. No mention of Heath's exciting news; Josh really could be a selfish prick.

'I was getting to that, Josh, but thanks for beating me to it,' Heath almost snarled. So, there *had* been conversations behind the scenes about the tour, and Josh had been made privy to certain things. His earlier comment now made sense.

Den held up his hands. 'Obviously, I knew about this because Heath and I have had to discuss things,' he said, a resigned expression washing over his face. 'If I'm honest, I was expecting it long before now. He's a father and wants to be there for his kids, hopefully, you can all understand that.'

Anouk cleared her throat. 'Congratulations, Heath and Agda, on your wonderful news,' she said and a rumble of assent travelled as the other members of the call added their congratulations. When things had quietened down again, Anouk added, 'Although girls can be trouble, can't we, Angel?' she said with a wink and a smile.

Angelia laughed lightly. 'Speak for yourself! Angel by name and Angel by nature,' she said, placing her hands under her chin and fluttering her eyelashes. Everyone chuckled along.

'Actually,' Anouk continued, 'I had the same announcement, about leaving the band. It feels like fate has other plans for us all now. Things happen for a reason; I'm a great believer in that. I've been working on some solo projects, and I would really like to give them a shot before I'm too old to have any success.'

'Do you need a manager?' Den asked, clearly only half joking. 'Because this trip to bloody LA has been a damp squib. I'm telling you it's getting harder to find raw talent. I think you lot are a dying breed.'

Bear ran his hands over his face. 'Erm… you're not going to believe this but—'

'You're quitting too,' Josh said, shoulders slumped, with a shake of his head and a deep sadness in his eyes.

Bear nodded. 'I'm tired, guys. So bloody tired. I want to buy a smallholding and just keep chickens, and shit like that. I'm in my forties, for feck's sake, and the rock star lifestyle is taking its toll. Let's face it, we've all got enough money now and there comes a point where you can have too much of a good thing. Let's leave things on a high instead of doing what so many bands do and going on long after we've drawn our pensions. I'd like to settle down, meet someone and maybe do the whole marriage thing before I look like Keith Richards. And before you say anything, I know I've got to find someone who'll put up with me first.' A few chuckles could be heard. 'Angel's diagnosis made me really think things through, you know? We lost Lorelie too young, and this all goes to show you never know what's around the corner. I don't want to wait any longer to start having a normal life. Well, as *normal* as it can be for people like us.'

Great, so her diagnosis had now caused the band to split. Heath must have noted the regret in her expression because he leaned closer to his camera and addressed her directly. 'Hey, Angel, none of this is your fault, okay? From the look on your face, I can guess what's going through your mind and you need to stop that line of thinking.'

'Oh, hell yeah, you do,' Bear added, eyebrows raised. 'I didn't mean to sound like I was blaming you, because I'm 100 per cent not, matey. I just think it's the right time. It sounds like we're all ready for this to end.'

'Not all of us,' Josh said in a surly tone. 'I can't understand why you're all making such rash decisions.'

Anouk was shaking her head and said, 'To be honest, Josh, I've been thinking about this for over a year but there was never a good time to say anything. We've been so busy and I didn't want to ruin things for everyone, so now does seem like the best time to call it a day when the majority are feeling the same.'

'Majority?' Josh scoffed and Angelia continued to remain silent, unsure how she felt and what to say.

'Dom? You're awfully quiet, mate,' Heath said.

Dom exhaled a long, loud breath. 'Sorry... I think I'm a bit shocked, but to be honest... *relieved*. Me and Rio have been thinking about getting married, too, and maybe adopting a wee 'un and we're not getting any younger. Plus, the lifestyle we currently have isn't really conducive to adoption. I'm not sure a tour bus and hotels are acceptable homes for a baby. So... I think maybe the time's right to say goodbye to Angel and the Fallen.' His voice broke and he dabbed at his eyes. 'We've had a bloody good ride though, eh?' Most nodded in agreement with him.

'So, the tour's already cancelled?' Angelia managed to ask with a wavering voice.

Den nodded. 'Aye, love, it is. We couldn't, in fairness, hold the venues to a contract when we weren't sure how you'd get on singing again. And the last thing we wanted to do was pressure you. We know how much of a perfectionist you are and how anything less than 100 per cent wouldn't be good enough for you. And we knew if we discussed this with you, you'd be racked with guilt, something we didn't want to happen, so we had to make a difficult decision. So... the plan is, there'll be a *best of* album using current recordings, and some of the unreleased tracks, and maybe some fan meet and greets around Europe on release, next year, for those of you who want to do that. And then... you all get to go and raise babies and chickens and whatever the hell else retired rock stars do. All we ask is that you keep this to yourselves until we've put out a press release. Let's keep our united front, Josh, I'm looking at you.'

Josh didn't speak, instead he clenched his jaw and glared at the screen as Angelia wondered what was going through his mind.

* * *

When the call ended, Angelia sat in stunned silence for what felt like an age. The screensaver on her laptop rotated photos of her and the band in candid shots, and it finally began to sink in that her singing career, as she'd known it at least, was over. A range of emotions vied for dominance but the one she hadn't expected was relief. She no longer had to figure out what to do about the band. Nor did she need to feel guilty or responsible for the other members. She just had to figure out what to do with the rest of her life.

She picked up Scrappy and sank her face into his fur, letting the tears fall until the dog's coat was damp. He tried to lick the tears from her cheeks and wagged his tail, almost as if willing her to cheer up. But this was it. The dream was over.

Eventually she made her way downstairs and into the living room where her mum and dad were watching a film.

'Hey, love, what's wrong? What's happened?' her dad asked as he stood and walked over to envelop her in his arms.

'It's over,' she sobbed. 'The band has split.' She collapsed into her father's arms as the sadness and sheer relief she felt overtook her whole body and she succumbed to it.

18

Sleep evaded Angelia yet again. She lay listening to Scrappy's cute little snores as she tried to relax. But the more she attempted to sleep, the less she was able to. It was just before 4 a.m. and her room seemed small and closed in, and for the first time ever she missed the expanse of her Frognal Rise apartment. At least there she could pace and listen to music to soothe her soul any time of day or night. Here, sound carried and she didn't want to wake her parents. But she needed to escape. To get some fresh air. She climbed carefully out of bed so as not to disturb Scrappy and pulled on her jeans and a sweater. She picked up her trainers and tiptoed out of her room, stepping over the creaky floorboard on the landing, and made her way downstairs.

Once she had made it safely to the kitchen without anyone hearing her, she grabbed her car keys and the shop keys from the hallway rack, slipped her feet into her shoes and opened the front door. After closing it gently behind herself she climbed into her car.

She released the handbrake and rolled the car down to the bottom of the driveway and as far away from the house as she could do safely, then fired up the engine. Keeping a check on her rearview mirror, she drove away towards Glentorrin. It seemed the obvious place to go. Maybe she could go to the shop and gather some inspiration for the renovation. Maybe something about the place soothed her like her music had back home. There was definitely something magical about the place as it kept drawing her back.

As Angelia drove, the sun was beginning to make its ascent, casting a warm amber glow over the coast that reflected on the water. The sea was fairly still, and the world was quiet apart from the odd jogger or dog walker, and, of course, the wildlife darting in and out of the hedgerows. A large barn owl flew low over her car, its wide, expanded wings cutting silently through the air as it eyed her suspiciously before seeking out a hiding place in an oak tree at the side of the road, its heart-shaped face peeping out through the branches.

She eventually pulled into Glentorrin and immediately felt her shoulders relax. What was it about this place? She parked the car in front of the shop and climbed out, stopping for a moment at the railing that surrounded the inlet of water the village was situated around. She inhaled the fresh, salty air and watched a couple of seagulls bobbing about on the water without a care in the world. The village was sleeping for now, but it wouldn't be long before the shop and bakery were buzzing with people starting their days. It was picture-postcard perfect at that precise moment and she breathed deeply, trying to memorise the feeling of peace.

As she watched the seagulls overhead catching thermal columns of air to float on, she began to replay the video call in her mind. So much had come to light in such a short space of time that it had felt quite overwhelming. Josh was getting married, Heath was going to be a dad again but this time to a wee girl, Bear wanted to keep chickens, Anouk wanted to be a solo act, Dom wanted to marry his boyfriend and adopt babies. And Angelia... What would she do? Who would she be? What would her future look like?

She had no clue. Absolutely none. But she knew she couldn't sit around doing nothing. It would drive her mad. But what was she capable of now? She had no degree. Could she go back to studying? How would she cope without the band? Her safety net? These past weeks had been strange, but she had always expected to be going back. She hadn't expected it to be over yet. Although, the relief she felt at knowing the decision was out of her hands was definitely there too. But she was Angel of Angel and the Fallen. She had been that person for a decade now. Who would she be from hereon in?

Her heart rate picked up and her breathing shallowed. She leaned on the railing for support as a wave of dizziness washed over her. Oh, God, what was happening? She squeezed the railing, the metal cold to the touch, but her grip weakened. She realised she had forgotten to take her medication in her rush to get out of the house. Fear gripped her. This feeling was new and terrifying. She tried to turn to walk back to the car where she had left her phone, but her legs were heavy and she couldn't make them move, try as she might.

Angelia grasped at her throat as her heart pounded so hard against her ribs, she feared it might burst through her skin. Stars danced before her eyes and her legs gave way beneath her. She tried to grip the railing again, but her fingers wouldn't bend. She fought for breath as tears welled in her eyes. This can't be it, she thought as she glanced hurriedly around herself. The sun was making its way above the horizon, but it was still so early. No one was around yet. Her legs gave way completely and she crumpled to the floor as her breathing became more erratic and difficult. Her eyes fluttered closed as she realised there was nothing she could do.

'Hey, hey, you're okay. An ambulance is on the way. Just stay with me,' an urgent male voice said as a gentle hand stroked her hair. She fought against the heaviness in her eyelids and gazed up into a familiar brown gaze.

'F... F...' She tried to say Ferris's name, but he shook his head.

'Don't try to speak. Just relax, okay? You're going to be fine. They won't be long.'

'Cry...' She tried to speak again, ignoring his instruction. 'Cry...' She pointed to her chest.

'Christ?' he asked. 'You want me to pray with you?'

'Sis...' she managed.

His eyes widened. 'Oh! Myasthenic crisis?' he asked with a strain of panic to his voice.

Knowing he understood but also wondering how, she closed her eyes just as she heard the siren in the distance.

* * *

Two hours later, Angelia walked out of the A&E department at Broadford Hospital to a quiet waiting room.

'Hey!' came a voice from the direction of the entrance. It was Ferris. As he walked towards her, she noticed his face was pale and his hair a little dishevelled. He was wearing jogging pants and a long-sleeved base layer kind of top.

'I followed the ambulance in my car. I wanted to make sure you were okay. There was talk of airlifting you to Raigmore, but I see they haven't needed to do that.'

Angelia glanced down at her feet. 'No, thankfully. I feel like such an idiot.'

His brow crumpled and he shook his head. 'Why?'

'It wasn't a myasthenic crisis. It was... it was a panic attack.'

His shoulders seemed to relax. 'Thank the Lord for that,' he said with a smile. 'They mentioned ventilators and induced comas and...' He grappled her into a hug. 'Thank goodness it wasn't a crisis.' As if realising his action may have been unwanted, he stepped back and his face flushed an almost fluorescent shade of pink as he reached to scratch the back of his neck. 'Oh, heck, I'm so sorry.' His eyes were filled with anxiety. 'I'm just so relieved. I've no nails left. Been sitting here worrying myself sick.' His eyes widened and he held up his hands. 'Not that I'm belittling a panic attack, of course. They can be horrendously frightening. I just...' He cringed as his words trailed off.

She smiled. 'It's okay, really. Thank you for being here and for waiting. And I'm sorry to have scared you like that.'

'No apology needed. Come on, I'll give you a lift back if you like.'

She nodded and followed him out to the car park. His car was an old Volvo in metallic green. He unlocked it and opened the passenger door and she climbed in.

Ferris started the engine and before he set off, he turned to look at her. 'Are you sure you're okay?'

She nodded. 'I am thanks to you.'

He smiled. 'I know you won't see it this way but... I think I was meant to find you today. I usually go out for my run much later, but I woke up at stupid o'clock and couldn't get back to sleep so I decided to go earlier. Under normal circumstances, I wouldn't have been there.'

Angelia smiled. 'Well, for whatever reason, I'm glad you were.'

He smiled. 'Me too. Now, where am I taking you?'

She sighed. 'Back to my folks in Portree if that's okay? Meghan is driving my mum down to collect her car, so I don't need to do that. But I'm in trouble, that's for sure.'

He cringed. 'Ah, so you've called them. I wasn't sure if I should've done that, or if the hospital would do it.'

'I called them as soon as the doctor explained what was happening to me.

I was so relieved it wasn't a crisis, but my mum and dad were furious and obviously really worried. They were hell-bent on coming to get me, but the nurse had already told me that the man who had come in with me had stayed. I guessed that was you, so I told my mum and dad I'd be okay to get home.'

They sat in silence for a few moments until Ferris broke it. 'Don't you get tired of the fame? Doesn't it get sort of lonely? I mean, I know you have the band, but don't you ever miss just being... *you*?'

She smiled but felt no happiness. 'It's not something I'll need to worry about for much longer.'

Ferris's brow creased. 'How so?'

'The band is no more,' she said with a wavering voice and a deep sigh.

He shook his head. 'I don't understand.'

She stared at her hands where they rested in her lap. 'Keep this to yourself, please, as there will be a press release but it seems my diagnosis has given people pause to consider their own futures and the band doesn't actually appear to be in any of them. Well, that is apart from Josh, the drummer, but he'll be snapped up by the Foo Fighters or someone equally as huge. He's very talented so he won't be out of the music industry for long.' She explained the plans of the rest of the band and when she had finished, he huffed air through his puffed cheeks.

'Wow. No wonder you had a panic attack. Not only have you had this major diagnosis to deal with, but the rug your future was resting on has been pulled out from beneath you too. I'm so sorry to hear that, Angelia. So sorry.'

She glanced across at him and saw genuine concern. 'Thank you. It was a bit of a shock. But... sort of a relief too. I was going to have to make a decision on what to do but now...'

'So, what will you do? Find another band?'

She closed her eyes briefly to fight the threatening tears. 'No point. I sang for the first time since my diagnosis the other night with my dad. I managed a couple of songs but that was it. I really don't see me being able to do full gigs again. My voice is pretty much gone. Or at least the strength to produce a good sound for long periods anyway. And the touring was exhausting for my other muscles, not to mention running around a huge stage, night after night.'

He fell silent, letting her words sink in and eventually said, 'So you're going to sell records instead of make them?'

She pursed her lips for a moment, confused by his words. 'No, no, I'm going to be a silent partner in the record shop. That's the plan, at least. I don't know anything about running a business. Collecting and listening to records is completely different to selling them. And I don't think it'd be a good idea for me to be too involved because I'm pretty sure the people of Glentorrin would hate to be swamped by fans of the band trying to get a glimpse of the singer that ruined everything for them.'

'Hey, stop that. You didn't ask for any of this. It's really *not* your fault, Angelia. And I can't think of a better way to live your life than doing something connected to what you love. I think you should at least consider it.'

She remembered the excitement she'd felt a short while ago when she had imagined herself behind the counter of a newly refurbished shop surrounded by rows and rows of albums, vintage pop and rock memorabilia mounted on the walls, alongside eighties and nineties band posters. Her stomach flipped again. It would be kind of cool.

'How did you know what I meant when I was trying to talk after I collapsed?' Angelia asked out of the blue.

'I told you I was going to do some research on myasthenia and that's exactly what I did. I wanted to understand it.'

She gave a light laugh. 'But why? You haven't known me that long, so why does it matter?'

He pulled over into a layby and turned off the engine. 'Angelia, can I make an observation?' Without waiting for her consent, he continued, 'You seem to have a surprisingly low opinion of yourself and that makes me both surprised and sad considering all you've achieved. I researched because I get the feeling you need friends who understand what you're going through. I'd like to think I could be one of those friends, and therefore I want to know what you're dealing with so I can help in any way you need me to.'

'You're a very kind man,' she said with a smile.

'I'm just a human being who doesn't like to see other human beings hurting,' he said with a shrug.

'Well, I think you're one of a kind. I haven't met many people who would go to all that trouble for someone they hardly know.'

'I just happen to think you're a nice person and I'd like to be your friend at a time where it's clear you're a little apprehensive about having them. Everyone needs friends, Angelia. But I understand it must be hard to trust people when you're so well-known. Some people can be cruel and take advantage but not all people. I'm not like that.'

She nodded but noted the sinking feeling in her stomach, why had that happened when he'd mentioned *being friends*? 'Well, thank you. But you're still not going to convert me.'

He laughed again as he pulled the car into the road once more. 'You're a strong-willed woman, MacAuley, I wouldn't dream of trying.'

19

The following day, Angelia was accompanied to the shop by Meghan and Scrappy to meet Bella Donaldson once more. She had emailed her mood board across, and it had been met with enthusiasm and eagerness, so she was keener than ever to get the wheels in motion. In the light of day, Ferris's words had really inspired her to consider the possibility of running the record shop she was creating; especially now the band was definitely folding. She felt she owed him a huge thank you for the things he had done in the short amount of time since she'd met him. Perhaps she could stop in at the church and take him a cake from the bakery, she thought.

Meghan took a seat on the window ledge of the shop with Angelia's laptop to do some admin, and Scrappy went on a sniffing mission just in case anything new had occurred since his last visit. Meanwhile Bella and Angelia chatted, both animatedly, about the plans for the shop. The ideas were coming together nicely. The place would be a tad twee and antiquey-looking, which was something Angelia loved the sound of, knowing she would never really have come up with any of it on her own, so she was grateful for Bella's vision.

The idea of almost having the place appear like a Victorian period film set that had been used for something like *A Christmas Carol* was both ridiculous and brilliant. It wouldn't be at all what people would be expecting from a shop selling relatively modern vinyl, so it was bound to attract attention. It would have bags of character and an 'olde worlde' feel thanks to the burgundy colour palette Bella had suggested. She had also sourced some chandeliers that would add an air of opulence to the place and would be a talking point seeing as such things weren't usually used in record shops. And the old cash register would be a feature, if not necessarily used for its original purpose; modern technology was far more efficient, even if it wasn't quite as pretty.

As they chatted, there was a knock on the door and Angelia turned to see a familiar face, its owner waving giddily at her.

'Ruby!' Angelia beamed at her friend as she stepped inside and the two women hugged.

'How are you doing?' Ruby asked. She narrowed her eyes. 'Are you okay after your visit to hospital? I can't believe that happened. You must have been terrified. I'm so sorry I wasn't here when it happened but I'm so glad Ferris was.' Ruby had always taken on the role of big sister, even though there wasn't much of an age gap between them.

Angelia nodded. 'I'm fine now, don't you worry. It's good to see you.'

Ruby hugged her again. 'You too, gorgeous. So, I'm guessing you're talking about the record shop plans.' Angelia nodded. 'Bella is so creative that whatever she comes up with will be incredible.'

'She's a genius. It's going to be such a beautiful shop and I can't wait to see it all come together now,' Angelia said, smiling at Bella.

'It's my first record shop so I'm going all out,' Bella said. 'Hey, we need to arrange another girls' night soon, Ruby. I think we're overdue. And I'm sure Angelia and Meghan would enjoy it too.' She turned to Angelia and told her, 'We've spent many a night at the Coxswain singing along to whatever performer Joren and Stella have booked. They get some really good musicians in.'

Ruby giggled. 'There's usually a glass of wine or three involved too.'

Angelia laughed along. 'Definitely sounds like fun.'

Ruby gave her shoulder a nudge. 'Aye but you'd show us all up so we might have to make sure you're barred next time there's a singer on.' Then, as if realising she had said the wrong thing, Ruby covered her mouth with her hand. 'Shit, sorry, Angelia, that was really insensitive, I'm so sorry, I wasn't thinking.' She reached out to touch her arm.

Angelia waved a dismissive hand. 'No, don't be silly. It's fine, honestly. You don't need to walk on eggshells around me. It is what it is.' She needed to nip this worry in the bud. The last thing she wanted was for people to be on guard around her.

'You're so strong, my lovely,' Ruby said with a smile and a brief glint of sadness in her eyes, but she brightened quickly and followed it with, 'But of course you always have been. Anyway, I'd better get going, I've a dance class to teach soon and I need to open up the hall and set up. I just wanted to come and say "hi". Let's catch up for coffee soon. Drop me a message when you're free again.' She hugged Angelia one last time. 'It's so lovely to have you here. I'm sure you're finding out for yourself but in my opinion, Glentorrin makes you feel like you're just a normal human being all over again. People just leave you to get on with life. Take it from someone who knows.'

'Yes, I'm certainly finding that too,' Angelia said with a responding smile.

Ruby nodded. 'You've made a great decision in coming home to Skye. Maybe you could actually move into the flat over the shop. Caitlin who owns the bakery lives with her husband and two kids over their shop and they've loads of space. Anyway, see you soon.' She breezed out, leaving the fresh, flowery scent of her perfume in her wake.

'I'll get going too,' Bella said. 'If you're happy to go ahead, I'll contact some of my regular contractors right away and see how they are for time.'

'I'm in!' Angelia replied. 'One hundred per cent!'

Bella smiled widely. 'Thanks for trusting me with this, Angelia.'

'Hey, thank *you* for the incredible ideas,' Angelia replied. 'It's going to be spectacular.'

As she watched Bella walking away in the direction of the police station, Angelia glanced across the village and spotted Ferris putting up posters. 'Meghan, I'm just going to nip over to the church. I won't be long. I just have to thank Ferris for his help when I had the panic attack.'

Meghan stood and gave a salute. 'Okay, boss, I'm right with you.'

Angelia held up a hand. 'Actually, I was going to go alone? You could stay here with Scrappy. I thought I'd take him a cake from the bakery as a thank you. I won't be long.'

Meghan gave her a knowing look. 'Oooh, okay. Cake for the hunky vicar, eh?'

Angelia laughed. 'He's just a friend, Meg.'

'Whatever, Trevor,' was Meghan's sing-song reply.

She stepped outside and turned left to walk along to the bakery. A delicious aroma of sweet pastries drifted through the air and into her nostrils, making her mouth water. Weirdly it smelled like freedom. Something she hadn't really experienced in years until she had arrived in Glentorrin.

The bell above the door jingled as she walked in and Caitlin, the pretty, red-haired bakery owner, looked up from a loaf she was packing in brown greaseproof paper. She smiled. 'Good afternoon, Angelia, what can I get you today?'

Angelia closely examined the cakes on display and her stomach growled in appreciation. All manner of muffins, pastries, doughnuts, gateaux and biscuits sat just waiting to be devoured. 'Hmm...' She tapped her chin. 'They're all so good and I'm enjoying making my way through them all.' She laughed.

Caitlin smiled as she placed a wrapped loaf in a paper shopping bag. 'I'm glad to hear that. You're quite the regular customer now. What's taking your fancy today?'

'Ah, well, today is different. I'm not just buying for Meghan and me. This is mainly a thank you. Maybe you can help? It's for Ferris, have you any idea what he likes?'

'Ah, now the good curate adores a choux bun filled with fresh cream,' she said, pointing to the huge chocolate-topped pastries. They looked so light and fluffy and were one of the delights Angelia was yet to try herself.

'Perfect. Could I take five, but could you put one of them in a separate box? I'll treat myself, my folks and Meghan to one too.'

'Absolutely. How are things going along the road?'

'Great. Bella's ideas are so good. I can't wait to see it all come to fruition.'

Caitlin smiled. 'It's good to know someone had the vision it needed. It's a shame for it to have been empty for so long but the whole absentee owner thing has been a nightmare from what I understand. Years that went on for. You came along at the right time.'

'It's a beautiful old building. But then again, it's a beautiful wee village.'

Caitlin gave a light laugh. 'Just watch yourself or you'll fall in love with the place and the people, like so many others before you.'

'I think your warning may be a bit late,' Angelia replied.

When the cakes were packaged up, she thanked her and left to head to the church. She now saw at close range the posters she had seen Ferris putting up. In fancy lettering they stated:

Glentorrin Summer Concert
14 June

She guessed this was the concert the choir were rehearsing for prior to losing their director and pianist. Such a shame.

The large oak door was unlocked, just as it had been on the first day she had discovered it, so she pushed it open and walked inside and along the stone aisle towards the chancel to see if she could locate the vestry. There was no sign of Ferris, however, and a twinge of disappointment tugged at her insides.

The Yamaha keyboard the choir had been using was standing there and Angelia ran her fingers across the top of it. She hadn't played since her diagnosis, which wasn't that long ago but she missed it all the same. She noticed it was plugged in and so she placed the cake boxes down on the closest pew before pulling out the stool and taking a seat.

She played a C major pentatonic scale from C to A and back again. The acoustics in the church gave the resonance of the notes a richness she immediately loved. She played it again, only this time she sang along with each note as she hit the corresponding key. She was happy to find the scale easy to sing and it spurred her on.

Thinking about Ferris and his dog Judy, she began to play the opening bars of 'Over the Rainbow' and smiled as the sound echoed all around her. She closed her eyes as she continued to play, letting her relaxed fingers dance gently across the Ivorite keys. The mineral-reinforced plastic had been created by the music company to mimic the feel of ivory when the harvesting of the original material had been, rightfully, banned.

Seeing as she was alone, she took a deep breath and began to sing, the beautiful, yet somewhat melancholy lyrics, of the song falling from her lips as she remembered them with ease. Her voice wasn't as strong as it once had been and as she sang, her eyes welled with tears when the words took on a new meaning for her. They spoke of dreams coming true which resonated within her. Her dreams had come true but now things had changed, and those dreams that had once been a reality were now somewhat out of reach. No amount of wishing on stars would change that.

Once the song ended, Angelia rested her hands in her lap and wiped away a few escaped tears. A spontaneous and unexpected round of applause from an unseen observer made her jump and she leapt to her feet and swung around to find Ferris standing halfway down the nave. As he clapped, he walked slowly towards her, a sweet smile turning his mouth up at the corners but his eyes glinting with unshed tears.

He took a seat on the pew closest to her and shook his head. 'That brought back so many wonderful memories. Thank you,' he said with a wavering voice.

'Sorry, I-I didn't think anyone was here,' she replied.

'No apologies necessary. It was absolutely beautiful. Made me think of my lovely mum.'

She smiled as she wiped more of her own tears away. 'Thank you. It felt good. *Really* good.'

He narrowed his eyes. 'I thought you said you'd lost your voice.'

She shrugged. 'I have really.'

He leaned forward, resting his elbows on his knees. 'That's not how it sounded to me. It actually sounded like you'd found it again.'

She recalled the recent occasion where she had tried to sing with her dad and it had made her sad that she couldn't carry on as long as she had wanted. 'If I keep singing it'll probably disappear and I'll sound like I'm being strangled all over again.'

'Or maybe you're giving yourself the chance to relax and think about something other than how you feel you're letting everyone down. The plans for the record shop seem to excite you and that's such a good thing. You light up when you sing, Angelia, but it doesn't have to mean you only get that feeling when you're playing stadiums. Have you ever thought about writing songs for other artists? So many singers do it. Or maybe just singing for fun for a change? Not that stadiums aren't fun, I'm sure they are, but... maybe this myasthenia diagnosis doesn't have to be the end of your singing career. Maybe it's just a side road that gets you to the same destination only via the scenic route.' He laughed out loud. 'Good grief, listen to me trying to sound like I know what I'm talking about. I'm pretty rubbish at metaphors.'

She thought about what he had said and a smile spread across her face. 'You're better than you think you are. What you've just said actually makes perfect sense. I haven't written for other artists, but I could definitely do it. I have folders full of songs I've written and never recorded. It would mean I still get to keep doing what I love, just indirectly. Like the scenic route you mentioned. Also, Ruby suggested movie score writing which is something I'd like to try too.'

His face brightened and a handsome smile lit up his features. 'Really? Well… that's brilliant.'

'I really need to stop looking at this as an end-of-the-road situation, and instead look at it as a diversion,' she said, knowing he had hit the nail square on its head. 'There are many routes to get to most places, and you don't always have to follow the map exactly as it's drawn, do you?'

He beamed. 'Definitely not. You have the most incredible talent, Angelia, and the world needs that.'

She shook her head as her eyes welled with happy tears this time. 'Thank you. I mean it, I've said it to you a lot since I met you, but I'll say it again, thank you.'

'And I'll say again that no thanks are needed. I'm always happy to help.'

'So, what's this summer concert I'm hearing about? I've seen the posters around the village. Although I have to say, I'm surprised there's no Highlands Games.'

'Oh, we have those too but they're in August. This is the early summer music and dance extravaganza. A new initiative sparked by Ruby and her dance students. It's a way to get the kids and adults of the village out and about doing something other than playing on their phones. It's not a competition or anything quite so serious but instead a way for people to come together and showcase their God-given gifts.'

'That sounds like something Ruby would set up,' Angelia replied with a smile.

Ferris tapped his chin and opened his mouth to speak but as if he thought better of it, he closed it again and covered it with the same hand.

'What?' Angelia asked. 'Just say it. You're the king of epiphanies at this point.' She laughed. 'What could go wrong?'

He glanced around conspiratorially for some reason, and it made Angelia giggle. He paused again and she wanted to shake the words out of him. 'Seriously, Ferris, what?'

'Look, it's none of my business and you can feel free to tell me to get lost but... You need music in your life and... the village choir needs a leader.' He held out his arms. 'Someone who understands the music and can advise them. Someone exactly like you. You saw what they were like on the night we met. They're a great bunch but without direction they're horrendous, in the best possible way.' He laughed. 'I've been stepping in up to now but I've no idea what I'm doing. I'm happy to play the keyboard but they really need someone who can arrange music and help them figure out harmonies. I'm nowhere near good enough for that. But while you're here it would be something to distract you from your worries and it wouldn't put loads of strain on your voice. Plus, you'd be doing them a huge favour. And me. What do you think?' He stepped back a little as if waiting for a firework to explode and covered his mouth again.

Angelia opened and closed her mouth as she fought to find an inoffensive way to say *thanks, but no thanks* but then she stopped. What would be wrong with helping out? Meghan would probably enjoy it too. What could possibly go wrong? It actually sounded like fun, and she certainly could use some of that in her life.

'I'll do it,' she said.

'I mean, you don't have to... sorry?' His eyes were wide with evident shock.

She lifted her arms and let them flop to her sides. 'I said I'm in. I'll do it.'

'Oh, my word! That's incredible! Thank you.' He stood and walked over to hug her where she stood by the keyboard. *Ugh, he smells divine, pardon the pun*, she thought, and his cheek was smooth against hers.

He stepped back quickly. 'I really need to stop doing that. My apologies. You'd think I'd had no training on appropriate behaviour towards parishioners.' He rubbed both hands roughly over his face.

Angelia laughed. 'They train you in that kind of stuff?'

'In a way, yes. So, I'm really sorry. It won't happen again.'

She smiled. 'It's really not a problem. And technically I'm not a parishioner.'

'Fair point. Okay, so, are you free tomorrow evening? That's when we're getting together again.'

At that moment the church door creaked open and Meghan shouted, 'Angelia, are you in here?'

Angelia rolled her eyes. 'Yes! I'm fine, don't worry. Just lost track of time, that's all.'

Meghan walked towards them with Scrappy trotting beside her. 'Thank God for that, I was beginning to think I was gonna get my arse handed to me for losing you. Shit, excuse me, father.' She cringed and gave a little bow.

Angelia and Ferris exchanged an amused glance and he turned to Meghan. 'You're forgiven, my child.' He made the sign of the cross and sucked his cheeks in, trying not to laugh.

Angelia gasped. 'Ooh, I almost forgot, I brought you a choux bun. Caitlin at the bakery said it was your favourite.' She leaned down and picked up the smaller box and held it out to him.

He took it and his face tinged a little pink. 'That's really kind but you didn't have to...'

'I owe you thanks for so many things since I arrived that a cake feels a little bit insignificant.'

He shook his head. 'Absolutely not. You've tasted Caitlin's baking so you know there's nothing insignificant about it. Excuse the terrible pun but it's almost a religious experience.'

Before she could comment, Meghan interjected. 'Erm, I don't mean to break up the party, guys, but we probably should get back up to Portree. I've got a video call arranged with Ezra, and I can't do that while I'm driving.'

Ugh, young love. Angelia sighed. 'Okay. But we're coming back tomorrow evening,' she informed her assistant with a wide smile.

Meghan shrugged. 'Fine with me. But why are you grinning like that?'

With a smile directed at Ferris, Angelia said, 'Because, Meghan, you and I have just joined a choir.'

20

Angelia awoke after the best night's sleep she'd had in a long while, feeling somewhat refreshed and wide awake. It was a step in the right direction, she figured. Scrappy was nuzzled into her side, snoring away, but must have sensed her awake state as he suddenly sprang to his feet and, with a frantically wagging tail, he stood on her chest and stared down at her, eyes bright and tongue lolling out. After several attempts to excitedly stick his tongue up her nose she managed to push herself up to a seated position.

'Get on with you, you wee dafty,' she told him as he flopped onto his back, exposing his belly for her to rub. 'What's got you so excited today, eh?' *Perhaps*, she mused, *he can sense my upturn in mood.* There was a tap on her door and she called out, 'Come in if you've brought coffee!'

The door opened and her dad poked his head around. 'Ah, sorry, there's a pot of coffee downstairs though, along with another surprise.'

Angelia was filled with intrigue. 'Oh? What surprise is that?'

Her dad chuckled. 'If I tell you, it's not a surprise, is it? Although I would get dressed if I were you,' he said, nodding at her fluffy pyjamas. And with that he left and closed the door.

A little puzzled, Angelia pulled back her duvet. 'Cryptic, eh, Scrappy? Come on, we'd better get dressed then.' She climbed out of bed and quickly ran to the bathroom to shower then, once dried off, pulled on some jeans and a sweater. With hurried steps she skipped down the stairs and into the kitchen, Scrappy running ahead. He started barking excitedly and as she rounded the corner she realised very quickly what the surprise was. Standing there, leaning against the countertop, with Scrappy in his arms was Ed, a wide, beaming smile on his face. He placed the little dog on the floor and opened his arms ready to envelop her.

'Ed!' she squealed and ran into his embrace. 'What are you doing here? You weren't coming for a week or so!'

He kissed the top of her head. 'We broke early and I got the first flight I could. I was desperate to see you. It's been too long.'

She pulled away and gazed up into his friendly green eyes. 'It really has. How long are you able to stay?'

He shrugged. 'A few weeks maybe.'

She hugged him again. 'That's brilliant. But how did you get here from the airport?'

'Hired a campervan.'

She laughed. 'A campervan?'

He smiled. 'Always fancied trying one and I figured you wouldn't have the space with Meghan being here too. It's parked at the end of your driveway, because…' He cleared his throat and in his best Michael Caine impression, à la *The Italian Job*, continued, 'Someone has parked a yellow Mini where I was going to park. Thankfully nobody has blown the bloody doors off it.' Angelia burst out laughing. She had missed him and his daft sense of humour so much. 'Anyway, nothing was going to stop me from visiting you. I had to come and make sure you're okay.' He held her at arm's length; his eyes filled with a combination of worry and concern. '*Are* you okay?'

She smiled. 'I'm getting there. Admittedly, it's been tough. I've been feeling a bit lost and wasn't really sure what I was going to do with myself but Ferris, my new friend, has been amazing. I can't explain why it took a relative stranger to talk sense into me, but talking to him has really helped.'

Ed's brow creased and he shook his head. 'Ferris? Who's that?'

Angelia gave a light laugh. 'He's the sort of trainee minister I mentioned.'

Ed's eyebrows rose. 'Angelia MacAuley, have you been going to church since we spoke?'

'Not exactly. I mean… I've been *in* the church, like I told you, it's where I met him, but I haven't "attended church",' she said while making inverted commas in the air.

Ed shook his head, frowning again. 'But, again, you don't *do* churches. So how did you end up hiding *in* one? Wasn't there a pub or a shop?'

'Come on, I'll pour us some coffee and tell you all about it, and the record shop, too.'

'Oh yeah, the record shop. I can't wait to hear all about that. Dead exciting. And so bloody perfect for you. I feel like I've missed loads of stuff.'

She poured two steaming mugs of aromatic, fresh coffee and placed them on the kitchen table then proceeded to tell him all about Ferris and their first meeting, then the record shop and finally the choir. Ed listened intently, smiling and laughing when appropriate.

'I've got my first meeting with the choir tonight, why don't you come along? It should be fun. They're mostly women but there are a couple of men too. I only know this from the night I took refuge in the church to escape the group of teenage fans. Ferris has some great ideas, and I think this is one of them. I feel like my life has a direction again.'

Ed nodded. 'Well, I need to meet this incredible trainee minister that's had an amazing influence on you in such a short amount of time. You friends with a vicar though, Angel.' He shook his head. 'I think it's quite funny.'

'I thought you might. And don't worry, he's not all preachy and "I want to convert you" or anything like that.'

Ed laughed. 'Why did you say that like the vampire off *Sesame Street*?'

Angelia laughed too. 'No idea.'

* * *

After a lazy day of lounging around at home and filling Ed in on all the details of the band and their apparent split, and each member's future plans, it was time to head to Glentorrin again to attend the choir rehearsal. Angelia was nervous but excited too. She wasn't really sure what to expect from the group of people seeing as she hadn't really heard much of their singing, instead she had witnessed rather more of their arguing and disagreements.

Meghan stayed home to give the friends some time to catch up, and Ed drove them to Glentorrin in the campervan. As directed by Angelia he parked beside the hall.

'This is a cute place,' Ed said as he climbed out of the van and took in his surroundings. 'It's like a painting.'

'Yes, it's lovely and it has everything you need too. Pub, bakery, museum, shop. All the essentials,' Angelia said as she too glanced around the place that was becoming very familiar.

Ed grinned. 'I like your priorities. Pub at the top of the list.'

'Come on, let's go in and I'll introduce you to Ferris.' Angelia led the way, followed by Ed, as she pushed through the large oak door. She had been in church more times in the last few weeks than she probably had in a lifetime, she thought.

'Ah, here she is, everyone, right on time!' Ferris said, gesturing towards her. A group of people were gathered in the chancel area where the keyboard still stood.

Ed stopped briefly and when Angelia turned, she saw something undecipherable in his expression. He didn't look exactly happy, that one thing was certain. He looked a little surprised and confused.

'Are you okay?' she whispered.

As if coming out of a trance, he shook his head and plastered on a smile. 'Sorry, yeah, all good.'

When she reached Ferris, he gestured to the gathered group. 'Everyone, this is Angelia MacAuley. Some of you have already met her and I know some may recognise her, it's only to be expected, but let's not get bogged down with her notoriety, shall we? And let's not go bragging to all and sundry that she's here in Glentorrin. She's here for a break of sorts and doesn't need to be hounded by fans. So, let's respect Angelia and be grateful that she has been willing to step into the breach at such short notice. Angelia, this is Glentorrin Village Choir, it's been going for around six months now and they're supposed to be singing at the annual village show in a few weeks. Allow me to make some more detailed introductions.' He pointed to a familiar blonde woman. 'You already know Bella Donaldson, and I believe you're a regular at Caitlin's bakery these days.' He grinned at her. 'I think you met Jules who runs the Lifeboat House Museum, next to her is Reid, her husband who's an incredible artist—'

'And who can't really sing, so is here purely to make up numbers,' Reid added and everyone laughed.

Ferris continued, 'Then there's Kenneth who owns the village shop, and his wife Morag—'

'Who organises Kenneth,' Morag added.

More giggles and an eyeroll from Kenneth who said, 'I wish I could say she's joking but she's not.'

Ferris chuckled and carried on, 'The very trendy young woman at the front there with the fabulous purple hair is Isla Douglas, who, if you can believe it, is Bella's *granny*.'

Isla patted her hair and feigned embarrassment. 'Young woman indeed, Reverend Blaikie, you do flatten me.'

Bella leaned towards her and, with a smile, whispered, '*Flatter*, Granny, you do *flatter* me.'

Isla rolled her eyes and through clenched teeth hissed, 'Aye, that's what a said, hen.'

Trying not to laugh, Angelia realised that Ferris had continued introducing people to her, but she had missed a fair few names thanks to Granny Isla's comedic moment.

She cringed. 'I'm so sorry but it may take me a while to remember all of your names.'

A young man, whom she thought she recognised as one of the teenagers who she had seen walking their dogs in the village, said, 'Don't worry, Miss MacAuley, we'll keep reminding you if you need us to. Oh, and thank you so much for helping us.' He clamped his mouth shut and glanced around before adding, 'And can I just say I love Angel and the Fallen, I have your posters on my wall at home, but I can assure you, you won't get any trouble from me. And I won't go telling people you're here. We're sort of used to famous people in Glentorrin. Oh, and I'm Evin MacKinnon, by the way.'

Jules put her arm around the young man who was around an inch taller than her and gave him a squeeze, a look of immense pride in her eyes. Angelia surmised she must be his mum.

'Okay, Angelia, I'll hand the floor to you to give a quick introduction for those members of the choir who maybe haven't encountered you before,' Ferris said, holding out his hand.

Angelia cleared her throat and felt her face heating. She could address a crowd of thousands in an arena but talking to a group of twelve or so people suddenly felt quite daunting. 'Hi, everyone. As Ferris said I'm Angelia. I'm originally from just outside Portree in the north of the island where I grew up, living with my mum and dad. Music is my true passion, and I play a variety of instruments and read music too. I started to study music at the

Conservatoire in Glasgow but that was cut short when I... well, when...' She knotted her fingers in front of her.

'You can say it, Angel,' Ed interjected. 'It was cut short when you landed your dream job as lead singer for the incredible rock band Angel and the Fallen.'

Angelia smiled nervously. 'Yes, when that happened. And by the way, this is one of my best friends, Ed Halsall, he's a fantastic musician too. He's played for some of the biggest orchestras in the world. So he's far better than me.'

Ed shook his head. 'Not entirely true. And anyway, we're not here to talk about me, go on.'

'Erm... I came home to Skye because...' Angelia glanced sideways at Ferris who gave an encouraging nod and smile. 'The band decided to take a holiday, and I figured I'd make the most of it and come and visit my folks.'

'Aye, dearie, you've to make the most of them,' Isla said with a nod and a sympathetic look to her face. 'Parents are *verra* important.'

Angelia smiled. 'I agree. I've also just bought the shop along the road from the bakery.'

'Oh, aye and my Arabella's working her magic on that for you, isn't she? She's *verra* talented, my Arabella,' Isla said proudly. 'She can give that Lawrence Lulu Lemon a run for his money, I'll tell you.'

Angelia wasn't sure at first who Isla meant but when the penny dropped, she had to try her best not to laugh. 'Oh, yes, that's right. Her designs are fantastic.' She held her arms out. 'And that's about it really. So, what do you need from me?'

Bella said, 'We need someone to guide us on the best songs for a relatively new choir to sing and how to come up with the harmonies.' She glanced around at the others who all nodded their agreement. 'Our last leader was great but unfortunately, she isn't available now and we didn't really solidify a set list. Apart from Christmas carols we have one song, "Love Shine a Light", which none of us actually like.'

Angelia nodded. 'And I understand you're to perform at the village show in June, so carols aren't really appropriate, I suppose.' She grinned. 'Okay, so how long a slot do you have?'

Caitlin told her, 'It's a thirty-minute slot before Ruby's dancers.'

'Great!' Angelia said. 'Do we have any other sheet music or song sheets to have a go at?'

Isla rolled her eyes and huffed as she folded her arms across her chest. 'Amelia, our former director, was a huge fan of ABBA but no one wants to hear songs about chicken tikka, do they? I'm more of a Harry Styles fan these days, thanks to Arabella. And I do like a bit of Florence and her machine.'

Angelia, fighting threatening laughter again, said, 'I love Harry Styles too. He's a nice guy and a lot more talented than people give him credit for. And Florence is an amazing vocalist, although her songs may be a little too obscure for such an event. How about Queen?'

Isla pursed her lips. 'Personally speaking, I liked her, although I wouldn't say I was a royalist. Not sure about King Charles yet but I'm prepared to give him time. Why do you ask, hen?'

Angelia couldn't help giggling this time. 'I was referring to the band, Isla. Freddie Mercury?'

Isla laughed and slapped her thighs with her hands. 'Och, that would make more sense. Although maybe best not to try to get us to perform that Bohemian rap song. I'm not sure we're up to that! All that "*scare a moose, scare a moose*", and all the harmonies might be a bit much, even for Glentorrin.'

'Noted. No moose scaring or crazy harmonies,' Angelia said as she shared an amused glance with Bella.

* * *

The first rehearsal went quite well considering Angelia hadn't done anything like direct a choir before. They had selected Harry Styles's 'As It Was' and Queen's 'You're My Best Friend' as starting points, the music for which Ferris had pulled up on his phone while the members of the choir had used their own phones for the lyrics.

Angelia found herself laughing with the singers on many occasions when lyrics were misheard or notes were completely missed, and she couldn't remember feeling this relaxed in weeks. She managed to arrange the singers into their vocal ranges from Reid as baritone and Isla and Morag as soprano and everything else in between. The evening flew by.

The mixed-age group of people thanked her profusely at the end, saying how much they had enjoyed it; that it was much more fun than when Amelia had been running it; she had, allegedly, been a tad too serious and obsessed with the seventies, making only one allowance for the Katrina and the Waves song but only because it had been a Eurovision song contest winner and that had been her other passion. The members had, apparently, thoroughly enjoyed having a say in which songs they would sing rather than being dictated to.

Once the choir had left, Ferris walked her and Ed to the door. He held out his hand to Ed. 'Good to meet you, Ed. Thanks for coming.' He turned to Angelia. 'That was amazing, Angelia. They clearly love you. But why wouldn't they?' He glanced at Ed and cleared his throat. 'Anyway, thanks again for helping with this. I think they may try to kidnap you when it's time for you to go back to London.'

Angelia left the church with a smile on her face, feeling like she had really achieved something for the first time in a while.

21

As they travelled back to Portree at around 9 p.m. that night, Angelia shared her plans for the record shop with Ed. He was keen to visit it as soon as possible.

'I have to admit I'm a bit jealous. I'd love to own a record shop. And how cool were those people in the choir? Such a great bunch. You did such a great job tonight. Anyone listening in would be shocked that they had only just learned those songs. They sounded awesome.'

It had been such fun; much more so than Angelia had expected. And her condition hadn't reared its head either, which was a bonus. Perhaps there was something to be said for being relaxed.

She thought back to some of Isla's comments and couldn't help giggling again. Working with the choir was going to be interesting if only for her malapropisms. 'They are lovely, aren't they?' she said, more to herself than anyone else. 'Isla's hilarious, but I don't even think she does it on purpose.'

'Yes, she's a gem,' Ed said. 'The chicken tikka comment almost choked me. I'm not sure how I kept it together after that.'

'And the moose scaring,' Angelia said, laughing. 'She's so serious when she says things though. She's either an accidental genius or a cunning one who knows very well what she's doing.'

'Sadly, I think it's the former rather than the latter,' Ed replied, grinning, then fell silent for a while and seemed deep in thought.

The sun had begun its descent which, Angelia recalled, tended to occur later and later as May progressed. The weather was dry and the sky overhead was an inky blue that faded to lilac, then pink, then orange. The mountains were now a mere silhouette of jagged edges. She had missed this; missed the beauty of Skye and its ever-changing colour palette.

'You didn't tell me Ferris was hot,' Ed said out of the blue.

'Sorry?' Angelia asked, quite surprised at his comment.

'When you talked about him, I expected him to be some bald fat bloke with protruding teeth who spoke with a lisp.'

Angelia gasped but laughed all the same. 'I never even described him so how did you come to *that* particular conclusion?'

'I suppose I just—'

'Stereotyped him?' she said. 'And badly.' She shook her head, but soon realised she too had done the same when she had met him.

He chuckled. 'Maybe a tiny bit. But I didn't expect him to be that good-looking. You don't expect religious people to be attractive.'

'That's a little unfair, Edwin Halsall.'

He poked her leg lightly. 'Ooh, you used my Sunday name. Am I in trouble?' Angelia shook her head and smiled. After a few moments, Ed spoke again. 'Are you and he...?' His question trailed off and he turned to stare out the window at the road, clearly not wanting to know the answer to his incomplete question.

Angelia narrowed her eyes and prodded him back with her finger. 'Are he and I *what*?'

He glanced at her briefly again. 'Is there something there? Between you and Ferris the vicar, I mean.'

Angelia rolled her eyes. 'I've only known him for a few weeks and we're friends. Although why should that matter to you?' she asked, a little befuddled.

Ed shrugged. 'No reason. I'm just being nosy.'

'Well, don't bother. There's nothing to tell. Anyway, why don't *you* tell *me* about Ava.'

Ed stiffened. 'What do you want to know?'

'How did you meet her? What's she like? Are you guys serious? You didn't even tell me you were dating anyone, so I know nothing, remember? I had to hear it from Fee and then when I talked to you on the phone you couldn't wait to hang up.' She knew she sounded a little wounded and surly about not being kept in the loop.

He held up a hand in a defensive motion. 'Okay, okay, jeez.' He gave a deep sigh. 'She's Australian. I met her when I travelled to Sydney with the Chamber Orchestra. She plays the cello. She's nice.'

Angelia laughed with incredulity. 'That's just a repeat of what Fee told me. And if I was Ava and I heard that *that's* how you talked about me I'd dump you.'

Ed scrunched his brow. 'What? I said she's nice, how is that a bad thing?'

'Nice is such a *meh* kind of word, Ed.'

He laughed without humour. 'Well, what else is there to say?'

'What colour hair has she got? Is she tall? Short? Curvy? Slim? What do you like about her? There are so many more superlatives you could've used other than *nice*.' She shook her head in exasperation.

'She's short, slim and pretty with long black hair, her parents are Japanese, and she's sweet, better?'

Angelia huffed. 'Fine, I get the feeling you don't want to talk about her.'

Ed paused and tapped his fingers on the steering wheel and clenched his jaw. 'It's not that… it's just… we broke up. That's sort of why I'm here early.'

Guilt niggled at Angelia, knotting her stomach. 'Oh, shit, sorry, Ed. Maybe you should have just said that though, eh?'

He shrugged. 'Maybe. Sorry. It's no big deal though. We weren't that serious.' She could see from the sadness in his expression that he wasn't being entirely truthful.

'Why *did* you break up?' She knew the question was possibly a step too far, but the words were out before she could stop them.

He narrowed his eyes briefly and shook his head. 'We wanted different things, I suppose. Why does anyone break up?'

'Is there any chance you might get back together?'

He shook his head. 'Nope. Definitely over.'

His curt answers told her it was time to stop pushing. And why, she wondered, was she so bothered anyway? She reached out and squeezed his arm. 'Well, I'm sorry to hear you broke up, even though it did mean I got you here early.'

He smiled but it was fleeting. 'Thanks.' He fell silent again for a few moments until he turned to her again. 'How about you? Seeing anyone?'

'Nope. My love life is non-existent, as usual.'

'I saw the shit in the paper about you and *Josh*,' he said, saying the drummer's name as if it left an acidic taste in his mouth. 'Has he been in touch much?'

Her heart sank and it was her turn to stare out the window now. 'No. I try not to think about Josh,' she replied flatly.

The rest of the journey was made in a heavy, weighted silence that neither of them seemed able to break.

* * *

After she had updated her parents excitedly about the choir practice, they all watched an episode of *Shetland*, another of her parents' favourites. Angelia had preferred the books to the TV drama, having read them on tour when her mum sent them a while back. Her mum had agreed that the books were better. Meghan, however, agreed with Angelia's dad about the show being brilliant.

After they had watched another episode, with Scrappy asleep beside Angelia on the sofa, she walked Ed out to the campervan.

'Are you sure you're going to be okay out here?' she asked, folding her arms around her body. It was almost midnight now and there was a nip in the air despite the fact it was spring.

He shrugged. 'Absolutely. It'll be an adventure. Speaking of which, when do your parents go away?'

'They leave on Monday to go down to Heathrow, but they fly out Wednesday the twenty-eighth for three weeks. They're going to travel on the Rocky Mountain Railroad which I'm a tiny bit jealous about. I know I told them they had to go but I'll miss them like mad. It's been so good being home with them again.'

'I know what you mean. I miss my mum and dad too,' Ed said with a sigh as he stared off into the distance and shoved his hands into the pockets of his baggy jeans.

'And yet you chose to come here instead of going home to Hampshire.'

He pursed his lips for a moment. 'Yes, but unlike yours, my folks are so hard on me. Always have been. As soon as I get home, they start asking when I'm going to apply for bigger orchestras, or higher paying, more prestigious work. I think they like to live vicariously through me which is an awful lot of pressure. And if it's not that it's, "*when are you going to settle down and get married? We'd love some grandkids while we're still young enough to enjoy them*",' he said in an almost mocking tone. 'Honestly, I can't win. I do love them, don't get me wrong, and I really *do* miss them but it's easier to be away from them than it is to visit home more than once a year. Coming to see you was definitely the better option.'

'Well, I'm glad to have you here,' she said, hugging him. 'I hope you manage to sleep okay.'

He removed his hands from his pockets, pulled her into his embrace and squeezed her tightly, giving a small laugh. 'Believe me, when you've slept on as many airport floors as I have a camper is the epitome of luxury.' She smiled up at him, then turned to walk away. 'Hey, hang on a sec, I've got an idea.'

His words stopped her in her tracks, and she turned to face him with eyebrows raised. 'Ooh, that's dangerous,' she replied with a grin.

He tilted his head. 'Funny.' He eagerly took a step towards her. 'Seriously, I was thinking, why don't we head down to Glenbrittle for a few days while I've got the van? From the pics I've seen online it looks stunning. There's this great campsite by the water out in the middle of nowhere. We'd be undisturbed, I'm sure. We could visit the Fairy Pools and do some hiking. Get some fresh air. Scrappy would love it.'

She laughed. 'You do know it'll be midge central, don't you? It's *May*, Ed. On Skye? Do you want to get eaten alive?'

'Pfft, we can take some of that stuff that repels them, you can buy it online. How bad can it be?'

She shook her head. 'God, you're such a towny. It'll be horrendous. It'll be heaving with people, because it always is, and I can tell you now Meghan won't go for it. Imagine how cramped it would be and how bored silly Meghan'd be if she came with us. We'd be reminiscing about uni days, and she'd just be sat there swatting midges.'

He shrugged, disappointment in his eyes and she hated that she had put it there. 'I just thought it'd be nice to spend some time, just the two of us. We haven't done that since that time the three of us were supposed to go camping during our second year at uni. Remember? Fee had food poisoning, so it ended up just me and you? We took my car out to Loch Doon and star gazed.

Best night ever.' There was a hint of melancholy in his voice, or maybe even regret. 'Anyway, never mind. It was just a thought. Goodnight, Angel.' He climbed into the van and after one final raise of his hand in a salute, he slid the door closed.

When Angelia got back into the house, she kissed her mum and dad goodnight and went to her room. Scrappy was already curled up on his own side of her bed, fast asleep. She changed into her pyjamas and climbed in beside him carefully so as not to disturb the snoozing canine, and she lay down and thought back to that September camping trip in 2014 she had almost forgotten about...

* * *

'This place is stunning,' Ed said, shielding his eyes as he climbed out of the car on the shore of Loch Doon. It was September 2014 and the weather was unseasonably warm. He wore a slate-grey Hozier T-shirt that fit tight over his biceps and broad shoulders; he'd had a Hozier obsession back then which had meant they had listened to the artist's self-titled debut album for the whole journey, both belting out 'Take Me to Church' and then skipping back to the start to sing it all over again.

Standing there on the shore was magical. The sunlight danced on the water as if it was made up of a billion tiny mirrors glinting and the sky over head was a vivid cerulean that almost looked photoshopped.

Angelia inhaled lungsful of the fresh air and thought to herself that you could be forgiven for thinking you were much more than an hour outside of the bustle of Glasgow. 'Glorious,' she said simply, because the word seemed to sum up the place quite succinctly.

Ed turned to face her. 'I just love Scotland. The fact that wild camping even exists is amazing. And look at that! That castle looks fascinating. We'll have to go and have a closer look.'

'Come on then,' she called out. 'We can get the tent out later, let's make the most of the weather because who knows what could happen with that in an hour.' And she headed off, jogging in the direction of the medieval structure. Ed caught up to her as she paused at an information board to read about the castle. 'Wow, it says here that it used to be somewhere else, an island in the loch somewhere over there.' She pointed in the direction the details denoted. 'But then in 1935 the loch was dammed so, because of the rising water, they took the stones *one by one* and rebuilt the castle here.'

'Bloody hell, that must've taken ages. Good that they didn't let such a wonderful piece of history go forgotten, though.'

They walked around the perimeter of the castle and Ed snapped photos on his phone of the view out over the loch. She even caught him snapping photos of her when he thought she wasn't aware.

Once inside the partial structure it was clear to see it must have once been an impressive place to behold. The holes for the joists for an upper floor were visible, as were the arched spaces that were once windows.

Ed joined her and shook his head. 'Wow, the painstaking way they must have worked to take each stone and note where it should go, only to carry it all the way over here and place it down in the exact spot it needed to be. Like a giant LEGO set.' He chuckled. 'One way to work up an appetite, I suppose. Speaking of which, I'm starving, shall I go light the barbie?'

Angelia laughed. 'You're always hungry.'

He patted his flat, lean stomach. 'I'm a growing lad.'

'Oh aye, and it's a wonder you're not growing outwards with the amount of scran you put away; you wee *gundy-guts*.'

They set up their two-man tent and Angelia took the old picnic blanket she'd bought in a charity shop and laid it on the ground. They then ate grilled sausages dipped in the sachets of ketchup Ed had pocketed on a trip to a fast-food restaurant at lunchtime. At said restaurant he had eaten two burgers, a portion of fries, a doughnut and had guzzled down a large cup of cola in the time it had taken Angelia to eat one solitary burger.

Once they had polished off the remaining barbecued sausages, Ed produced two bottles of merlot from his backpack which they proceeded to drink straight from the bottles. Then, as the sun descended beyond the distant mountains, Ed retrieved both of their guitars from the boot of his car, and they sat side by side strumming a variety of tunes together by the glow of the fire.

'We should write a song together,' he blurted as if a light bulb had just pinged on above his head.

Angelia giggled. 'All right, Bob Dylan.'

'No! I mean it. How cool would that be? We could play it for Fee when we get back.'

She shook her head, a little giddy from the alcohol she had imbibed. 'What would we write about?'

He fell silent and gazed up at the canopy of stars twinkling above them. 'The night sky, the universe, the cosmos.' He lowered his face and fixed his bright green eyes on her. 'Us.'

She tilted her head. 'Us?'

He placed down his guitar and slid closer to her. 'There *could* be an us.'

She smiled and nudged him with her shoulder. 'There already is an us, you wee dafty,' she said, the heat of the fire, or more likely the wine, warming her from inside.

His face remained stoic and his lips parted as he gazed deep into her eyes. 'A different kind of us,' he whispered as she watched the reflection of the flames dance in his irises.

She had always thought Ed was handsome. He was stereotypically good-looking with his thick mop of wavy brown hair, tall lean body and dreamy green eyes that could hypnotise if you stared into them too long. She had always admired Ed's sense of humour and love of adventure. His ability to lift her mood when she was feeling down. She had found him very attractive too and had harboured more than just a crush for a long while, if she was completely honest. But there was a line you didn't cross with friends, wasn't there?

Okay, so his lips looked incredibly kissable in that moment, and he smelled deliciously masculine, a mixture of fire smoke and red wine, but if they kissed there would be no going back. *What would Fee think, when she found out?* Would she feel like a third wheel? A spare part? That wouldn't be fair. Kissing Ed would be selfish. She had thought about it on many occasions but had always assumed he was keen on Fiona, and saw her as bestie and nothing more, so she had managed to gloss over her attraction; push it to the back of her mind for the greater good. For *The Three Amigos*.

Until now, that is.

And as his lips closed in on hers, she felt helpless to stop it. In fact, she wanted it. She didn't fight. She didn't keep Fiona in her mind. She simply let him kiss her, and she kissed him back with just as much fervency. As her heart pounded and skin heated, he slipped his hands into her hair and inhaled as if pulling her deep into his body. He moaned against her mouth and whispered something about wanting this for so, *so* long. It dawned on her that she felt the same. This deep need for him. Someone she had fantasised about kissing, and more, if the truth be told. And now it was happening. But what would happen when the alcohol wore off? Would they still be the same? Could they work as much more than friends? She tried to fight that fear and push it down, as far down as it would go and just relished the feeling of his hands on her body, his lips on hers.

Riiiiing! Riiiing!

The kiss was interrupted by both of their phones alerting an incoming group call on WhatsApp.

Fiona.

They each picked up their phones and stared at their individual screens. Then they simultaneously looked to each other. There was a shared gaze. A split second and an infinitesimal shake of his head, followed by an apologetic frown.

'Hey, Fee! How are you feeling?' Ed asked as he accepted the call, stood and ran his hand back through his hair.

'Like my stomach is trying to vacate my body through my throat,' Fiona replied. 'I've never felt so ill. I wish I could be with you guys. Don't have too much fun without me, will you? You can't be the *two* amigos. It doesn't have the same ring to it.'

With his pained eyes fixed on Angelia for a brief moment, Ed replied, 'Don't be daft, Fee. The Three Amigos are forever, right, Angelia?'

Without realising, somehow on autopilot, Angelia had also accepted the group call. She forced a smile and nodded. 'Absolutely... *forever.*' But a stinging sensation began behind her eyes. It was over before it began. *The Three Amigos*, she thought. Was he actually in love with Fiona as she had always suspected? She had never commented on it because it was clear Fiona didn't feel the same. But it would explain his change in mood as soon as he heard her voice. Maybe the alcohol had played a bigger part than she cared to admit and she had been a substitute for the one he really wanted to kiss.

She concluded that must be the case because it was like a switch had been flicked and what had happened in the seconds before had been a dream. There may have been a physical attraction there but evidently it wasn't enough. The subject was never broached again and Angelia often wondered if she had in fact imagined it.

And they never did write that song.

22

On Monday morning, Angelia got up extra early to wave her parents off on their trip. Her head was still fuzzy from sleep, but she had awoken to an exciting message from Bella saying she was going to meet with a contractor at the shop in the afternoon, and asking if she'd like to come down to Glentorrin to be present. Angelia had replied to say Bella could go ahead without her. She had already given her a spare key and had approved all the plans they had discussed, so her being there wasn't really necessary. She had read the reviews so she knew she could trust Bella.

Now here she stood at the front door, in her pyjamas trying not to yawn as her mum clung to her hand.

'Are you sure you'll be okay, sweetie?' her mum asked, her eyes glassy. 'I feel so bad leaving you at a time like this. And we're going to miss your birthday.'

She smiled in what she hoped would be a reassuring manner. 'Honestly, Mum, you don't need to worry. There'll be other birthdays. And I'll be fine. Ed's here, and Meghan. And nothing bad has happened so far since I've been home.' *Apart from the group of fans recognising me, the Monty Python paps and a massive panic attack, oh, and my band and career collapsing around my ears*, she thought but didn't mention any of it.

'Come on, love, we really need to go,' her dad called from where he stood by the taxi. He had already said his goodbyes and had asked, once again, if

Angelia was sure she didn't want them to stay home, but of course she wouldn't allow them to lose all that money they had invested in their trip of a lifetime.

Her mum pulled her into a strong embrace. 'I love you and I'm so proud of you,' she said with a wavering voice.

'I love you too. But please try not to worry. Just go and have an amazing time. You've dreamed of this holiday for so long, please don't let worrying about me spoil it.'

Her mum pulled back and cupped her face in her free hand. 'I'll try, darling.' She gave one last smile and turned to dash towards the waiting cab. Then, as the car pulled away, her mum waved until she could no longer be seen.

Angelia closed the front door, and Ed pulled her into a hug. 'Are you okay?' he asked with a kiss to the top of her head.

Angelia nodded. 'I'm fine, honestly. Absolutely fine.' She needed to change the subject. 'Bella's meeting a team of contractors at the shop today, fingers crossed they can take the job soon. Although I'm not holding my breath. It's a pretty long shot, I suppose, and I'm guessing I may be in for a fair wait.'

'Let's hope she can pull some strings then, eh?' Ed said, releasing her from his arms. 'It's going to be so bloody cool when it's done.'

Meghan cleared her throat. 'Hey, sorry to interrupt you, guys, but I've... erm... I've had a call from my aunty. My mum was taken to A&E last night and now she's in hospital having major surgery.'

Angelia gasped and covered her mouth with one hand. 'Oh no, Meghan, what on earth happened?'

Meghan's face was unusually pale, and she leaned on the wall to steady herself. Angelia had never seen her looking so vulnerable. 'She, erm... she had a heart attack.'

Angelia strode towards her and hugged her. Meghan melted into Angelia's arms and sobbed.

'You need to go home, Meghan. You need to be there.'

Meghan nodded silently into her shoulder and clung to her for what felt like an age. Then, as suddenly as it had all happened, she straightened her spine and wiped roughly at her face with her sleeve. 'I'll call Den. They can send Austin... or Chad... or—'

'Look, I'll call Den,' Angelia insisted. 'You just get your things packed and go. Please. Never mind any of the other stuff. Den will understand. Just go.'

Meghan, for once, didn't argue. She simply nodded, turned and walked towards the spare room, lifting her phone and swiping at the screen as she went.

Ed rubbed his hands roughly over his face. 'Shit, what a morning. Poor Meghan. Can I do anything?'

Angelia smiled. 'There's nothing to do. Let's just let Meghan get sorted and we can deal with the rest later.'

Meghan packed and arranged a hotel room for that night in Carlisle, roughly the halfway point of her journey to Cardiff. As she was leaving, she hugged Angelia tightly. 'Thank you, Angel. I appreciate you being so understanding. I'm sorry to dash off like this.' Her voice wavered.

Angelia shook her head. 'Hey, you don't need to apologise. Our parents are so important.' She remembered Isla's words at choir practice. 'You've got to make the most of them. Are you sure you're okay to drive though?'

Meghan nodded. 'Yeah, I'll… I'll be fine, lovely. I'll be careful, don't worry. I feel like I'm abandoning you.' Her voice wavered again.

Ed slipped his arm around Angelia's shoulder. 'Honestly, it's fine, Meghan. I'll look after her. You concentrate on yourself and your mum.'

Meghan glanced up at Ed. 'Thank you, Ed. You're such a good friend.' She turned her attention back to Angelia. 'Looks like you're in safe hands,' she said with a look that Angelia recognised but chose to ignore. *Ever the matchmaker*, she thought.

Angelia hugged her once more, her heart squeezing in her chest. 'Please keep me posted on how your mum's doing. I'll be thinking of you.'

Meghan nodded, her eyes filled with tears and worry, lifted her bag and walked to the yellow Mini.

Back inside, Ed walked through to the kitchen and returned with two mugs of coffee. 'I figured you'd need this.'

She closed the door and took a mug, inhaling the earthy aroma and feeling a sense of calm wash over her. 'Thanks. You know me so well.'

'So, who do you think they'll send to replace Meghan?' Ed asked as he sipped his coffee.

Angelia tried to act nonchalant. 'No one. Because I'm not calling Den.'

Ed's eyes widened. 'Oh, right.' He nodded.

'I need to get used to not having an assistant now the band has finished so there's no time like the present, eh? And I don't need to be watched and wrapped in bubble wrap, Ed, like I'm somehow more important than other people. I'm not. I'm human like everyone else and I just want to be normal again.'

He held up his free hand. 'Hey, you're preaching to the choir.'

Angelia looked up and fixed him with a determined gaze. 'So... what do you say we take that camping trip you talked about?'

His eyes brightened. 'Seriously?'

'Seriously. I mean we'd have to be back for Friday because it's choir practice then, and again on Saturday and I can't let them all down.'

Ed fist-bumped the air. 'Hell, yes!'

* * *

The hour-long journey to Glenbrittle later that day was fun, like old times. They sang along to Hozier, of course, although Angelia not so much this time, but she enjoyed Ed's dramatic delivery of 'From Eden', complete with hand gestures that made her giggle. Thankfully he kept his eyes firmly on the road ahead. They made a stop for Scrappy to have a bathroom break and for Ed to call into the nearest shop to gather provisions, although he'd been excited to inform her there was a café and shop on the campsite if they needed anything else.

The sky was heavy and grey for the whole journey, but Angelia wasn't going to let it dampen her mood, and anyway, it only added to the drama of the scenery that surrounded them. The wildflowers in the hedgerows, dog violets, blackthorn and cowslips in their pinks, whites and yellows, were a bright, cheery contrast to the otherwise murky colour palette. But ultimately this was a taste of freedom she didn't often get, and she wanted to make the most of every second. She fought the urge to stick her head out of the window to feel the breeze on her face like a puppy experiencing life for the first time.

It was raining heavily when they arrived at the Glenbrittle campsite, but it was still quite busy. Ed pulled the van into a space close to the beach and the shower block which was, surprisingly, a little quieter.

'We'll camp here so you have quick access to the loo and showers. You can keep your hood up and head down so no one will know it's you,' he said, clearly having thought things through, which she appreciated. 'And hey, less midges thanks to the rain. Bright side and all that.' He grinned. 'Come on, I'll get the kettle on.'

He climbed out of the van and walked around to the sliding side door that led into the main body of the camper. Inside was quite spacious for a two-berth vehicle. There was a countertop with a small sink, a two-ring stove and a fridge underneath, all situated opposite the door, and to the right was a double seat that flattened out into a bed. Scrappy was asleep in his red tartan harness, clipped onto the seat until Ed climbed in at which point he awoke and wagged his tail until Ed gave him a scratch behind the ears.

'Hey, little fella, you looked all snuggly there, sorry for waking you.'

Angelia was able to swivel her passenger seat around without getting out of the van, which was handy considering the deluge outside. She unclipped Scrappy, removed his harness and placed him on the floor where he rolled around excitedly on his back trying to bite his tail until he exhausted himself, sighed, and decided on nap number twelfty-eleven of the day.

Once Ed had dried his hair off with a towel, he switched the gas on and fired up the heater to take the chill from the air. 'I'm so glad you agreed to this,' he said, rubbing his hands together and blowing into them. 'Once we've had a cuppa, why don't we get our coats on and take Scrappy for a walk on the beach? There's nothing quite like a refreshing walk in the rain.'

'Sounds good.'

Phone signal had been intermittent on the way down so as soon as she connected to the site Wi-Fi her phone pinged with several messages and a couple of missed calls. Most of which were from Josh.

> JOSH
>
> Hey, Angel, just checking in as I haven't heard from you in a while. Are we okay?

Then,

> JOSH
>
> I just don't understand why we can't all go on as we did before. We could still tour. Just maybe not as often. You'll get better maybe if you exercise your voice more.

Had he even listened when she had explained her diagnosis? He clearly hadn't done the same research as Ferris, which, considering Josh had known her a hell of a lot longer *and* professed to love her, was a tad disappointing. If he had he'd have known that exercising her voice was the last thing that would help.

The next message read,

JOSH

I miss you. And I'm sorry I didn't handle this whole myasthenia thing very well. I just hate the thought of you being ill. It brings back painful memories of Lorelie, you know?

Again, she thought, *I'm not ill. Not like Lorelie was. This is completely different. And way to make it all about you, Josh*. Then came,

JOSH

Have you forgotten about your old pal Joshy already? Because I can't stop thinking about you, Angel. You're constantly on my mind and it's hard for me. I think we need to talk.

Good grief, talk about mixed messages, she thought.

'Bloody hell, who are all the messages from?' Ed asked as more pinged through. 'Are they from Ferris?' He sounded strangely sad as he asked the question.

She shook her head even though he now had his back to her. 'Josh.' She cleared her throat. 'They're from Josh.'

Ed turned. 'Oh, right. Missing you, is he?' This time his voice was laced with disdain. He had never hidden his feelings about Josh Baron and the way he dangled Angelia on a string like a puppet; well, that's what he'd said about their situation anyway. She had never really looked at it that way. Perhaps until recently at least.

'Apparently so,' she replied flatly. She reluctantly hit reply.

ANGEL

Hi, Josh. I'm away just now camping with Ed. Signal isn't great. I'm fine though. Angelia.

She kept the reply short and to the point and left it at that. No more messages came.

'I don't get guys like him,' Ed said after a few moments. 'He has this amazing girlfriend who's stuck by him all this time, even when the rumours were flying about you and him. Yet he still clings to you. It's as if he doesn't want you but he doesn't want you to move on without him. And that's shitty on you *and* Nancy, in my opinion.'

He was right on all points, Angelia feared. Just then another message came through.

FERRIS

Hey, Angelia, how are you doing? I thought you might like to know that I saw a few of the choir at church yesterday and they all had such great things to say about you. I'm so glad you took on the role. Anyway, if you get a chance this week, I can be free for coffee and a chat. We could discuss plans for the choir going forward maybe? Although I understand you may not be on Skye forever, that's possibly wishful thinking on my part. For the choir I mean. Anyway, let me know if you're free. Ferris, Curate Extraordinaire.

He finished his message with a smiley face that had a halo above it, and it made her smile. She hit reply.

ANGEL

Hi, Ferris, or should that be Mr Extraordinaire? Actually, I'm playing truant this week. Ed and I have escaped to Glenbrittle for a few days of rain, or midges, or maybe both, who knows with Scottish weather? Fear not though, I will be back in time for choir on Friday. Not long until the show so we need to make every rehearsal count. Angelia

The icon flashed to indicate Ferris was typing a reply. Was he going to question the lack of a mention of Meghan?

FERRIS

Ah, yes, I did wonder if you'd abscond, and Glenbrittle is a rather beautiful location to choose. Meghan called into the church on her way off the island. I was very sorry to hear about her mum and told her I'll pray for her. She asked me to be extra vigilant at choir practice in case any paparazzi showed up when the press release is made about the band, although she wasn't sure when that would be. I had a sneaking suspicion you might accidentally on purpose 'forget' to let your management know you were flying solo. Whilst I completely understand your desire for freedom and a 'normal' life, I can't help worrying that you underestimate your value. Please be careful. See you Friday. God bless.

So only a hint at a lecture. That was better than she expected. She'd wondered if Meghan would feel it necessary to inform him. She shook her head and placed her phone back in her pocket. 'Shall we stick the coffee into those two travel mugs I saw in the cupboard, and head out for some fresh air now?'

Ed turned and smiled. 'You must've read my mind, MacAuley.'

The rain had slowed by the time they had climbed over the low dune and arrived on the beach. The volcanic sand was even darker than it would normally be, thanks to the weather, and the Black Cuillin mountain range, serving as a backdrop to the beach and campsite, appeared even more imposing due to the same factors. Scrappy, now off lead, ran towards the water's edge and away again as soon as the waves appeared to chase him. His tongue lolled out and his eyes were bright. He didn't care about the rain; he was living his best life.

'This place is amazing,' Ed said as he clung to his coffee cup. His hood flapped around in the breeze and his eyes were filled with wonder.

'It's beautiful,' Angelia replied. 'I'm not sure why I haven't been before.'

Another message pinged to her phone but this time it was Bella.

BELLA

Hey, Angelia. Great news! The team can start this week! They had a job just cancel so the timing is perfect. Structurally the building is sound, as you know from the original survey, and the site manager says the work is pretty superficial which is more good news! If you're okay to go ahead with the plans, and the attached quote figure is agreeable, just let me know. Of course, I have the spare key from when I showed them around this afternoon so I can deal with entry, I'm sure you're busy.

She clicked on the link in the message and was pleasantly surprised, rather than shocked, at the figures she saw there. So, the record shop would be up and running sooner than expected. Her stomach flipped with excitement and she replied immediately.

ANGEL

Excellent! I can't wait. Please accept before someone else snatches them up! I'm away just now but home Friday for choir. Signal is a bit hit and miss but message or call if you need me and I'll get back to you as soon as I can. Angelia.

She lifted her head to see that Ed and Scrappy had wandered on, so she jogged to catch up with them and grabbed Ed's arm, linking hers through his. 'The shop's a go!' she squealed. 'They're starting this week! *This week*, Ed!' She wobbled his arm and jumped up and down, and he laughed.

'You'd better get some decisions made then, MacAuley! Do you see yourself as a rock legend running a record store? Or as a silent partner, living the life of luxury while someone else runs it for you?' She chose to treat the questions as rhetorical, mainly because she was rather torn about the whole thing, and they carried on walking as the rain became heavier once again.

After they had walked the full length of the long beach and back again, they eventually returned to the van where Ed set about preparing a platter of crackers and cheese, pâté and French bread, and poured two rather large glasses of his favourite red wine. He flicked through his Spotify account and chose a mellow, chilled-out playlist by Zero 7 and they ate mostly in companionable silence, only commenting on how delicious the food was when they did speak.

'Do you want to know the real reason Ava broke up with me?' Ed asked out of the blue as he dried the last of the dishes Angelia had washed, and placed it in the overhead cupboard.

She looked up at him. 'Only if you want to tell me,' she replied.

He picked up his wine glass and sat on the sofa, so she followed suit and sat beside him, ready to listen.

He stared into the ruby-red liquid for a few moments, silent with his thoughts. 'It's silly really. But she found a heart-shaped photo in my wallet and realised I was in love... *am* in love with someone else.'

Angelia's heart sank a little. So, he *was* in love with Fiona all this time, as she had suspected. Was he about to confess it? She steeled herself. Even after all these years, Ed's smile still made her heart flip but she couldn't let that show. What good would it do? And anyway, she was an expert at heartbreak.

She chose to pre-empt him, selfishly to soften the blow to herself. 'Look, I think I already know who you mean. And I'm so sorry, Ed. Unrequited love is horrendous. I've been there so I know.'

His eyes widened and he opened his mouth to speak but frowned and closed it again. He swallowed and blinked rapidly. 'You do?' He closed his eyes and exhaled. 'Of course you do. And it's okay. I just thought I should tell you. Get it out there, you know?'

She reached out and squeezed his arm, sadness knotting her stomach, but she wasn't sure who she pitied more, him for loving Fiona when she was with Marcus, or herself for loving him. 'How long have you felt this way? I'm guessing it's quite a long time.'

His eyes seemed glassy in the low light. He smiled but it disappeared quickly. 'Since uni. Since my first day at uni to be exact. I saw you and Fiona walking through the campus, before I met either of you and... that was it.' He shrugged as if defeated. 'I made it my mission to bump into you both on that night out during freshers' week. And I suppose, seeing as we're being honest, I should own up and tell you I acted a lot more drunk than I actually was. I thought it'd be disarming. It gave me the perfect excuse to hang out with you both and to get to know you. Does that make me a total shit?'

Angelia smiled as she thought about the lyrics to Taylor Swift's 'Mastermind'. 'Not at all,' she replied. 'Cunning maybe, but not a total shit.'

He laughed and swiped at tears that had escaped from his eyes. 'God, look at me. What a wuss. Don't go telling Fee, will you? I'll never live it down that I cried like a baby.'

She rested her head on his shoulder. 'I won't breathe a word. I've suspected it for a long time, to be honest.'

He stiffened. 'You have? And you never said anything?'

She lifted her chin to find him staring down at her. 'What could I say? I couldn't do anything to help.'

He shook his head as deep sadness took over his expression. 'No, I suppose not. I just wish...' He shook his head. 'I just wish things were different.' His chin trembled and her heart ached for him.

She had never seen him like this. She'd never listened to him pour his heart out. But then again, she was kind of glad about that because she'd had feelings for him for so long that hearing him declare his love for someone else would have been awful, just like hearing Josh talk about Nancy had once been, in fact. Yes, she realised, by falling for Josh she had inadvertently replaced one unrequited love for another, and that said a lot about her really. Perhaps she was terrified of loving someone who actually loved her back because that hurt was something she could control even less.

'Welcome to the club,' she said with no little sadness to her tone as Zero 7's 'Somersault' played in the background.

23

The conversation ended as quickly as it had begun as they finished the bottle of wine and once they had both been to the shower block they laid out the two sleeping bags as Scrappy curled up in a ball in his makeshift bed on the floor. They hadn't spoken much since their heart to heart and Angelia felt bad that she couldn't do, or say, more to help her friend. In the night she found herself reaching for his hand when he was asleep and thinking about what could've been if things had, indeed, been different.

The following days of their trip seemed to go back to normal, and they chatted and laughed as they walked. She remembered how much she loved spending time with him, how easy he was to be around, and realised how grateful she was to have him in her life, even if it wasn't perhaps the relationship she had once hoped she'd have with him. She could certainly pick them, she thought; the arty, handsome types whose hearts were always elsewhere.

The Fairy Pools were just as she remembered. Beautiful, but busy, with what felt like a million other tourists. The attraction was unsurprising. The waters were so clean and clear that light caused colours to reflect deep down on the submerged rocks, creating a blueish hue which appeared magical and otherworldly. Some pools were skirted by waterfalls that would have been at home in the Brazilian rainforests.

On this occasion the weather was doing its best to prove just how Scottish it was as the heavens remained open and the sun barely came out for the whole time they were there. This wasn't such bad thing, however, because it meant her hood remained up and she, incognito. And, of course, midges didn't much care for the rain.

Scrappy was yet again having the best time. They'd had to keep him away from the smaller pools as he had already tried to jump in and the smell of wet dog wasn't something they wanted to leave in the hired campervan. At one point Angelia almost came a cropper on a slippery rock and was en route to landing headfirst in one of the larger pools, she squealed as it all seemed to happen in slow motion but at the last moment Ed rescued her from a fate worse than soggy clothes and yanked her back into his chest. *My hero*, she thought with a smile as she gazed up into his verdant eyes. He returned her smile and helped her back onto a steady footing.

They reminisced about university and about Angelia's auditions for *Scotland Rocks* and shared stories from their more recent trips around the world until it was time to head back.

'Thank you for not hating me,' Ed said as they drove the winding roads towards Portree on Friday morning.

Angelia turned in her seat. 'I could never hate you, Ed. Don't ever think that I could. It's been so good to really catch up and spend time together.'

He smiled but there was a tinge of sadness visible in his features again. 'It has.'

* * *

'Okay, we're doing this a little differently to the versions you may have heard. We're starting with the chorus rather than the first verse. It's more impactful that way,' Angelia informed the choir. 'Isla and Morag, you sopranos come in on four, and sing solo for the first four lines and then everyone else comes in all together on the last line of the chorus. We hold the word "need" for four beats, and then my baritones, you take the first verse. Sound good?' A rumble of agreement travelled the church.

Isla put up her hand like a nervous schoolgirl. 'I... I'm sorry but I don't know if I'm good enough to start this off, though, Angelia dearie,' she said, a worried crease furrowing her brow. 'I think Mick Jagger will be rolling in his grave when he hears it.' She shook her head.

Bella gasped. 'I sincerely hope not, Granny. And I think that would be pretty tricky too.'

Isla turned to her granddaughter. 'Aye, well, there's no much room in a coffin, I suspect.'

'It's not that, Granny.' Bella was giggling now.

'Was he cremated?' Isla asked, scowling.

'Erm, *no*!'

'What is it then?' Isla said, as serious as ever.

'Because he's not actually dead!'

Isla's eyes widened. 'Oh! Is he not?'

'He's very much alive and kicking, Isla,' Ferris added, grinning.

'Actually, Isla, from what I know of Mick, and it's not much admittedly,' Angelia said, 'but I reckon he'd be impressed by your talent. In fact, I might get Ed to record it on his phone so I can give him a call and play it for him,' she said with a wink. 'Also, I think he's around your age.'

Isla waved her hand as she laughed. 'Och, don't you dare! I'm a married woman, you know. I can't have some rock god sweeping me off ma feet.' The whole place erupted in laughter.

They ran through Ed's rather apt suggestion, considering their recent conversation, of the Rolling Stones' 'You Can't Always Get What You Want' and it went surprisingly well. Angelia glanced over at him where he stood with his mic'd electro-acoustic guitar and they shared a heartfelt smile.

'Are you going to sing at the concert, Angelia?' Evin asked at the end of the session.

'Angelia's here to help us all, son, not to perform for free,' his dad, Reid, informed him.

Evin sighed, disappointment evident in his downturned expression. 'That's a shame in my opinion. I think it'd be the highlight of the show,' he said defiantly.

Ferris glanced worriedly at Angelia and then back to Evin. 'Erm... I'm sorry, Evin, but it's not quite as easy—'

Angelia interrupted Ferris with, 'It's okay, I'm happy to explain.' Ferris nodded and gestured for her to go ahead so she continued, 'What I'm about to tell you all will soon be public knowledge, but I'd really appreciate it if you could keep it to yourselves just for now.' The group shared concerned glances, but each agreed to do so. 'The thing is, I've been diagnosed with a condition that affects my muscles, including my vocal muscles. When I do repetitious things like singing, walking and even smiling, for extended periods the symptoms worsen. That's really why I'm here on Skye. That and, of course, the fact my folks live up by Portree.'

'And that you've bought an awesome shop,' Ed added.

Angelia giggled. 'Yes, that too. So please forgive me if I choose not to sing at the concert. It's not because I don't want to, believe me. Singing is my greatest passion. It's just... not as easy as it once was.' Her voice broke and she cleared her throat as her eyes misted over.

Evin stepped forward from his position and Angelia thought he was going to walk out. Had she embarrassed him? Made him feel bad? She really hoped not. But instead, he stopped right in front of her and, after the briefest of pauses, he enveloped her in his arms and hugged her.

'I'm so sorry, Miss MacAuley. I'm so, so sorry.'

Her eyes welled with tears and she hugged him back. Then, one by one the rest of the choir stepped forward and joined the embrace until it was one mass of people with her in the centre. The compassion she felt at that moment almost brought her to her knees whilst simultaneously lifting her spirits higher than she had ever experienced.

'Thank you,' she whispered. 'Thank you all *so* much.'

At the end of the rehearsal, once everyone had left the church and Ed had gone to bring her car across, Ferris stood with Angelia by the church door.

'You were very brave tonight,' he said as he reached out to touch her arm.

'I didn't feel brave. I felt like a gibbering wreck,' she replied with a laugh.

He shook his head. 'No, you were amazing. You're always amazing, Angelia.' He fixed his gaze on her and smiled. 'Always.'

Ed opened the door and paused, glancing between them. 'Sorry, am I interrupting?'

As if snapping out of a trance, Ferris said, 'Oh, gosh, no. Sorry, just getting caught up in the events of the night. See you both tomorrow?'

Angelia nodded. 'See you tomorrow, Ferris,' she almost whispered before following Ed out to the car.

As they travelled back north once more, Angelia pondered the events of the evening. 'I think I'd like to sing at the concert,' she said.

Ed frowned. 'But... I thought you didn't want to? Don't feel pressured.

They all completely understand, you know. I've never felt so uplifted by a group of people, Angel. They really do get it. There's no expectation on you. None at all.'

Angelia nodded. 'I know. And that's why I want to. Because they lifted me up tonight too.'

After a pause, Ed said, 'He adores you, you know. Ferris, I mean. I think Evin does too, but who wouldn't? You're adorable,' Ed said and Angelia giggled. 'But joking aside, I think he's falling for you. Again, Ferris I'm talking about.'

Angelia turned towards him. 'Do you really think so? But I've only known him, what, a few weeks?'

Ed shook his head. 'Means nothing. When you know, you know. And I definitely get the feeling he knows.'

* * *

Messages had been flooding in from her parents with photos of each stop on their Canadian adventure and Angelia looked forward to each instalment. Calls were limited due to time differences, but the regular updates were wonderful. They both looked so happy and had clearly met some interesting people on their travels.

Meghan had been in touch, too, to say her mum's surgery had gone well and she was on the mend. These messages were so welcome but on Sunday Angelia got the message she had been both dreading and anticipating after her message to Josh about her trip. A demand for her to join the inevitable Zoom call she had hoped to avoid.

Ed gave her a pep talk just before she was due to join the call. 'Don't let them make you feel bad for not telling them about our camping trip. You're entitled to do what you want when you want to do it now. The band is no more. They don't own you. Now here, Dutch courage,' he said, handing her a glass of wine. 'I'll be downstairs if you need me to kick some virtual butt.' He left her to it and she logged on.

'Hello, Angelia, thank you for joining us,' Den said, his face deadpan.

Heath was there too but no one else, which added to her state of nervousness. She was definitely in for yet another dressing down. 'Hi, Angelia. Good to see you. You're looking well,' Heath said, his face also a mask of serious civility.

'Thanks, I'm feeling great just now.'

Den's jaw was ticking under his skin. 'I suppose you're aware that Meghan's mum is out of the woods.' As he spoke, he steepled his fingers and perched his elbows on the table in front of his tangerine-hued face.

Angelia nodded, her heart pounding. 'We've kept in touch, yes. I'm so relieved for her and her family. It's really good news.'

He narrowed his eyes. 'And your camping trip. How was that?' he asked with a knowing glare and a tilt of his head. He just needed a cat to stroke, and he'd be the perfect Bond villain.

'Oh... erm... I...' She remembered Ed's words and straightened her spine. 'It was great, thanks. Really good fun.' She forced a smile.

Den pursed his lips and his eyes remained unblinking. 'Hmm. It would have been good to have heard it direct from you, rather than to have Josh messaging us, panicking about you being unsafe.'

Angelia sighed. 'I wasn't unsafe. I went camping with my best friend. And anyway, the band has folded so I need to get used to being out without a driver or an assistant, or security, don't I? And I'm on the Isle of Skye, Den, it's hardly the crime centre of the world. I'm sorry but you're being ridiculous and as the band is no more you don't really get to have a say about what I do and don't do now.'

Den sat, wide-eyed, in a stunned silence which was a first, while she herself was quite proud of the fact that she hadn't used a single swear word. *Ferris would be proud*, she thought.

Heath pursed his lips, evidently amused by the whole situation. 'Just to let you know, Angel, the press release is going out tomorrow so expect some attention on social media. I imagine we'll all get tagged in stuff, good and bad. There'll be lots of speculation regardless of what we put out there. The fans will have questions, and some may not take so kindly to the news of the split. And even though you're on Skye, just be prepared that the press might arrive and try to get information from locals. Maybe just let your friends and family know to point them to the band's website or the management's.'

Angelia nodded. 'Fine. I will. Thanks for letting me know.'

'I've emailed you a copy of what's going out. Let me know if there's anything you want to add or remove.'

After an awkward pause, Heath said, 'I know Den maybe came over quite harsh about this whole thing, Angel...' Den opened his mouth to speak but Heath continued. 'Come on, Den, you did a bit. But the thing is, you're like a kid sister to us in the band. We just want to make sure you're safe. You've gone from being escorted around big cities by bodyguards to camping out with your friends. It's a massive change. And as safe as you feel, things do happen in the most unlikely of places. We just want you protected, even if the band is no more, okay? We love you, that's all.'

A lump lodged in her throat as she realised how much she missed the guys. 'Yeah... well... I love you too.' She sounded like a stroppy toddler.

Heath pursed his lips and then burst out laughing. 'God, I miss you, kid!' he said. 'Den, I think she's right. We need to move past this. The last thing I want is for the band to part with any animosity. Can we just drop it and move on?'

Den held up his hands in a surrendering motion and sighed.

Heath continued, 'Look, while I've got you here, I wanted to ask something a bit left field. I'm asking on behalf of Anouk because she's otherwise engaged.' He leaned forward and whispered, 'She's on a date.'

Angelia was delighted for her former bandmate. 'Ooh, exciting. What do you need to ask? Fire away.'

'The thing is... I'm joining Den in band management as part of his team and Anouk is my first artist.'

Angelia widened her eyes and clapped her hands together. 'That's amazing, H, I'm so happy for you! But... what does that have to do with me?'

'Well, the thing is, *my client*,' he said with a glint in his eye, 'wants to know if you'd like to collaborate on some songs for her solo album. She loves your songs and she's desperate to work with you. She says it can all be done remotely and you can do things at your own pace. No pressure to tour unless you want to join her when the time comes, of course, because she would absolutely love that. You'd be credited as a co-writer obviously, so would be entitled to royalties. You don't have to give her a decision right away, but it looks like we're about to do a deal for her to sign with Blue Demon Records, so it'd be a real boost to her if you'd work with her.'

Her throat tightened again and her eyes stung. 'Really? She wants me on her first solo album?'

Heath nodded. 'Hey, she's getting in before the world realises you're available. You've no idea how in demand you're going to be as a songwriter. If that's something you feel you want to pursue. Anyway, have a think about it and let me know.'

Angelia laughed and wiped tears of joy from her cheeks. 'I don't need to think about it. I'm in.'

24

June arrived and brought its best and brightest outfits along; the sun was out, the sky was blue, the hedgerows were buzzing with life around a multitude of coloured blooms, and the birds were having their own choir practice. The songs Angelia had selected and had been rehearsing with the choir were really taking shape and she was giddy with excitement. With the show in a few days' time, her excitement was tinged with a little sadness that it was going to be over soon.

After what had felt like so much bad news in the last few months, she now felt like life had taken a turn for the better. Meghan's mum was out of ICU and was set to make a full recovery, although there would be strict lifestyle changes, but Meghan, who had realised she needed to be around for her mum more, had relocated to Cardiff to work for a talent agency. Ezra had already bought a house on the outskirts of Cardiff almost as soon as he had met Meghan, so determined was he that they were meant to be, and now he and Meghan were stronger than ever and talking about moving in together. Meghan had promised to keep in touch and that made Angelia happy.

After the conversation she'd had briefly with Heath, Angelia had gone on to chat with Anouk on video call about their songwriting collaboration and had even sent her some demos of songs she'd already written a long time ago. Anouk had loved every single one and had asked if she could use some on her album to which Angelia immediately agreed.

Anouk had signed on the dotted line with Blue Demon Records, and the world had finally been notified, via the band's website and a general press release, that Angel and the Fallen would be no more. Angelia had felt it important to have her diagnosis mentioned in the press release as myasthenia wasn't such a well-known condition and after doing her own research on the condition she was living with, she wanted to use her platform to raise awareness. She had anticipated heavy fallout, and for people to be angry about the band's unexpected demise. But to her surprise and relief, she received nothing but support on social media. The story had made the headlines in all the papers too; both broadsheet and tabloid, and from what she had been told, and witnessed for herself, almost everyone was sympathetic.

There was, of course, a small cohort who bemoaned her condition online and insinuated it was all down to overindulgence in illicit substances but in response to this, Heath had recorded a video that was put out, addressing their *true fans* in which he decried such rumours and made it clear that drugs had *never* been a part of Angel and the Fallen.

The most touching occurrence was that other people with myasthenia gravis wrote letters of encouragement to her personally, and these arrived in sacksful to her parents' house via the band's management company. She read as many as she could and was humbled by some of the stories of people overcoming the worst symptoms to raise money for myasthenia research. She vowed, then, that she would do whatever she could to spread awareness about the relatively unknown condition and even spoke to Den about the band making a donation from the proceeds of their upcoming 'best of' release, to aid further research too. The rest of the band agreed.

An organisation that helped and supported people with the condition contacted her around the beginning of June, via Den, and asked her to meet with them to discuss being an ambassador. It was something she had been honoured to accept and had met with Kendric MacKinnon for an interview to start the ball rolling. It was a little surreal sitting on a couch in a TV studio to talk about something other than the band and being interviewed by a man she used to watch on her local channel presenting the weather. She had been incredibly nervous, but it had gone well.

On the back of the letters from other MG warriors, as she called them, she had decided she would definitely sing at the summer concert and had chosen one of the Angel and the Fallen ballads she had co-written. Only instead of the raucous, heavy guitars and rousing drum solo that the track originally showcased, she would sing a stripped-down version accompanied by Ed on his electro-acoustic guitar. They'd run through it at home a few times and it sounded good, even by Angelia's exacting standards. It was her intention to surprise the choir and the audience at the summer concert, which was approaching rapidly.

Meanwhile Angelia and Ed had spent almost every waking minute together. They had been on long drives to secluded beaches to picnic, and had visited the shop on several occasions, too, to oversee the progress. The only occasions he left her were when she met with Ferris for coffee and cake in their usual spot. But on those occasions, he never strayed too far.

On one visit to the shop that happened to be on her birthday, Bella had requested a meeting to discuss colour charts for the living accommodation. Angelia was struggling with the thought of letting the place go and to this end she had decided against the original safe and bland neutral colour palette and had chosen to decorate the place to her own tastes. Bella had brought samples of dark greens, blues and reds for her to look at, along with samples of William Morris print wallpapers.

Angelia pored over the samples but was finding it difficult to choose. They were all so beautiful.

'Which one do you like best, Ed? I think I'm leaning towards "Strawberry Thief" with the navy background,' she said as she flicked through the sample books.

Ed had been fidgety and kept glancing at his watch. 'Sorry, what?' he asked distractedly.

'"Strawberry Thief" in navy or red?' she repeated.

'Oh... I like the navy,' he said, walking over to the window. 'Why don't we go over to the pub for a drink and some lunch and we can decide there?'

'That sounds like a good idea,' Bella said. 'We can take the sample books.'

'Ugh... okay. We'll go to the pub. I don't know what's got into you today, Ed.'

He walked across and linked his arm through hers. 'Sorry. I think I'm just hungry,' he replied, pouting.

'You're always hungry. And always eating. I've no idea how you stay so lean,' Angelia said as he tugged her towards the door.

'I'll go ahead and get the drinks in while you lock up,' Bella said as she dashed down the stairs.

'I'll just have an orange juice!' Angelia called after her.

'Oh, come on, it's your birthday. Have a glass of wine at least,' Ed said as she locked the door to the shop.

'I need my wits about me, or I'll end up having wallpaper that's sky-blue and pink with yellow dots on.'

Ed laughed. 'I don't think you'll ever be *that* drunk.'

When they reached the Coxswain, Ed held the door and gestured for her to walk in first. As she did, she was greeted with a chorus of 'Happy Birthday' from the choir who were standing in front of the bar and being led by Ferris on the keyboard she recognised as the one from the church. Shocked, she covered her mouth with her hands and grinned beneath them like the Cheshire Cat.

When the rendition was finished, the whole pub began to clap and cheer and it was only then that she realised, as well as her new friends from Glentorrin, Fiona and Marcus, Meghan and Ezra and the band were there too. She was enveloped in a group hug and had to fight the threatening tears on receiving such a wonderful surprise.

The pub had been closed to anyone who wasn't a resident of the village or part of the invite list and Stella and Joren who owned the pub had prepared a buffet. Caitlin had baked the most incredible chocolate birthday cake that could rival anything seen in the most expensive patisseries in London.

Heath and Anouk performed a couple of acoustic songs, which her friends from the village loved, especially Evin, who was a little starstruck. Angelia introduced him and his girlfriend, Grace, to the band and made sure to take photos of him with them on his phone.

'Hey, how are you?' Josh asked when he found her at the buffet table while Nancy was talking to Ruby.

She nodded but her stomach clenched with annoyance. 'I'm good, thanks. You?'

He sighed. 'I know you're upset with me. I know I haven't been the best friend I used to be. But… it's been hard for me. What with your news and then the band folding. It's been… difficult,' he said with a shake of his head.

Angelia clenched her jaw. 'Don't you think it's been hard for me? I never asked for any of this. I didn't do it on purpose, you know.'

'I know, I know that. It's just... You mean so much to me and... I...'

'I don't mean enough to you for you stay in touch, Josh. You bailed when I needed you the most. That's hard to forgive.'

He closed his eyes for a moment. 'I know. I'm sorry. I just—'

'That's the problem really, Josh. You've said "I" so many times during this brief conversation that I don't want to listen to it any more.'

Someone tapped at the microphone near the bar, and everyone turned to see Ed seated at the keyboard.

He cleared his throat. 'Seeing as the musos in the room have been doing their bit I thought I should too. This piece of music probably isn't the most lively thing for a birthday party but... I know it's one of Angelia's favourites, so I'm going to play it anyway.' He closed his eyes and began to play Debussy's 'Clair de Lune' and tears spilled over from Angelia's eyes. The emotion and pain she'd felt during the conversation with Josh and the memory of the night she fell in love with Ed overwhelmed her and her heart ached.

Part way through the piece, with everyone in rapt awe of Ed's playing and the chosen music, Fiona came over and slipped her arm around Angelia's shoulder. 'He adores you, you know. Always has,' she whispered.

Angelia smiled. 'Josh?' she asked.

Fiona shook her head. 'No, you wee dafty, Ed.'

'I adore him too,' Angelia replied.

'No, I mean he *really* adores you,' Fiona said.

Angelia turned her head to stare at Fiona and widened her eyes as her heart tripped over itself. 'What do you mean?'

'He arranged all this,' Fiona told her.

'Yes but... he adores me as a friend, *right*?'

As Fiona was about to answer, Ed's piece ended and the pub erupted in raucous applause. And from that moment Angelia was whisked away, handed gifts and left wondering.

Ed had arranged a taxi to take them back to Portree at the end of the night and Marcus and Fiona accompanied them. Meghan and Ezra were staying at Morag's B&B and were setting off very early the following morning to get the train back to Cardiff, so they said their goodbyes outside the pub.

'I'm so glad your mum is getting better,' Angelia said as she hugged Meghan.

'Me too, it's been quite scary. But Ezra has been amazing.'

Angelia hugged him next. 'Thank you for looking after Meghan. She's so used to looking after everyone else it's good to know she has someone looking out for her.'

Ezra smiled. 'I have you to thank for us meeting. She's the love of my life.'

* * *

When she came out of the bathroom, Fiona and Marcus had already gone to bed in her parents' room. Scrappy had curled himself up on her bed and was fast asleep so before collapsing into bed Angelia knocked on the spare room door where Meghan had once slept but Ed had now taken up residence.

'Entaaaaar!' Ed called out, clearly a little sozzled.

'I just wanted to say thank you for tonight, you stinker,' she said, smiling.

'Ahhh, you're not easy to keep secrets from,' he said with a slur. 'But I managed this one!' He wagged his finger and gave a crooked smile. 'I'm proud of myself because I'm usually useless at keeping things from you. I've even confessed my biggest secret to you, remember. Fat lot of good that did me, though.' He smacked his forehead. 'Ugh, I'm too pissed. Must sleep.' He fell back onto the bed and before Angelia could say anything else he was snoring.

The following morning, Ed was surprisingly chipper and managed to cook a huge breakfast for them all and they sat around the kitchen table to eat. Angelia tried to make time to talk to Fiona again about what she had intimated the night before but there was never a time when Ed and Marcus weren't around.

Eventually a taxi arrived to take Fiona and Marcus back to Glentorrin to pick up their car and Ed got a lift with them to go pick up Angelia's car from the village.

As the taxi drove away, Angelia messaged Fiona.

ANGEL

We need to talk! I want to know what you meant last night. Has Ed said something to you?

Fiona replied straight away.

FIONA

No, it's just a feeling I get. He was always trying to be with us at uni and I've seen the way he looks at you.

Angelia's heart sank. She remembered the heart to heart she'd had with him at Glenbrittle and realised Fiona had got the wrong end of the stick.

ANGEL

Ah. I see. I'm sorry Fee but you're mistaken. I actually know it's you he's always loved. We've talked about it. And I've been seeing the way he's looked at you since we were at uni. It was you he was trying to be close to. Not me.

There was a long pause and then Fiona's reply came.

FIONA

What? Really? No way! Oh heck, poor man. Well don't I feel shitty now? He's like a brother to me and that's how I've always seen him. I felt sure I was right. Sorry about that, Angel. It's a good thing you don't love him then, eh? (winky face) Anyway, it was so good to see you. Can't wait to see the shop next time when it's not such a flying visit! Love you.

That was the end of the topic. Fiona had clearly been oblivious to Ed's feelings, and it didn't matter anyway seeing as she was head over heels in love with Marcus. The strange thing was, however, Ed didn't seem to be in any rush to return to the orchestra, but when she asked him about it, he quickly changed the subject which was a little odd. She wondered if perhaps he was reluctant to go back and be face to face with Ava; perhaps the breakup had hurt him more than he had let on. Although she felt sure he'd talk about things when he felt ready. And in any case, she was in no hurry to send him away. She wasn't exactly sure what she would do when he did leave. Having him around had been both reassuring and reaffirming. The only problem was her feelings for him had been rekindled in the process.

During the evenings that followed her surprise party, they sat and watched TV on the sofa together or read in that same companionable silence they had shared on their camping trip. She found herself watching him surreptitiously. She adored the way he played with his hair and chewed his bottom lip while concentrating. She loved the way he threw his head back and guffawed unabashedly at *Last One Laughing*, especially when his comedy hero, Bob Mortimer, was on the screen.

Why did all the men she liked have to be hung up on someone else?

* * *

It was Friday, the day before the summer concert, and Angelia and Ed made the journey down to Glentorrin to check on progress at the shop. The team of people Bella had arranged had been amazing. They had all been introduced to her and asked to sign non-disclosure agreements about what was going on and who they were working for. This had been handled by Den, and they had all signed without protest. Now every time she called in, they greeted her like an old friend.

They walked in through the front door of the shop and were met by the smell of fresh paint and wood stain which caused Scrappy to sneeze. A radio somewhere towards the back was playing The Darkness; a band Angelia had toured with and loved like brothers. Someone in the building was singing along, out of tune, to 'I Hate Myself', the falsetto parts were particularly cringeworthy, and Angelia made a mental note to email Justin Hawkins and joke with him that he had competition on a little island off the coast of Scotland.

Walking into the shop was like walking back in time. There were dark oak shelves to all the walls that reached two thirds towards the ceiling. The top third had been left for posters, and several cabinets had been built on the floor with slots ready for whatever albums would be stocked.

The carved oak counter was now situated towards the back of the shop floor and acted as a barrier which cut off the entrance to the private dwelling from the rest of the sales area, and the ornate old till was positioned atop it, so it was visible to everyone as an integral part of the shop's history. There was a modern point of sale system on order which was to be incorporated into a tablet positioned in a specially created pull-out drawer on the cashier's side, to keep the illusion of the 'olde worlde' feel.

The walls were currently being given their second coat of burgundy, and the shelves were being edged in gold paint. The stunning chandelier that Bella had sourced had been hung in a central position, but smaller lights had been hung on almost invisible wires to create enough light for browsing the records.

Over to the right was a block of three listening booths. These were small, soundproofed cubicles, each containing a turntable, a set of headphones and a chair. The idea was that people could try before they bought like they used to in the fifties, sixties and seventies. These had been one of the things Angelia was most excited about and seeing them come to fruition was mind-blowing. This place was so incredibly special.

Angelia was in awe of how much work had been carried out in less than three weeks and had already made a start on ordering stock from vintage and second-hand wholesalers online. Ed had loved being part of the stock sourcing for the shop and he had managed to locate an online vintage music poster site in the USA. His virtual cart was full in readiness for Angelia to give the go-ahead. All she had to do now was decide who would run the place. And the more she saw, the more she wanted that dream for herself. She had fallen in love with Skye all over again but most importantly, she had fallen in love with Glentorrin. Its people had hearts as big as boats, and they had accepted her and treated her like one of their own and it meant so much.

Bella arrived, tablet in hand, to do her own check on progress. 'Hi, Angelia,' she said with an air of giddy excitement. 'What are you thinking of the place now? I bet you're going to struggle to let it go. My money's on you staying and running it yourself.'

Angelia shook her head. 'I have to say, it's very tempting. It's incredible, Bella. The team have worked wonders, and I can't quite believe how quickly it's all coming together.'

Bella beamed at her in response. 'I know, Noel is a star when it comes to getting things done.'

A middle-aged man with greying hair walked into the room from the direction of the flat entrance. 'Did I hear my name mentioned?' His white coveralls were spattered with the same burgundy paint, and he was wiping his hands on a cloth that was hooked into one of the belt loops at the waist.

'You did, Noel,' Bella said. 'And it was all good, I can assure you.'

'You're happy then, Miss MacAuley?' he asked.

Angelia shook her head. 'Not just happy. Over the moon, Noel! And please call me Angelia. Anyway, I wanted to pop in and ask what you and the team are doing tomorrow night? Because if you're free you should come to the summer concert in the village hall. It's going to be a brilliant event. There'll be music, dancing and a few good raffle prizes too. All proceeds to the upkeep of the hall. And the drinks are on me for all of you, as a thank you for all your hard work.'

Noel smiled. 'That's grand, thank you. I'll tell the lads and lasses. It certainly sounds like fun. Are you doing a turn?'

Angelia glanced at Ed and then at Bella; her plans were still a secret from the choir, of which Bella was a member. 'Ah, I don't think so,' she lied but felt her cheeks burning.

He tapped his nose. 'Right-oh,' he said with a wink.

There was a tapping on the window, and they all turned to see Ferris waving. 'I think you're wanted,' Ed said. 'Shall I take Scrappy for a walk and meet you at the café in an hour?'

She smiled. 'Scrappy would love that, wouldn't you, lad?' she asked the dog who wagged his tail as if he understood every word.

'Come on, fella,' Ed said as he wandered out of the shop, acknowledged Ferris briefly and then continued across towards the pub.

'Right, well, keep up the good work,' Angelia said. 'And Bella, I'll see you tonight for our final rehearsal.'

'I'll be the one quaking in my boots,' Bella said with a giggle.

Angelia stepped outside to where Ferris was waiting. 'Hi, Ferris, how are you?'

He smiled. 'I'm... erm... I'm good, I think. I have news. Shall we go grab a coffee? My treat.'

'Sounds like a plan,' she said and followed him into the café, where she headed for their usual table which was tucked away in a corner. There were a few other people in there, including some of the locals who she had met. Evin and Grace were there, too, and waved at her. And as she walked past one of the tables, a teenage girl who was sitting with her parents, playing on her phone, looked up and gasped.

'Mum, it's Angel from Angel and the Fallen,' she whispered.

'Are you sure, love?' her mum asked.

'One hundred per cent. Can I go say "hi"?'

'Oh, no, love, leave her be. She won't want to be hounded by people. It wouldn't be fair.'

'But mum, she's—'

'No, Sarah, it's rude.'

Angelia remembered the similar situation she had been in when she had met Ruby for lunch and the young couple had clearly wanted to say hello. She stopped and turned to face the girl. 'Hi, Sarah, is it?'

The girl's eyes widened and her face turned cerise. She nodded.

Angelia smiled. 'It's lovely to meet you. Would you like a selfie?'

The girl looked at her mum, her eyes now filled with happy tears. Her mum stood up and held out her hand. 'Hello, thank you, I think you've just made her birthday,' the woman said.

Angelia shook her hand. 'It's really no problem. And it's your birthday, Sarah?' she said, addressing the girl again. 'Happy birthday. How old are you today?'

'Th-thank you. I'm thir... thirteen.'

'Oh, wow, I remember being that age,' Angelia said with a smile. 'What did you get?'

'Partly this holiday,' the girl replied, clearly still a little awestruck.

'She wanted to come to Skye because she heard you're from here,' the mum said.

Angelia was touched by that. 'Ah, well, Skye is beautiful so it's a good place to come on holiday. What else did you get?'

The girl, now overcome with emotion, wiped away the tears that had escaped down her face. She sniffed. 'Some money towards a guitar.'

'You've inspired her to take up music,' the dad said as he stood now too. 'She was diagnosed with ADHD a couple of years ago and has really struggled at school until she discovered your band. Since then, she's learned ukulele and started having piano lessons. She recently progressed from ukulele to guitar, but she's been borrowing one from school so we're saving up to get her a good one of her own, you know?'

'You're my hero,' the girl said and Angelia's heart swelled. 'We saw the interview on TV a couple of days ago that you did about your condition. You've been through such a lot and you're trying to help other people like you now. That's really brave.' The prerecorded TV interview she had done with Kendric MacKinnon had aired at the start of the week but Angelia had forgotten all about it.

'Well, Sarah, I think you're *my* hero. You've overcome some tough times, too, and look at you now. Learning all those different instruments is amazing. Where are you staying?'

'We're at the little campsite along the road,' the dad said.

'Tell you what, why don't you come to the summer concert tomorrow at the village hall? I think I have something you might like,' Angelia said.

'Can we, Mum? Dad?' Sarah asked, a pleading tone to her voice.

'I don't see why not,' the dad said.

'That's sorted then,' Angelia said. 'Now how about that selfie?'

When she went over to where Ferris was now seated, he smiled up at her. 'You really are wonderful, you know,' he said. 'Am I right in thinking you're going to give that girl a guitar?'

Angelia widened her eyes. 'How on earth did you guess?'

He shrugged. 'Because I'm learning what a special person you are.'

She picked up her mug and took a sip of coffee. 'I'm not special at all. I just feel like I've been so privileged and I want to give back. I have my old guitar at home; the one I learned to play on. It's been well-loved, but it was a good model back when it was bought so I think it will be a great starting point for her.'

'You'll need to sign it for her too. She won't believe it's real.'

Angelia felt her face warming. 'She seems like a lovely girl. Anyway, you said you had news?'

He sighed. 'Indeed, I do.'

'Well, come on, tell me. Although you don't seem too happy about it. Whatever it is.'

He lifted his chin to fix his gaze on her. 'I have very mixed feelings.'

'What is it?'

'I've been offered my own parish,' he said, staring down at the slice of Victoria sponge on the plate in front of him.

'Oh, that's brilliant. It's what you've wanted, isn't it?'

He nodded. 'It is. And I should be happy.'

She tilted her head. 'So why aren't you?'

'Because it's in Lerwick.'

Angelia gasped. 'In the Shetlands?'

He nodded. 'In the Shetlands.'

'Oh, wow, Ferris, you couldn't get much further away.'

'I know.'

'Don't you want to go?' she asked as sadness washed over her.

He lifted his chin. 'I can't imagine leaving here. It wasn't meant to be permanent, and I was absolutely fine with that at first but... Things have changed.'

She thought back to what Ed had said about Ferris and his feelings for her and wondered if perhaps she was the reason he was reluctant to leave. But that felt incredibly conceited and that was something she certainly wasn't. There could be a number of things that made him feel that way. His love for the local people for starters. She was about to ask him to elaborate when the door burst open and a woman barged in, knocking over tables and chairs in her wake.

'It's all your fault!' the woman screamed as she threw a bottle in the direction of Angelia, luckily it missed. She continued to shout, 'It's your fault Angel and the Fallen have split! After they plucked you from nowhere, this is how you repay them? You've ruined everything!'

Realising what was about to happen, Sarah's family and some of the people at the other tables stood to form a blockade and Ferris ushered Angelia out the back door followed by Evin and Grace who led the way around to the back of the bakery. Grace banged on the door and Caitlin opened it in a panic.

'What on earth's wrong?' Caitlin asked, peering outside with a worried expression.

'Mum, there's a lunatic woman trying to get to Angelia!' Grace said.

Caitlin's eyes widened and she gestured for them to come in. 'I'll give Inspector Donaldson a call.'

Within minutes, Inspector Donaldson and two further police cars were outside the café to deal with the drunken so-called fan who could be heard shouting and swearing, even from the bakery.

Angelia stayed out of sight in the back kitchen with the others, her heart pounding and a pit of dread in her stomach. After around ten minutes the bell above the bakery door jingled and then came a loud voice. 'Angelia? Are you in here? Are you okay?'

'It's Ed,' Angelia said. 'My best friend, Ed.'

'Come through to the back,' Caitlin called to him and when he arrived in front of her, Scrappy in his arms, he pulled Angelia into his side with his free hand.

His lip was bleeding. 'Are you okay? Are you hurt?' he asked, panic evident in both his wide eyes and strained tone. 'I was so worried when I saw what was happening with the police. They were dealing with a woman who was going mad throwing stuff and screaming, and I heard your name mentioned so I panicked and came looking for you.'

'I'm fine, honestly, no harm done. Ferris, Evin and Grace worked so quickly to get me out of there. I'm so grateful to all of you,' she said, addressing her rescuers. 'But what's happened to your lip, Ed? You're bleeding.'

Caitlin handed Ed some damp kitchen paper and he placed Scrappy on the floor and dabbed at his mouth first before pulling Angelia into his arms again. 'I'm fine, just got caught in the face by one of the missiles. It's nothing. Thank goodness you're okay, that's all I was bothered about. I'm sure I heard one of the officers say they were arresting her for disturbing the peace. They were slapping handcuffs on her and then I saw her being bundled into the squad car. Another officer said something about threatening behaviour and causing damage to property. Thank goodness you're safe. I'm so sorry I left you. It won't happen again.'

She reached up to touch his face where a bruise was becoming evident and guilt knotted her stomach. '*I'm* sorry this happened to you.'

25

When the coast was clear, Ed drove Angelia home and she stared out of the window, absentmindedly stroking Scrappy's head where it rested on her lap from his position in the passenger footwell.

'Well, I think I know what I need to do about the record shop now,' she said, her voice breaking and her heart sinking to a new low.

'What's that?' Ed asked.

She shrugged. 'I need to get someone in to run it, or maybe even sell it so I have no connection to it, and I think I need to go back to London.'

'Wait, *what*?'

'You saw what happened back there, Ed. The people of Glentorrin and the people of this island don't need that kind of thing happening on their doorstep. It's clear that me being here would cause too many negative issues. Obviously not everyone is okay with the fact that the band has folded, and they blame me for it. The last thing I want to do is bring trouble here. The lovely people don't deserve that. They don't deserve me and the problems I bring.'

Ed pulled the car into a layby and parked. He turned to her. 'Hey, look at me.' She turned slowly, her eyes now foggy with tears. He reached over and took her hand. 'This isn't you. This isn't how you think. And can I point out that Heath wanted to quit, Anouk wants a solo career, and Bear wants to keep bloody chickens for goodness' sake. If *you* want to run that record shop, then we'll make that happen. Don't go throwing that away because of a lone psycho with only two brain cells to rub together. This is the first time anything like this has happened, so you haven't caused anything negative. That nutcase has clearly watched that interview you did on TV, taken her brain out, got pissed and placed blame where there isn't any. The real fans don't think like that. It's stupid and so was she. The people of that village love you.' He pointed back in the direction they had travelled from. 'It's clear when we're at rehearsals how well thought of you are and how grateful they are to you too. But ultimately, Angel, you're one of them.' He shrugged as if it was obvious. 'And you deserve to be happy. You've had a hell of a lot thrown at you, but you still insist on putting other people first. Well, maybe it's time to do what *you* want. And if running a record shop or heading a choir in Glentorrin is what you really want then you should absolutely do it. I'll help in any way I can, you know that. But please don't give up because of what happened today.' If she'd had any doubt about her feelings for him before, they had just evaporated, which wasn't exactly helpful.

'It was so scary though, Ed. I've never really experienced direct hate from fans of the band, and it made me so sad that she sought me out. I hate to think what would have happened if the people in the café hadn't protected me. She threw a bottle. What if someone there had been hurt? There was a thirteen-year-old girl in there with her family.'

'Think about what you just said. They. Protected. You. They didn't all stand idly by while you were attacked, Angelia. They stood up for you. That speaks volumes. And Ferris is such a good bloke. I can totally understand why you're drawn to him. I think… I think he might be just what you need.' She opened her mouth to speak but he stopped her. 'Now, let's get home, chill out for a while and then freshen up because you have a rehearsal to get to later. And I need to call Fee and tell her you're okay because I made the mistake of telling her about the incident at the café and now, she keeps bombarding me with messages because I told her not to tell you I'd said anything. Good grief, what a tangled web we weave,' he said with a laugh and a shake of his head.

You're not wrong there, she thought and inwardly sighed as his mention of Fiona reminded her that her feelings were misplaced.

* * *

When they arrived home, Angelia went to the bathroom to splash cold water on her face. She was still a little shaken up after what had happened and each time she thought about it she began shaking again and was plagued by what ifs. What if the woman had found her when she was alone, what if she had hit someone with the bottle she had thrown, what if one of the kids had been hurt. When she was done, she made her way back to the kitchen and could hear Ed talking on the phone in a hushed voice.

'No, she's fine, don't worry. Honestly, she's still definitely shaken up but she's a tough person. She'll get through it, I promise... Yes, absolutely... I'll make sure to give him a call... Yeah, maybe I should press charges. Nah, it's fine... a bit swollen but nothing serious. The utter moron needs psychiatric help if you ask me. Okay... no worries. See you soon... bye.'

'Is everything okay?' Angelia asked as she took a seat at the table, presuming he had been talking to Fiona.

He smiled. 'Everything's fine. It was Ferris, he wanted to check that you're okay and ask if he was okay to give my number to Inspector Donaldson so he could call me about making a statement, but I've said I'll phone the station.'

Angelia crumpled her brow. 'I didn't know Ferris had your number.'

Ed scratched his head. 'Yeah, I gave it to him when I saw him after Meghan had left. I figured it was a good idea.'

'Ah, okay. How's your lip?' The skin near the cut now had a purplish hue and his lip was swollen.

He lifted his hand to it and gave it a prod. 'Oh, it's fine. I can hardly feel it, don't worry. How are you doing?' She nodded but her chin trembled and her emotions got the better of her. 'Hey, come on.' In one stride he was scooping her into his arms. 'Shhh. It's okay. You're okay. Which is more than that cow bag will be if I ever see her again.'

She smiled at his turn of phrase. 'Thank you for staying with me,' she said as she clung to him, inhaling his aftershave and relishing the feeling of his smooth skin against her cheek and his familiar strong arms around her.

He stroked her hair. 'I'd do anything for you, Angel. You know that.' Then after a pause he added, 'Best friends for life.'

* * *

That night, as she walked into the church for their final rehearsal, Angelia was surprised to see the choir already assembled. They were all deep in conversation about something that appeared serious and none of them seemed to realise she had entered.

When Isla spotted her, she glared at Ferris who was seated at the keyboard and hissed, 'The eagle is in the henhouse!'

Bella turned to her, and with a quizzical expression said, 'Pick a metaphor, Granny. Either *the eagle has landed,* or *the fox is in the henhouse.*' She shook her head and rolled her eyes but went back to her conversation.

Isla scowled at her granddaughter and then shouted, 'Oh, for goodness' sake, everyone, Angelia has landed in the henhouse!'

Everyone fell immediately silent and turned to stare at Angelia who giggled. 'Is everything okay?'

Ferris counted to four and began playing as the choir launched into a rendition of 'Stay Another Day' by East 17 and Angelia stood there, open-mouthed and a little watery-eyed. Their harmonies were a bit bizarre, but they sang with such passion that she couldn't help it when a few tears escaped.

When the song was over, she applauded and Ed joined in, adding a whistle for good measure. 'That was wonderful. But I don't understand, it's a Christmas song really and the concert is for summer. And we've already finalised the set list.'

Isla cleared her throat. 'Aye, hen, we know it's a Christmassy song. It's by that East Enders group. We performed it at the Christmas concert. But you see we wanted to sing it for you because of the words and the sentiment. I think I speak on behalf of everyone here when I say these last few weeks of working with you have been wonderful. And we're kind of hoping you might stay on the island and maybe… I don't know… open a shop selling vinolay flooring or something.' She smiled and gave a little wink. 'Although it's a strange choice for a former rock star,' she added, but quietly, and probably to herself.

'*Vinyl*, Granny. As in records that you play,' Bella whispered.

A puzzled expression briefly crossed Isla's face. But then in true Isla fashion she replied, 'Aye, that's what *ah* said,' through the corner of her mouth, without moving her head. 'Anyway, Angelia dearie, we know you're feeling a bit shaken up after that wee mad grouper tried to get to you. But we want you to know that we'd love you to stay, and you've not to let that thug derail any plans you might have had, that's all. We're used to celebrities on this island, you know,' she said with a glint in her eyes. 'And if this is somewhere you think you might like to make a new life for yourself then we'd be happy to have you, and we'd look out for you. And...' She glanced around at her friends. 'We're sort of, selfishly, hoping you might like to stick around and direct the choir too.' Everyone else enthusiastically added their agreement to this.

Angelia looked to Ferris who was smiling at Ed, and then she turned to Ed who was also smiling back. When he saw her looking at him, he simply shrugged but his smile remained fixed in place. He was clearly very pleased with himself; they both were. *So that must be what their phone call was about*, she thought. *The two of them have been in cahoots*. But she was so grateful they had.

'Thank you all so much. Your words, and song choice, mean the world to me,' she told them with a wavering voice. 'I have a lot to think about but for now, we've a concert to prepare for so shall we get some rehearsing done?'

The whole choir burst into spontaneous applause and for a moment Angelia felt like a football coach who'd just given a team talk. She took a bow and then took her position at the front of the choir.

Their version of 'You Can't Always Get What You Want' was her favourite of all the choices. She loved the sentiment of the chorus and especially the way it talked about maybe the thing you think you desire being out of reach, but perhaps instead the universe gifts you the thing that will actually help you move forward. That resonated within her. She had always thought that being a rock star was what she wanted and was what she was meant to be, but a diagnosis with a chronic condition and the last few weeks of working with the choir had shown her that life doesn't always have a singular path. Perhaps the little paths that run off at tangents were just as fulfilling if you either chose to veer off, or, in her case, were made to do so.

There wasn't an ABBA song in their set list, even though she had suggested it as an homage to their former choir manager who was apparently now fit and well and hoping to attend the concert. But the group agreed that audiences wouldn't particularly be fussed with songs about chicken tikka, or any other cuisine for that matter; but that was mainly Isla. And also, thanks to Isla, there was to be no moose scaring either. So, in addition to the Rolling

Stones, the choir had chosen 'Friends Will Be Friends' by Queen, The Beatles' 'Let It Be', 'Happy' by Pharrell Williams and 'A Sky Full of Stars' by Coldplay, simply because it mentioned the word 'sky'. And the set was to end with Katy Perry's 'Firework'; another uplifting song about being yourself and being happy. Angelia couldn't help but notice the song choices were all filled with not-so-hidden messages, maybe not purposefully chosen for that reason, but each song spoke to her all the same.

'You guys are incredible,' Angelia told them at the end of the final rehearsal. 'You've all put so much effort in and learned these songs in so few rehearsals, and I can't tell you how amazing that is. We used to rehearse for months before going on tour, but you guys have seriously worked wonders with everything I've thrown at you.'

'Reid, Evin and I have been having mini-practices at home,' Jules said. 'It's been a great way to have family time together.'

Evin laughed. 'Aye, we've been using anything and everything as microphones, wooden spoons, the vacuum hose.'

'The shower head,' Reid added and then blushed. 'But obviously no one else saw my solo performances.' Everyone chuckled.

'I think my Tam might be glad when it's over, to be honest. He's not down with the kids like me. He did ask me how on earth it was possible to be happy like a lounge without a ceiling. But I did tell him those weren't the words,' Isla said with a roll of her eyes and a shake of her head. The rest of the group shared smiles and glances, evidently amused at the irony.

'Well, you're going to blow the audience's socks off tomorrow night. And I want you to know I'm so immensely proud of each and every one of you.'

'Does that mean you might stay?' Evin asked, his eyes full of hope. His dad put his arm around his shoulder and kissed the side of his head.

Angelia smiled and tried not to think about what had happened earlier that day; she didn't want to end things on a low note. 'I have a lot of things to think about, Evin. But the fact that you all want me to stay is absolutely wonderful. You've made me so welcome. And you've made me feel like one of you. I can't tell you how uplifting that's been.'

***

At the end of the rehearsal, when everyone had gone, Ed went to bring the car around as usual. Angelia stood with Ferris by the door.

'Oh, I almost forgot in all the excitement this evening. Someone handed Ed's wallet in to me earlier. He must have dropped it in the kerfuffle outside the café this afternoon. Anyway, I'll go get it for you to give to him.' He headed off towards the vestry and returned moments later holding it aloft. He somehow tripped over his own feet, and the wallet went flying through the air and landed on the floor at Angelia's feet.

'Are you okay there, vicar?' she asked with a giggle. 'Been overdoing it with the communion wine, have we?' She bent to pick up the wallet which had landed open on the flagstones. Something caught her eye poking out of one of the card slots, and when she retrieved the wallet from the floor, she pulled out the item with intrigue.

She gasped. There in her hand was a heart-shaped photograph.

Of herself.

26

'Is everything okay?' Ferris asked. 'You look like you've seen a ghost.'

Angelia nodded absentmindedly, still trying to process what she was looking at. Ed's words rang around her mind. *She found a heart-shaped photo in my wallet and realised I was... I am in love with someone else.* But this photo wasn't Fiona. This made no sense. Why had he kept mentioning 'best friends' and why on earth did he tell her that Ferris was just what she needed?

'What is that?' Ferris asked, pointing to the photo. It was one that had been taken years ago on their camping trip to Loch Doon; one of the ones Ed must have taken when he thought she wasn't paying attention. Her chestnut hair had blown partially across her face, and she was reaching up to tuck it behind her ear. In the distance the sun glinted on the water as she was stepping from one rock to another. She wore a long-sleeved T-shirt, dark blue jeans and walking boots and had a checked shirt tied around her waist. She remembered it like it was yesterday.

'That's a lovely photo of you,' Ferris said, glancing over her shoulder. 'He clearly adores you,' he added with a hint of sadness.

Ed honked the horn as he pulled up and she quickly shoved the photo back in the wallet and turned to Ferris. 'Thanks for today. And tonight. And... for everything. I'll see you tomorrow.' And with that she turned and jogged out to the car.

When she climbed in, she handed him the wallet. 'This was handed in to the church. Ferris asked me to give it to you. You must have dropped it in the *stramash* at the café.'

He took the wallet. 'Oh, heck. I hadn't even missed it. That's not good, is it?' He laughed. 'I'll drop Ferris a message to thank him.' There was no mention of the photo. The thought must not have even crossed his mind.

Angelia was silent for the first part of the journey home, not knowing what to say about her discovery, and not really believing what it could mean. Perhaps she had completely misinterpreted things?

'Are you okay?' he asked as they passed through the village of Dunan on the shores of Loch na Cairidh. The view across to the tiny island of Scalpay, whose inhabitants numbered four last she heard, were always picturesque but even more so tonight as it was currently illuminated by nothing but moonlight. It was quite beautiful.

'Hmm? Sorry, yes, thanks, I'm... I'm fine. Just tired, I think,' she lied.

'Yeah, no wonder. Today has been quite a rollercoaster, eh?'

You can say that again. 'It has.'

'Your mum and dad land back at Heathrow tomorrow, don't they?'

'They do. It'll be good to see them. I think they're flying back up to Glasgow and staying there overnight.'

'It's a shame they won't see the show. But I'll make sure someone takes plenty of photos of the choir while we're on stage. And maybe some video footage too.'

She smiled. 'That'd be great, thank you.'

There was another brief silence until he said, 'Then I suppose I should go and see my folks.'

Her heart sank. 'Oh, you're leaving?'

He shrugged. 'Well, I should show my face. And you'll be fine when your folks are home.'

She couldn't answer him. Because she knew she wouldn't be fine when he left.

They arrived back at the house and Scrappy was excited to see them both. Angelia clipped on his lead. 'I'm just going to take Scrappy out for a wee walk. He's probably busting.'

'Here. Let me. You're worn out and I don't mind. You make a coffee while I'm out.'

She nodded and he left with the dog. She paced the kitchen as the kettle boiled. She needed to say something. She needed to at least check that her interpretation of the situation was right. Because if he left, she knew she would never have the courage to ask again and would forever wonder what could have been. She made a fresh pot of coffee and sat nursing a cup until Ed returned.

She heard the door open and close and Scrappy came running through from the hallway. She poured a mug of coffee for Ed and placed it on the table.

'The sky's magnificent tonight,' Ed said. 'Reminds me of the sky we had that night when we camped at Loch Doon.'

This was it. This was her chance.

'Erm... speaking of Loch Doon, Ed... I think we need to talk,' she said, her heart pounding and hands shaking.

He removed his jacket and placed it on the back of one of the chairs. 'Is everything okay?'

'I think so. But... Something fell out of your wallet tonight at the church, when Ferris passed it to me.'

He rolled his eyes and rubbed his hands roughly over his face. 'Oh God, was it the receipt for the campervan? Because I can—'

She shook her head. 'No, not that. But why would that be an issue?'

He cringed. 'Because it's a stupid amount of money to spend on something I won't be owning at the end of it. And I know you, you'll want to give me something towards it but the answer's absolutely no, Angel. And in my defence, it's been worth every single penny, even if I haven't slept in it every night. It's been worth it because...' He shook his head. 'It's just been worth it.'

'Can I ask you something, and will you promise to tell me the truth?'

He gave a nervous laugh. 'Erm... I suppose that depends...'

'Why are you in no rush to go back to the orchestra?'

He pulled out a chair and sat down, his expression filled with regret. 'I don't want to tell you because A, you'll think I'm insane, and B, you'll be angry with me.'

'Try me.'

He stared into the mug of coffee in front of him and fell silent for a while. 'I... erm... I quit.'

Angelia wasn't expecting that. 'What? Why? What happened? Was it because of your split from Ava?'

He lifted his chin and fixed a sorrow-filled gaze on her. 'No. Nothing like that. She and I weren't long-term. Well, not as far as I was concerned anyway. But no... she wasn't the reason.'

'Then what was?'

He closed his eyes and inhaled a long, deep breath before opening them again. 'Because I was worried about you.'

Angelia shook her head, filled with incredulity. 'Why would you do that?'

'Because you're my best friend in the world, Angelia. And you were going through something huge. And I was racked with guilt that I'd been such a shitty friend over the last few years. I needed to be here for you with no distractions and nothing to force me to leave. To make sure you had someone if you needed it. Fiona has her life in Edinburgh and her and Marcus are solid. I knew she couldn't be here even though she wanted to. Not long-term anyway. So, I quit.' He shrugged as if it was the most common-sense thing he'd ever said and done.

She sighed and lowered her head. 'You didn't need to do that, Ed. I'm not ill and I don't need—'

'Wrapping in bubble wrap, yes, I know that. I've always known how strong you are, Angelia, that's never been the issue. This was about me. I... I needed to be where you are. That's all.'

'You know that night after I had performed my first-ever gig with the band, and you said you had something to tell me? What was it?'

He sighed and stood, walked over to the countertop and leaned on it but wouldn't make eye contact. 'I can't remember, that was years ago.'

She stood and walked over to him. 'Come on, think. It was definitely something important.'

He turned to look at her now, his eyes glassy. He chewed the inside of his cheek. 'There's no point,' he whispered.

'Shall I tell you what fell out of your wallet tonight?'

He frowned. 'Okay.'

'It was a heart-shaped photograph... of me.'

He shrugged. 'Okay, and? You already knew about that. I meant to get rid of it after we talked on our trip but... Sorry, I'll throw it away now.'

He moved to get past her, but she put her hand on his chest. 'What did you think I meant on that night we talked?'

He fixed his green gaze on her now, anger evident in his narrowed eyes and furrowed brow. 'Why are you doing this to me? I didn't think you were cruel, Angelia, but this is pretty cruel.' He scoffed. 'Do you want me to spell it all out for you? Huh? Is that what you want?'

She nodded. 'Please, yes.'

He rolled his head back and growled at the ceiling. 'For pity's sake. I fell in love with you the first day I laid eyes on you at university. I engineered the whole being drunk thing just to get close to you. You know all this, though.' He lifted his arms and when she didn't comment he let them flop back down to his side again. 'But then the three of us seemed to become this trio. We even had nicknames for ourselves. It was clear we were only ever going to be friends, and to be honest that was fine. It hurt and it wasn't what I really wanted but it was fine. Because it meant I got to have you in my life. That night we spent at Loch Doon is one of my favourite, and at the same time, my most hated memories. Because when I kissed you...' He closed his eyes again and his chin trembled. 'Because when I kissed you, it almost felt like you loved me the same. But then Fee rang and... I suppose I knew things would go back to how they had always been. The Three Amigos...' He stopped talking but she waited, she knew there was more to come. She had to fight the urge to fling her arms around him, but she wanted to be sure because everything so far had been past tense.

'Then that night you were about to go away with the band I almost told you how I felt but it didn't seem fair to put guilt on you when you were going away. You didn't feel the same, so you didn't need to know. And I didn't want it to look like I was saying I was in love with you because you were going to be famous. So, it was better to say nothing than have the *slightest* chance of you thinking that way. And ever since then I've kept my distance in many ways. Self-preservation, I suppose. You fell in love with Josh, or rather *deeper* in love with him, seeing as you've always been crazy about him. I remember the posters on your wall at uni. And I tried to move on. I did move on, for a while. Then I heard about your diagnosis, and it all came flooding back. And I felt shitty for the years I'd hardly called or emailed.'

She narrowed her eyes and her heart sank. 'So, you felt sorry for me?'

He placed a hand on each of her arms and gazed into her eyes. 'Not at all. Like I said, you've always been strong. I wanted to be in your life again, have you in my life again, that's all. I suppose I wanted to protect you, which I *know* you don't need.' He laughed. 'Didn't stop that instinct kicking in, though. But no, Angelia, it wasn't pity that brought me here. It was love.' He released his grip on her arms. 'But you've got Ferris, so I'm surplus to requirements really, if we're both honest. And he's a great guy. I actually really like him. He's given you such confidence. He's helped you to realise you have so much more to offer the world. I wish I'd been the one to do that but you can't always get what you want.' He laughed. 'And now you've got this potentially incredible life ahead of you, and I'm genuinely happy for you. Because I've only ever wanted you to be happy.' He swiped at the tears that had trickled down his face. 'Look, crying like a baby again.'

'Can I speak now?'

'Oh, go on then, I suppose,' he said with a forced chuckle.

'I thought the photo in your wallet was of Fiona.'

'Eh?'

'I thought it was Fiona you loved. I thought, all these years, that you thought the kiss was a huge mistake and it almost broke my heart.'

He shook his head and his brow furrowed. 'What? No… but the night we were at Glenbrittle, when I told you about Ava finding the photo of you, you said you understood *unrequited love*. I took that to mean my love for you was unrequited. Like it was your way of letting me down gently.'

She smiled. 'I didn't know the photo was of me then, remember?'

His eyes widened. 'Wait… what are you saying?'

'What I'm saying, Ed Halsall, is that I've loved you since we met too. Only I thought you didn't feel the same. I transferred that love onto Josh because clearly, I hate myself.' She laughed. 'But having you around these past few weeks has brought everything back. All the feelings I had are still there.'

He smoothed her hair away from her face. 'Angelia MacAuley, are you telling me you love me?'

Angelia stood on her tiptoes. 'I'm telling you I've always loved you.'

His hands slipped into her hair and as if in slow motion his lips connected with hers in a passionate, heartfelt kiss, only this time she knew for sure it was mutual.

27

The morning of the concert arrived, and Angelia awoke to Ed's arms wrapped around her. She smiled and snuggled deeper into his embrace. They had missed out on so much time but would spend the rest of their lives making up for that. She had messaged Fiona the night before and sent a photo of her and Ed together. Fiona's response?

FIONA

> So I was right! I bloody knew it! It's about blooming time! You two have been skirting around each other for years and now I finally get what I've wanted for all this time! I'm so bloody happy right now!

They had both laughed and had both been equally as surprised at her response. She'd never said anything to either of them until the night of Angelia's birthday but then again, she'd been in a tricky situation, they both agreed on that point.

Her phone pinged and she shuffled over to pick it up. There was a message from Josh with a video attachment sent to the group chat. She frowned and pushed herself to a sitting position before hitting play.

On the screen were her, Ed and Ferris playing a song together and singing in the church as the choir looked on. They were running through 'Friends Will Be Friends' to show the arrangement they had come up with. It had been filmed from the back of the church near the doors. The message that accompanied it said,

JOSH

This is what I woke up to on TikTok. So, you lied. You can clearly still sing. Here you are with your own little fan club audience. You just wanted to quit the band. You should have had the guts to just say that, Angelia. You're a coward. Thanks for nothing. In fact, no, thanks for something, and that's you ruining my career because you got tired.

Anger bubbled up from deep within and her eyes stung with angry tears. She forwarded the message to Heath and Den.

Ed sat up, rubbing the sleep from his eyes. 'What's wrong? What's happened?'

She jammed the phone towards him and he took it. His eyes widened. 'What the hell? Who filmed that?'

'No idea. But that's not really the point, Ed. How dare he?' she hissed. She hit record to make a reply by voice note.

'Josh, it's Angelia. How the hell dare you question me and accuse me of lying? You have no bloody clue what I've been through. How scared I've been. How much courage it's taken to even attempt to sing since my diagnosis. You haven't done one single iota of research into my condition like any normal friend would, like all my other friends have, even ones I've only just met. You're presuming so much and not even asking me for my side. Well, that's it. I've had it with you. You can sod right off.' As if a fire had been extinguished, the love she thought she'd once had for Josh Baron was doused in one fell swoop. He was a selfish, self-centred arse, only bothered about himself. Thank goodness she hadn't wasted any more time pining over him.

A few moments later a message came through from Heath.

HEATH

Oh no, he didn't just send that. (face palm emoji) he's such an idiot. Leave it with me. You sound incredible in that video by the way. Very proud of you. H.

* * *

The village hall was decorated with flowers and bunting in readiness for the concert, and every seat had been booked. Angelia had arranged for Sarah and her parents to come to the hall early and meet her in the kitchen area so she could see them in private.

'I want to thank you all for your help the other day at the café. It must have been terrifying for you all and I'm so sorry you had to experience that,' Angelia told them.

'Hey, no thanks needed,' Sarah's dad said. 'We wouldn't stand by and watch that lunatic intimidate you like that. I'm just glad the café had a back door for you to escape through. I hate to think what might have happened to you if it hadn't.' He shivered.

'So, Sarah, have you had a lovely holiday? Apart from that incident, of course.'

Sarah nodded. 'The absolute best holiday of my entire life,' she replied.

Angelia beamed. 'I'm so glad to hear that. Now, I've got a wee gift for you.'

Sarah's eyes widened and her face flushed pink. 'Oh, gosh.'

Angelia reached into a tall broom cupboard and took out a guitar case. 'In this case is the first guitar I ever owned. It's the one I learned to play on,' she told Sarah as she opened the case. 'I want you to keep going with your lessons, and then the next time you come to Skye, you and I are going to play a song together in my record shop, okay?'

Sarah's eyes welled with tears, and she let out a sob as Angelia handed her the guitar. The front was covered in flower motifs, interspersed with old band stickers and when Sarah turned it over there was an inscription written in silver Sharpie.

To Sarah, my hero, happy playing, all my love, Angelia

'I can't even speak,' Sarah said through her tears. Angelia, Sarah's mum and dad and Ed all laughed, none of them had dry eyes at this point.

Sarah's mum hugged Angelia. 'Thank you so much for this. I can't tell you how grateful we are. You really are a wonderful person.'

Angelia shook her head. 'It's my absolute pleasure. Please keep in touch and let me know how the lessons are going and make sure to practise often, okay? And look after that guitar.'

Sarah nodded as she wiped her eyes with a tissue her dad had passed her.

'I'll treasure it forever. And then maybe one day, when I'm famous, I can give it to another girl like us.'

Angelia sniffed and wiped at her eyes. 'I think that's a wonderful idea. Now, why don't you go on and enjoy the show, eh?'

Sarah and her parents left the kitchen, and Angelia took a moment to compose herself.

'Are you okay?' Ed asked as he put his arms around her. She nodded.

There was a knock on the door and when Ed opened it Ferris was on the other side. Angelia gasped. 'Oh, sorry, I'm coming.'

'Erm... could I have a word with you, Angelia, in private, please?'

Ed smiled and squeezed her arm. 'See you out there.'

Once Ed had left the room, Ferris cleared his throat. 'I just wanted to say... I wanted you to know that I'm taking the job in Lerwick.'

Angelia nodded but sadness washed over her. 'I see.'

He took both of her hands. 'I want you to know that your friendship means the world to me and so does your happiness. I think it's possibly obvious that my feelings for you have grown since you've been here, and now that I know how you feel about Ed, I think maybe I need a fresh start of my own. But please know that I'm not running away from you, or Ed. Quite the opposite. I'm running towards whatever God has planned for me next. Because, in a way, I'd like to think that God put me in your path for the very purpose of helping you to see how you really feel, and for you to find what will make you happy. If that's the case, then I'm so glad He did. Now what have you decided to do about the record shop? Please tell me you're going to be the one running it.'

She beamed. 'I am. I'm so excited for this next chapter of my life, Ferris. We talked about it for hours last night. Ed's going to run the shop with me and I'm going to write songs for other artists too. I'm already working with Anouk from Angel and the Fallen and there are a number of others who Heath has put me in touch with.'

Ferris shook his head. 'Incredible. I'm so glad. Is Ed not going back to orchestra work?'

'He's in touch with the chamber orchestra again about doing some local shows but he's also going to go into music tuition. A couple of the locals have asked him, and he's said he'll help them. Inspector Donaldson, I mean Harris, I can't get used to calling him that,' she giggled. 'He's asked Ed if he'd like to join the Glentorrin Four as their guitarist is moving away to the mainland for a promotion.'

'Wow, it's all happening. And it's all wonderful.'

'Oh, Ferris, I can't thank you enough for everything you've done for me. And your friendship too. I hope you'll stay in touch with us.'

Ferris smiled. 'You can't get rid of me now. I want to preside over your wedding,' he said. 'Because mark my words, there'll be a Halsall–MacAuley wedding. I just know it.'

Angelia's eyes welled with tears for what felt like the hundredth time that day. 'Deal,' she said. 'But that will depend on when he asks me because I'm an old-fashioned girl at heart, so I won't be asking him, that's for sure.'

Ferris narrowed his eyes. 'Well, if you want my opinion, I don't think you'll be waiting very long and that's all I'll be saying at this point in time. Now could I maybe hug you?'

She giggled. 'I think that's allowed.' He pulled her into his arms and embraced her. 'You're a very special person, Angelia MacAuley. Don't ever underestimate your value.'

'Thank you, Ferris.'

'Ahem, I think you maybe mean Reverend Blaikie of Lerwick Parish,' he said, grinning and brushing invisible dust from his shoulders.

She wagged her finger at him. 'Oh yes, of course, pardon me, that's what I meant,' she said with a warm smile.

'Now, come on, let's get this party started.'

* * *

The main lights were dimmed and the stage lights illuminated. The choir stood there before Angelia in their rainbow-coloured T-shirts and jeans; Granny Isla's was, of course, purple to match her hair. Angelia had played many shows in huge stadiums, but she couldn't remember ever being this nervous. This night meant so much more to her than any of the others had.

She smiled widely as she counted in a low whisper to four, just loud enough for the choir to hear her and when she gave the hand signal, Isla and Morag sang the opening lines of their arrangement of 'You Can't Always Get What You Want'. The audience sat in complete rapt silence and looked on in awe as the rest of the choir joined in, and then a thunderous applause travelled the room before the baritones took over for their first verse.

Each song went so well and was filled with such energy and passion that Angelia felt like she was floating six inches above the stage. After every single song the audience cheered and whistled their appreciation. And at the end of their spot the crowd were up on their feet as the choir took their final bow of the evening.

The night went on to be one excellent act after another, with Ruby's dancers wowing the audience, a young lad playing the bagpipes and bringing a tear to every eye as he played 'Amazing Grace', and many more, each person putting their heart and soul into their performances.

At the end of the evening, Ferris took to the stage. 'Ladies and gentlemen, boys and girls, I want to thank you on behalf of all the performers this evening. It's been a magical concert and I'm sure you will all join me in saying thank you and showing your appreciation once more,' he said and a round of applause echoed around the crowded room. When the applause had died down, he smiled. 'Now, we saved one last performance for you. One you're not expecting. But please welcome to the stage Ed Halsall on guitar and the one and only Angelia MacAuley on vocals.'

The place erupted as Angelia and Ed walked out onto the stage. She couldn't help the emotion that washed over her as she peered out at the smiling faces. People were up cheering and whistling, and the sound almost beat every stadium she had ever played.

When the audience had calmed down again, Angelia took to the microphone. 'Thank you all so much. If you'd have told me at the start of this year that I would be directing a choir, I would have laughed and said you were crazy. But these past few weeks have been some of the best of my life. You may already know that earlier this year I was diagnosed with an incurable, sometimes quite debilitating condition. At that point it felt like my life was over. I was lost, terrified and had no idea where my life was going to go. But then I came home to Skye, and all these incredible things started to happen. I met some wonderful new friends who showed me that I still have so much to offer. That I still have a purpose. They gave me the strength to imagine my life as something other than the lead singer of Angel and the Fallen and now, I'm looking forward to the future. So, thank you, Ferris, Ed and Glentorrin Village Choir. This one is for you. It's called "Only When I Dream".' Another round of applause rang out and then the audience fell silent as Angelia began to sing her own lyrics that had taken on a whole new meaning to her.

As she sang, she saw Ed in her periphery watching her, a serene smile on his face as he plucked the strings of his guitar with mastery. He had written in a new guitar solo to give Angelia a break to rest her voice and as she turned to smile at him her heart flooded with adoration.

She knew it would be easy to dwell on all the time they had wasted but there was no point, because she knew that her future was with Ed and it would happen in Glentorrin and she couldn't have hoped for anything more perfect. She would still have music in her life, but it would be on her terms and at her pace.

The song ended and the place erupted once again. Every single person was up on their feet. She glanced at Ed, who gestured to the front of the stage. 'Take a bow, Angelia.'

She stepped forward and with tears streaming down her face took her bow, knowing it wouldn't be the last as she had thought not long ago. She gestured for Ed and Ferris to join her, and they both put an arm around her as the three of them bowed again.

She turned to Ed and smiled as he wrapped her in his arms. 'I'm so proud of you,' he whispered. 'And I'd like to ask you a question, but I'm worried it might be too soon.'

She gazed up at him as the applause died down, knowing full well what the question was, and shook her head. 'We've known each other forever, Ed, it's not too soon.'

As the audience looked on, he took the microphone from its stand and lowered himself to one knee. A collective gasp of realisation travelled the room as he gazed up at her. He spoke into the microphone. 'Angelia, we've been friends for so long that I can't actually remember much about the time before we met. But I want the rest of our forever to start as soon as possible. So, Angelia MacAuley, will you run a record shop on Skye with me for as long as we both shall live?'

She giggled as tears spilled over from her eyes and replied, 'I will.'

He smiled. 'Oh, and maybe would you marry me too?'

The room was silent as if every single person was holding their breath. Angelia took the microphone from his hand and said, 'One hundred million per cent, yes!'

The room erupted with cheers and applause and Ed stood to scoop her up in his arms, literally sweeping her off her feet.

In the space of only a few months, Angelia MacAuley had been broken and built right back up again. She had thought her career was over, until she realised all she needed was a new career, she had thought she needed love, until she realised it was there all along. She just had to reach out and let it in.

EPILOGUE

The middle of August was warm and the shop looked incredible. The people of Glentorrin had given encouraging comments about the exterior and the fact that Angelia had installed the most beautiful hanging baskets filled with vibrantly coloured blooms.

'It will be a real asset to the village, and the island,' she had been told.

'It's about time we had something funky here,' Evin had said to her and Ed when they had been out walking Scrappy. 'I can see me needing to get a job to subsidise my new hobby.'

'Well, maybe you could help us on Saturdays if your mum and dad say it's okay,' Angelia had suggested.

Evin's eyes had widened and he had almost knocked her off her feet with the hug he gave her.

The evening before the official opening had been a busy one. Angelia had spent it opening boxes and checking the stock within them was in good enough condition. Ed had been up a ladder most of the night clipping posters to a magnetic strip that Noel had installed just under the cornice. He had done it for free as an apology for one of his workers filming their rehearsal and posting it on TikTok. Angelia had told him it wasn't necessary and that she wasn't angry about it. She had made him promise not to fire the person in question, too, which had taken some convincing, but a promise had eventually been forthcoming.

There were some absolute classics amongst the artwork Ed had sourced and it was exciting to see them being hung. Each poster he had opened when they arrived had sparked a reaction in him like a kid on Christmas Day. Her favourite was a tour poster from 2013 that featured The Fallen Angels when Lorelie was still alive and long before Angelia knew what was going to happen in her future. Only this one had a special notice on it that read:

NOT FOR SALE

There was no way she was letting that poster go, not for all the money in the world.

Ruby and Mitch had brought sandwiches and Caitlin had brought cakes, and they had drunk prosecco and listened to some of the albums Angelia had sourced on the sound system that had been installed. Later, Evin, Jules and Reid had called in to wish them luck and had brought fresh flowers and a bottle of champagne, too, and Angelia had presented Evin with his name badge for when he started his Saturday job, something he apparently couldn't stop talking about.

Angelia's mum had helped her to place the albums in the holders in alphabetical order, her favourite thing to do thanks to being a bookseller, and her dad had helped unboxing band memorabilia to place on the oak shelving to be sold, while Bella handled the items that were going to be for display only. Angelia had used many of her incredible contacts to source these particular items. Amongst which was a pair of wristbands that Rufus Taylor from The Darkness had worn, and a framed silver-grey tie that Justin Hawkins from the same band had sported on the cover of their *Dreams on Toast* album.

Of course, there was a signed guitar from Heath and a collection of signed plectrums from Anouk and she had offered to do an album signing at the shop when her debut was released. Bear had sent a signed photo of him shirtless wearing wellies and standing in a chicken coop on the smallholding he had bought in the Lake District. In the photo he was holding onto Bertha, his favourite Marsh Daisy chicken. She was his prized bird because Marsh Daisies were apparently rare and endangered, so he had vowed to breed her and increase the UK population. He looked ridiculously happy... and a bit ridiculous.

Dom and Rio had said they would visit soon but they were in talks with a potential surrogate for their first child. In the meantime, Rio had provided some gloves worn by Taylor Swift on her Eras tour and Dom had sent the T-shirt he had worn on the cover of their Come What May 2023 tour. He and Rio had already eloped and married in secret in Sicily. Josh... well, Josh had been a little quiet since his outburst. But Angelia had received an invitation in the post for his upcoming wedding, so she felt it was probably a good idea to forgive him and move on. She had sent an RSVP accepting the invitation.

Evin had produced a poster to advertise the opening of the record shop. The shop's name, Vintage Vinyl Emporium, was printed at the top in the same font as the lettering on the shop's frontage, and featured the mural that his dad had painted on the wall above the listening booths. The mural featured music icons past and present all standing together as if being photographed for a magazine. They all looked happy and relaxed with their arms resting casually around each other. Stars that had never met in real life all gathered together in Reid's special creation. Buddy Holly standing by Kurt Cobain, Freddie Mercury leaning on Louis Armstrong, Amy Winehouse laughing with Janis Joplin. It was a real feature, and Angelia knew that many people would visit solely to photograph it. It had already been featured on the recent update TV interview she had taken part in with Kendric MacKinnon and had quickly garnered some wonderful comments online.

The morning of the opening had arrived, and Angelia, who hadn't really slept, lay there in their luxurious bedroom, in the stunning flat above the shop as Ed slept. She was plagued with nerves. Would it be a success? Would any idiots try to spoil it? Meghan had promised she and Ezra would arrive early that morning in plenty of time for the opening. They had booked a room at Morag's B&B. Fiona and Marcus were already there and were using Glentorrin as a stopover on their Highlands and Islands tour thanks to it being the school summer holidays and Ferris had even travelled down from Shetland to be there for the opening day.

Ed awoke and pushed himself up on his elbow to look down at her. 'Morning, beautiful,' he said as he placed a kiss on her forehead. 'I'm guessing you haven't slept much.'

She shook her head. 'To coin a Granny Isla phrase, I'm absolutely putrefied.'

Ed laughed. 'Oh, heck, that won't do. Come here, let me take your mind off everything for a while.' He pulled her on top of him and kissed her deeply. She melted into his arms and let him whisk her away out of the stratosphere.

* * *

The blinds were down in the shop and Angelia was watching the clock, which featured Elvis Presley wearing a blue chequered jacket; his legs swung from side to side in a pendulum motion to count the seconds. It was coming up to nine o'clock.

Meghan was in assistant mode, standing by the door, old habits definitely died hard there. Angelia's mum and dad stood towards the back of the main floor, Scrappy by their feet wearing his Axl Rose-style bandana, and Bella glanced nervously around, evidently still checking for snagging issues, of which there were none.

Ed walked over to the stereo system and selected a record from some he had pulled out earlier. He wouldn't tell her what he was choosing, and she said she didn't mind as long as it wasn't Angel and the Fallen because that would seem conceited and a bit obvious as the first customers, if there were any, walked in the door for the first time.

'Here we go, folks. The first official song,' he said as he placed the needle on the record. 'I feel like one of those wedding DJs,' he said with a chuckle. 'This one goes out to all those making a fresh start today,' he said as the intro to 'Unwritten' by Natasha Bedingfield began to play. Ed walked over and took her in his arms and spun her around before pulling her close and kissing her. 'Ready for your big day?' he asked.

Angelia couldn't have loved him more if she'd tried. It was the perfect choice of song, and he was the perfect man. 'Ready,' she replied.

'Okay, Ferris, open the blinds,' Ed said.

'Aye, cap'n.' Ferris flicked the switch on the wall and the window and door blinds ascended. At that precise moment, Angelia's mum turned the key in the lock and opened the door.

Angelia gasped as she saw the queue of people reaching from the shop right across to the village hall.

'Well, Miss MacAuley,' Ferris said with a wide smile. 'Looks like you made the right decision.'

And there was no doubt in her mind, as she shared an excited smile with Ed, that she had.

* * *

MORE FROM LISA HOBMAN

ACKNOWLEDGEMENTS

Writing a book about something so personal is both cathartic and emotional. I was diagnosed with MG back in 2003 and sadly, at the time, it took away my singing voice. Singing had been both my job and my passion for many years and losing that was like losing a part of myself. Over time, however, with the support of my family and friends and with the right medical assistance I was able to revisit singing again and subsequently joined both a choir and a trio. I even had the wonderful experience of performing on stage at a music festival. I don't sing as much these days but that's simply because I don't have the time! I therefore want to thank my wonderful mum and dad, my husband and my Gee, and my awesome friends and business partner, Claire, as well as those medical professionals for their encouragement and understanding, especially when I hit the low points after my diagnosis. I now know this condition has given me strengths I didn't realise I possessed.

In my books you usually meet a little canine friend and this one is no different. Scrappy the miniature schnauzer was named by my lovely competition winner Kathryn Vox. So thank you, Kathryn!

I would like to say huge thanks and send hugs to my wonderful friend and beta reader Christine. Your help is always invaluable, and I appreciate you so much!

I am always in awe of the team at Lorella Belli Literary Agency and the work they put in for their authors, so thank you, Lorella and team, from the bottom of my heart.

Last but by no means least, I want to say a massive thank you to Caroline and everyone at Boldwood for your patience and support. We got there!

ABOUT THE AUTHOR

Lisa Hobman has written many brilliantly reviewed women's fiction titles – the first of which was shortlisted by the RNA for their debut novel award. In 2012 Lisa relocated her family from Yorkshire to a village in Scotland and this beautiful backdrop now inspires her uplifting and romantic stories.

Download your exclusive bonus content from Lisa Hobman here:

Visit Lisa's website: www.lisajhobman.com

Follow Lisa on social media:

facebook.com/LisaJHobmanAuthor
instagram.com/lisahobmanauthor
tiktok.com/@lisahobmanauth

ALSO BY LISA HOBMAN

The Skye Collection Series

Dreaming Under An Island Skye

Under An Italian Sky

Wishing Under a Starlit Skye

Together Under A Snowy Skye

Happiness Under a Summer Skye

The Highlands Series

Coming Home to the Highlands

Chasing a Highland Dream

A Highland Family Affair

Shooting Stars Over the Highlands

Snowy Surprises in the Highlands

Standalone Novels

Starting Over At Sunset Cottage

It Started with a Kiss

A Summer of New Beginnings

What Becomes of the Broken Hearted

www.ingramcontent.com/pod-product-compliance
Lightning Source LLC
LaVergne TN
LVHW030914080826
845145LV00012B/2891

* 9 7 8 1 8 0 6 3 5 0 1 1 7 *